Grumpy Cowboy
BODYGUARD

Jax KANE

WHERE DANGER
MEETS DESIRE

Contents

Chapter 1
Cowboy, City, Chaos

I slipped out of the SUV while my security detail argued about where to park. Neon streaks curled against my neck, the bow sat like a billboard on my head, and oversized sunglasses swallowed half my face. People turned when I passed, the way they always did when the costume did the talking first. I told myself I loved the ripple that followed me across a plaza. It sounded like applause if I pretended hard enough. Under the noise, loneliness hummed like a low note only I could hear.

Downtown smelled like cinnamon and car exhaust. A busker played a bruised guitar under a mural of angel wings. A little girl pointed at me and tugged her mother's sleeve. I lifted a finger to my lips and the girl grinned as if I had handed her a secret. I wanted to keep walking and not be recognized at all. I wanted to leave the bow at the bottom of a trash can and keep only my real name.

I hugged the edges of the crowd, imagining a version of myself who ordered tea without a bodyguard, who did not need to smile for strangers or pose for a phone thrust at my face. The pavement glittered with spilled sugar from the donut stand. I let the random churn of voices soak into my skin until my heartbeat steadied. Freedom like this came in tiny crumbs and I had to snatch it while I could. A sidewalk. The sounds of a song I did not have to sing. My palms stopped sweating. I laughed at nothing and felt thirty seconds younger.

Then a shadow paused at my side. I pretended not to notice at first. Maybe they were just a stranger, just someone else wanting a latte. I breathed in chai steam from someone else's cup and counted to five. The shadow did not move on. The prickle at the back of my neck returned, the one that said I had been seen, not for myself, but for the clothes I wore, the brand painted larger than my life ever could be.

The coffee shop's door chimed and released a sigh of cinnamon and milk into the street. I queued like everyone else. Head down. Phone up. I picked a song that always steadied me and let it run while I stared at the menu I already knew by heart. The barista looked tired and kind. When it was my turn, she called me ma'am without lifting her eyes. It felt like a blessing.

I ordered a dirty chai and paid in cash from the tiny pocket in my skirt. No assistant. No clipboard toting expenses. No manager fretting about memes. I leaned against the front window as I waited and watched the street like I was a regular person. An old man fed crumbs to pigeons. A boy on a scooter dragged his foot making sparks. I pretended to be a woman who had nowhere urgent to be. A woman who could text a friend and ask her to meet for pancakes. A woman who could say I do not want to talk about work and have anything else to talk about.

My drink arrived with a heart in the foam. I wanted to take a picture but didn't. I wanted to drink without seeing my own face on a stranger's screen. I lifted the cup and felt the heat sink into my palms. The first sip loosened a knot under my ribs. I almost believed I could be invisible inside a city that never stopped staring, looking for the famous.

Then I felt it again. The weight of someone's attention at my shoulder. I glanced at the window and watched his reflection. He pretended to study a poster about a jazz festival while he drifted an inch closer. I did not want to be paranoid. I did not want to hear manager Richard's voice in my head telling me why I needed a leash. I stepped away from the window and out into the sunlight. The man moved when I moved. My stomach cooled. The tea suddenly tasted like a promise I had already broken.

It happened the way it always happens in the cautionary clips. A jolt at my shoulder. A slick hand. The whisper of leather sliding free. My purse vanished from under my arm, a flash of gold chain flicking against my wrist, and the thief sprinted into the plaza. For a beat I did nothing. People shouted. Someone laughed like it was part of a street show. I tasted metal. Rage flashed, hot and real. I ran.

He cut through a knot of tourists and took the stairs two at a time. I followed with my drink sloshing up the rim and down my knuckles. Another voice called my name and phones swung up as if they had been waiting for a cue. My heart kicked hard, and my legs answered. I heard a high girl scream and a woman yell get out of the way. The city blurred into blocks of color. The bow on my head bounced and turned into a metronome clicking to the beat of my feet.

I did not call for help. I did not look for a bodyguard. I wanted this to be mine. The thief glanced back, saw me closing the gap, and pumped his arms faster. He probably wasn't expecting a dancer's strength hidden under my glittered tights. He veered toward a fountain where kids waded with rolled-up jeans. Spray turned the stone slick. I almost lost my footing, caught it, and slid past a family who would probably upload our collision before I caught my breath. The chain of my purse flashed again at the thief's side like a dare.

I cut left to intercept and he juked right. I felt the old pulse that came before a stage dive, that sense of falling and flying at the same time. The plaza tipped into a roar. It should have lifted me. Instead, it made the ground tilt. I did not think about what was in the bag. I thought about a hand that had touched me without asking. It triggered ancient rage. This angry stranger was not me but I knew her and I ran faster.

The thief clipped a stroller and stumbled. He recovered in the same motion and lunged toward the street. Tires chirped. A horn bit the air. Then a shape cut through the crosswalk like a blade. A man in boots and a worn hat stepped into the thief's path and met him with a shoulder. They hit hard. The thief bounced, tried to pivot, and the man wrapped him up with a wrestler's efficiency, one arm clamped under the thief's elbows, the other braced for leverage. The purse flew. A phone clattered. People gasped. The cowboy did not so much as wobble.

I slid to a stop as everyone else froze. The sound shifted from chase-noise to spectacle-noise. Someone yelled 'get his face'. A camera operator jogged backward with his rig balanced on a shoulder. I watched the cowboy pin the thief with two clean moves, then straighten without grandstanding for the crows. He looked like a wall lifted from a ranch and set down in a city that did not deserve it. Sunlight shown like dust on his shoulders. His hat cast a hard shadow that hid his eyes for a second.

He bent, picked up my purse by the strap, and checked the clasp like he had handled way more delicate things than this. He did not ask if it was mine. He did not pose with it. He held it with the certainty of someone who already knew the answer and turned until he found me in the mass of lenses and open mouths. Our eyes met across a strip of sun, and I felt heat slide along my skin in a line that did not belong to embarrassment or anger.

The thief writhed on the concrete. The cowboy shifted his weight and ended the writhing with a knee and a quiet instruction the thief could not ignore. A siren wailed somewhere close. Someone started clapping and the crowd obediently joined in. I stepped into the circle before it swallowed me. My pulse still raced, although the danger now looked like microphones.

He handed me the purse without ceremony. I wrapped my fingers around the strap and checked for the little scratch on the clasp that told me it was mine. Though, who else's it could have been escaped me. I was just looking for something to focus on other than this confident stranger. I nodded and pushed my sunglasses down my nose to see him better. I expected smirk or swagger or at least stunned recognition. I found a face built out of angles and patience. His eyes were hazel with a slice of green that caught the sun. He took me in with one look and did not blink. It felt like a measuring that had nothing to do with fame.

I was confused. Everyone recognized me, wanted something from me, leveraged their moment with me to try to elevate their status in the limelight. I mean, that whole cowboy schtick had to be some wanna-be actor's attempt to get noticed in this town, right? Then why wasn't he posing? Why was he looking at me so calmly like my star-power meant nothing to him?

"Hold on to your things, princess." He said it flatly, like a rule, not a flirt.

The word landed on my skin like a slap I had not earned. Princess was a label the machine had glued to me and lacquered until it would not peel. Hearing it in his mouth made my cheeks heat. I lifted my chin and almost said I am not your princess. The crowd pressed closer. The thief groaned and tried to buck again. The cowboy shifted a fraction and settled him back into the pavement.

I tried to gather my dignity the way I gathered the purse strap into a tidy loop. It did not cooperate. Gratitude wrestled with irritation inside my ribs. I hated that I had needed help. I hated that he had given it so easily. I hated that the princess word had stung because it was true in all the ways I didn't want. I realized I was still staring and he was still watching me. The corner of his mouth seemed to want to lift but did not. I didn't have a canned reaction I could spit out to his stationary calm, and it was flustering the heck out of me.

Police spilled into the edge of the scene and a reporter stuck a microphone toward my lips. I swallowed the exasperated sound I wanted to make and turned so the camera would get my good side. The cowboy stood, not beside me, but slightly in front, as if his body had decided where to belong without asking me. My gratitude shifted, reluctant but real. I clutched the purse but refused to thank him out loud.

The circle broke into sectors. Press. Police. Bystanders who were probably already editing captions in their heads. A teenager shouted my name and the flock answered by chanting it. I felt the old autopilot slide into place. Smile. Shoulders down. Tilt the chin. Make it look easy. The cowboy hat beside me pulled attention like a magnet. The cameras did not care which of us had almost been hurt. They cared about the image we made together. *Opposites.* I could almost see the memes building themselves over people's heads while they filmed us.

I could almost hear Richard's voice cataloging the publicity angles in my ear even though he was not here. He would call the save a gift. He would want me photographed under the cowboy's arm. He would try to book the man on morning shows and find out whether he knew how to string words together without appearing stupid or cussing.

The thought made me want to throw the bow from my head into the fountain and sink after it.

A reporter asked how it felt to be rescued in such dramatic fashion. I said I was grateful to the brave bystander and happy everyone was safe. The line sounded polished because it had been sanded by years of practice. I tried to catch the cowboy's name as he spoke to the police and failed. He stayed quiet while the police lifted the thief and read him words that sounded rehearsed and small after so much drama.

Phones lifted higher. Someone asked about my upcoming CD release. Someone else asked if my new cowboy boyfriend would be coming on the tour. I laughed in a way that let them print the laugh without calling it cold. I had no boyfriend. Definitely not part of the Forever Innocent brand I was saddled with. The cowboy tracked the crowd like a hunter listening for a branch to snap in a field. When people reached toward me, his palm rose demanding space without touching anyone. They obeyed him more than they obeyed me or even my usual bodyguards. I hated that. I also loved how safe I felt for a breath that did not belong to the cameras.

While the police tried to bundle the thief into a cruiser, he twisted and slipped through a gap. The officers grabbed for him, and he lurched in my direction with an ugly grin. It happened so fast that the people filming didn't even lower their phones. He leaned toward me, and I caught the sour stink of sweat and fear.

He said it under his breath, mouth barely moving, like a prayer spoken to a single god, me. "He said not to hurt you. Yet."

The word 'yet' slid under my ribs and lodged against my spine to send chills racing. For a second I did not process the rest of the sentence. *He?* The shape of a person who did not exist in front of me. The idea of a mouth that had ordered my purse taken as a rehearsal for something stunned me. I forgot to breathe. The cowboy did not. His hand closed on the thief's collar and the man lost his air and his grin at the same time as he was nearly lifted off his feet. The police moved in. The cowboy did not look at me right away. He looked beyond me, past the press and the fountain and the pigeons, as if the thing he needed to see did not stand in the open.

Then he turned his head, and I saw the shift in him. His jaw set. The softness that had almost happened at his mouth vanished. He wore a face I had seen on men who guarded doors I was supposed to pass through with a smile. He was a man who understood threats, security, protection. He didn't have to tell me in words. I recognized the type.

I knew I should tell the police exactly what I had heard but my tongue stuck. Heat climbed into my throat and settled into my ears as I debated. I swallowed and tasted chai and fear at the same time. I was afraid to voice it, to make it any realer.

The cameras kept filming because fear looks good on a screen. I closed my eyes for a count of two and opened them to find the cowboy watching me with that same measuring look. In it I saw a question. I nodded once to say I was okay, and his shoulders lowered by a hair in response. It was an oddly close moment to have with a stranger, but I felt like he saw me. A chill shook me because no one ever looked past the brand name 'Isla Dove', past the glitter and the bow on my head. Yet, he had, immediately.

The thief vanished into the cruiser with a slam. The chant around us lost volume and turned into a hundred small conversations. I did not want any of them. The cowboy stepped close enough that I caught the scent of sun and soap and old leather. He did not touch me. He did not have to. His voice landed like a line drawn in chalk around my feet.

"Looks like your label was right."

I hated that sentence. I hated that it made me feel nine again, sneaking into a room I was not supposed to enter. I hated that it acknowledged a fear of mysterious notes and shadows I had been naming for weeks and laughing off the next day. A tiny spark of relief flared inside me anyway. Not because anyone deserved to be right. Because someone else had finally said it out loud.

I looked up at the hat, at the curls of blond hair escaping it and then at the eyes under it. Hazel with green like a field after rain. I wanted to ask how he knew. I wanted to ask who he was. I wanted to ask why the world quieted when he stood between me and the lenses. Another reporter leaned in with a question that tasted like bait. I did not answer. I let the cowboy absorb the noise for a second and found my breath again.

My security reached the edge of the crowd with faces I knew. Their mouths opened. My name rose as a scold and an exasperated sigh. I did not turn. I kept my eyes on the man who had cut through a city and a problem at the same time. I did not say thank you. I did not need to. I think he heard my shoulders drop. The plaza tilted back to level. The fear stayed. So did the strange cowboy who had just stepped into my story.

Chapter 2
Cowboy
Contract

The rental SUV smelled like leather wipes and stale coffee. I had parked it far enough down the street that the mansion's gates looked like a movie set, all gold trim and fake grandeur. Sierra Bravo Security's file sat open on the seat beside me, the words blurring into bullet points I already knew by heart. Protect the client. Investigate credible threats. Maintain cover.

In this case, that meant moving into the pop princess's castle and playing her boyfriend for the cameras. Babysitting duty dressed up like security. I hated jobs like this. Too many handlers. Too many eyes. Too much pretending. Real danger did not care about glitter or hashtags. It cared about openings, about weak points in schedules and walls.

I rubbed a hand over the stubble on my jaw, wondering what kind of world I had stepped into this time. She was not a diplomat or a business magnate. She was a singer whose stage clothes looked more like a child's costume trunk than armor. The board at Sierra Bravo did not waste their best men on circus assignments unless there was more to it. And the file outlined credible stalking and escalating threats that her own manager was ignoring. Her record label had contacted Sierra Bravo, going over her manager's head. He was unaware of my real purpose. I had to embed, watch, and if necessary, take down any threats. They'd chosen me because I was an unknown in this L.A. market, an out-of-stater. Definitely off the Colorado range out here.

There were three possible shadows listed in the file. A rabid fan, one Brian Avery who had sent her gushy mail, left presents at her mansion gate and showed up everywhere she was. Jenna Marks, an ex-backup singer fired for "malicious behavior" whatever that meant and then rehired to play in her band for reasons that escaped Sierra Bravo and certainly me. She was listed as jealous and still a potential threat. And then there was Richard Clark, Isla's own manager. He was in towering debt. Enough to make him a saboteur or a potential weak link. It was no secret that with a new Isla Dove CD to be released within the week, sales would skyrocket if tragedy were to strike down the star. Shares from those sales would go far toward eliminating Richard's financial problems. And, of course, with any mega-visible personality there was always the reality of a host of people out to make a name for themselves by being her killer or kidnapper. Privately, with the image of Forever Innocent Isla and her schoolgirl dress up, I'd put money on a whole lot of predators anxious to steal her away to some concealed lockup for their fun and games.

She had a host of her own security, of course but the threats kept getting through. Like the purse snatcher with his message. The simple fact that her "bodyguards" had allowed her to get away from them to get that chai and get her purse taken was proof enough to me that she needed me. Probably wasn't going to like me much because I was going to set hard rules, but she was going to get through her concert and CD release party alive. That's all that mattered.

The SUV ticked as the engine cooled. I checked my sidearm, concealed under the denim of my jacket, then studied the mansion again. Cameras glinted on the roof, but half the ground-level hedges had gaps wide enough to crawl through. Sloppy. Hollywood liked appearances more than strength. And a hedge was not a fence to start with. I blew out a breath and shoved the file back into its folder. Whatever circus waited behind those doors, it was mine now.

And I had to ignore the fact that this was Isla Dove, my little sister's favorite singer. A sister I had lost due to my own negligence. I had walled off those memories and those songs that she played over and over until I screamed at her to play anything else. I'd give anything to hear her humming them again. But, who wouldn't? That's what grief did. Made you regret everything you did, didn't do, said. I had to ignore the past and focus on my job, as I had every day since. It was the only way to combat the guilt.

Manager Richard Clark opened the door himself, sweaty handshake and teeth too white. He smelled like the kind of cologne meant to cover late nights and cheap liquor, but it never fooled anyone who had spent time in a barracks. His grin clung to me as he ushered me into a living room that looked borrowed from a catalog and not lived in. He launched into a pitch before I even set my boots on the marble.

I was scanning as I entered. Too many entrance points. And I sure as hell hoped that back glass wall was bulletproof. Otherwise, it was a goddamn shooting gallery along this whole side of the house. How was I supposed to protect this girl in here? Maybe we'd be moving to a concrete bunker.

Richard called Isla's stage persona the Forever Innocent brand. He described Isla Dove like a soda flavor: bows, glitter, sequins, bubblegum songs, purity, a smile that sold T-shirts. Every word landed like static in my ears. He bragged about how her breakout ballad had stayed on top of streaming charts for years and was still playing strong. My chest tightened. That was the song my sister played on repeat, her headphones bleeding the melody through her door. The memory turned my jaw to stone.

I kept my face locked down, but Richard must have seen something. He smirked, thinking it was disdain over the music genre. He kept selling, spinning fantasy to a man who had no interest in what he was selling. Maybe he thought I'd be impressed with her mega chart success or world tours. I had my own world tours carrying an M4 and my mega success was surviving as a field bomb tech. He ignored the way my eyes swept the room for exits, knick-knacks I could turn into weapons in a heartbeat, the way my attention kept snagging on doors that did not close properly, on curtains that would hide a man with a gun or knife.

"It is all about image," Richard said, voice slick. "And you, cowboy, are part of that image now."

I muttered that a lie this big was dangerous in a world full of predators. He waved me off with a laugh, like predators were only used in movies. My fingers curled against my thigh. I wanted to remind him that predators were real, and that his star client was already prime bait.

The floors shone so brightly I could see my reflection in them. My boots tracked grit across the marble. The Stetson stayed on my head because I did not care when it crashed into the chandelier. Richard stared at me like he was seeing mold on a loaf of bread.

"We will need a make-over," he muttered finally, voice pinched.

He circled me as if he were choosing fabrics. He gestured at my shirt, my hat, the plain leather belt that had been to places I was sure he'd never heard of. He smiled like he had already ordered a stylist. I let him talk. When he finally looked me in the eye, my stare shut his mouth. Years of field work taught me that silence spoke louder than posturing. I did not need to puff out my chest or threaten him. I only needed to make it clear that I would not be handled or changed. I wasn't here to be part of his Isla brand machine or her glittery sidekick. He broke eye contact first, fidgeting with his cufflinks. He might be thinking make-over but he was about to meet irresistible force.

"This is Beverly Hills," he muttered, not quite brave enough to meet my eyes again. "Appearances matter."

"Staying alive matters more," I said flatly. His smile faltered for half a second before he pasted it back on.

The chandelier swayed faintly overhead from my knocking it. I didn't reach up to steady it. The windows framed the hills in expensive glass, but I saw the vulnerabilities instead. High ground for anyone with a scope in the back. Shadowed corners perfect for lurking. I felt the familiar itch along my spine, the one that meant I had stepped onto a battlefield even if no one else noticed the battle lines. Hollywood could try to position me as a boyfriend, but it would not change what I was here to do.

The door at the far end swung open on a laugh that cut through the air like a bell. She walked in wearing a skirt that belonged in a high school costume shop and lips glossed to a shine. She downright sparkled. Sequined skirt, glitter shoes, neon midriff shirt with some shiny thread sewn into big flowers. Her neon-streaked hair was caught up in twin pony tails on either side of her head that reflected the light like fishing lures. They'd be cute – on a six-year-old. She tossed her bag onto a chair and stopped when she saw me.

I expected innocence. The file had painted her that way. What I saw instead was vulnerability. A grown woman wrapped in neon and glitter, a target dressed like a doll. My stomach tightened.

She took me in with a glance that lasted half a second too long. Her green eyes landed on the hat, the boots, the way I stood with my weight set like I had no plans to move. Her mouth quirked and she said, "Did the Wild West lose a sheriff?"

The laugh from Richard was too loud, too eager. I grunted. It was all I gave her. I did not trust my voice not to betray the punch she had landed without a word or meaning to. She was arresting. Stunning in a way that irritated me. I reminded myself that she was not mine to admire. She was my assignment. And I had seen plenty of beautiful distractions before. They always came with trouble attached.

We went in to sit across from each other at a long dining table that I doubted had ever been used. Another man was already seated. He hadn't been in Sierra Bravo's file. He wore an expensive blue silk suit over a white linen shirt but no tie. I wasn't sure what he was trying to convey by that. Too important to worry about the complete outfit? Wanting to convey some casualness? He was perfectly tanned, polished nails, a shark's shallow smile. Richard introduced him as Lucas DeWitt with a rapid eye twitchy hurry that told me Lucas had the power in the room.

"I just want to make sure our princess is protected and that you understand the brand here, son." Lucas said with a smile that didn't come anywhere near his dark eyes, "She is Forever Innocent. Isn't that right, Isla?"

"Of course." Richard spouted before Isla could even get in her eye roll, "And that's all in the contract here."

Richard spread papers between us on the table while I stared at Lucas, trying to figure his position in all this.

"It's a huge house. Plenty of bedrooms." Isla giggled but I heard an edge to her voice.

I didn't know who it was aimed at. Maybe me.

"What's your stake in this?" I asked, not taking my eyes off Lucas'.

"I'm simply the promoter." He said spreading his hands as if innocent, though I hadn't accused him of anything, "I've invested a small fortune in reserving all the concert dates and venues. Can't have anything disrupting the schedule."

'Like the star getting killed,' I thought.

Richard jumped in to explain the contract terms like he was arranging a business merger. I would move into Isla's mansion. I would pose as her boyfriend until the CD launch was over. Great. Jake Dalton, Isla's eunuch boyfriend. I wondered how fast that would sink. It wouldn't take long for the media to track into my past and find a history of bodyguard, military and a few girlfriends with steamy stories to tell. But Sierra Bravo knew that and sent me here under my own name. So be it.

My jaw clenched. Playing pretend had never sat right with me. The soldier in me wanted clarity, not theater. But the assignment was not optional. Richard just didn't realize he was playing along with Sierra Bravo's script. I'd let him deal with any media fallout from a man suddenly living with their "innocent" Isla.

Isla crossed her arms and slouched in her chair. Her eyes flicked to mine every few seconds, sharp with challenge. She did not like the idea any more than I did. Sparks jumped between us, not friendly, not soft. Maybe this 'innocent' brand was just advertising nonsense. Not that it mattered to me. I was here to protect her. Not develop a relationship of any kind.

"Fake boyfriend," I muttered under my breath. The words tasted bitter. I would much rather come in overtly as a bodyguard.

Her mouth curved in a smirk that dared me to break eye contact first. Richard ignored us both, talking about publicity angles and again about a makeover. I barely heard him. He could chatter on all he wanted. I was not changing anything. The tension across the table between Isla and I was thick enough to cut.

The pen felt too light in my hand. I signed because Sierra Bravo expected me to, each stroke of ink a chain link pulling tighter around my wrist. Isla leaned forward, her chin resting on her hand, watching me with something that was not quite disdain anymore. Curiosity lived in her eyes. Distrust too.

I did not like how aware I was of her presence. Of the way her perfume clung to the air. Of the way her laughter earlier still seemed to echo in the room. The contract was supposed to be business. My reaction was leaning towards personal.

I reminded myself that chemistry was a distraction. A dangerous one. I finished the last signature, capped the pen, and pushed the papers back across the table without looking at her again. Still, I felt her gaze on me, a weight I couldn't shrug off.

My phone buzzed in my pocket. I pulled it free under the table, thumb unlocking the screen out of habit, in case it was a Sierra Bravo alert. The text glowed bright against the dark: *Stay away, cowboy. Or she pays.*

The timing was too sharp. Too personal. Whoever sent it knew exactly where I was, who I was with, and what I had just agreed to. My stomach tightened, the soldier in me snapping into readiness.

I lifted my eyes to Isla's. She tilted her head, lips curving into a half-smile that was equal parts defiance and dare. The contract lay between us, signed and binding, but it felt like something heavier had been written in the air.

I slid the phone back into my pocket, my pulse steadying in the way it always did before setting out to defuse a bomb. She thought this was still about playacting for cameras. She was wrong.

I scanned the room. Richard was still talking about brand angles, haircuts and clothing. Lucas was looking at Richard. Isla was still watching me with that half-curious expression. No one else seemed to notice that open war had been declared.

Chapter 3
Pop Princess, Pretend Love

My house felt like a beehive, buzzing with too many people and not enough air. Stylists darted around with curling irons and powder brushes, tugging me this way and that while my assistant, Lily, yammered on about rehearsal schedules. Glitter spilled across the vanity, sequins stuck to the soles of my feet, and I wanted to scream. Somewhere behind me, Richard was droning about tonight's interviews, but his voice blended into the chaos like static.

And then there was him. Jake Dalton. My brand-new shadow, standing in the corner like a storm cloud in boots and denim. Arms crossed, jaw locked, eyes scanning every movement like we were in a war zone instead of my Beverly Hills mansion. He wasn't like the other bodyguards, the ones who faded into the background until I forgot their names. No. Jake filled the room just by standing still, and every stylist kept sneaking glances at him like he was something they couldn't quite believe.

I tried to ignore him. I told myself to focus on the mirror, on the neon curls bobbing around my face, on the ridiculous oversized bow Lily clipped into place. But the weight of his stare followed me with every turn. He didn't see Isla Dove, Pop Princess. He seemed to see underneath, and I hated how naked that made me feel.

When I tripped over a pile of shoe boxes and muttered a curse, he finally spoke. "Careful," he said, voice low, edged with command. Not mocking, not amused. Just a soldier warning me about potential land mines. My skin prickled at the low sound of his voice.

I wanted to tell him to shove his cowboy concern somewhere dark, but instead I bit my lip and kept moving. The last thing I needed was this grumpy stranger unraveling me before I even hit the interviews.

By the time I made it downstairs, Jake was already there, planted by the double doors like some watchdog carved out of stone. Sunlight cut across his shoulders, glinting off the worn buckle of his belt, and for one dizzying second I thought he looked almost... heroic. Then he opened his mouth.

"You left that back window unlocked." His tone was flat, like he was announcing a death sentence.

I stopped short, clutching my glitter-studded phone like a shield. "So?"

"So, anyone with half a brain could walk right in," he said, hazel eyes narrowing. "You want to make it easier for a stalker? Or do you just enjoy tempting fate?"

Heat flared in my chest. Who did this cowboy think he was? My father? My warden? I was used to paparazzi, not prison guards. "Maybe I like a little fresh air," I shot back, lifting my chin.

He didn't blink. "Fresh air won't save you when someone slides a knife between your ribs."

My pulse skipped, just once, before anger smothered it. I hated that he could get under my skin so fast. I hated that a part of me knew he was right. So, I did what I always did when cornered. I went for sarcasm.

"Relax, Sheriff. Not everyone's out to get me. Some of us just want to live without armed cowboys pacing holes into our floors."

That earned me a muscle ticking along his jaw. Small victory.

I stalked past him, my heels clicking on the marble. But even with my back to him, I felt the weight of his presence, the heat of his disapproval. Like a brand seared into my skin. Opposites didn't just attract, I realized. They collided. And I had met my high-speed collision course.

Richard hovered in the foyer like a frantic stage director, waving his phone while barking orders as the stylist fussed with my hair. "Hand in hand. Big smiles. They need to believe this is real."

Real. The word curdled in my stomach. Nothing about this felt real. Not the bow pinned too tight against my scalp, not the sequined skirt that rode up my thighs, and definitely not the flannel shirt draped over my shoulders like more borrowed costume. His flannel.

I tugged at the sleeves, inhaling the faint scent of leather and cedar. The smell was maddeningly 'him', solid, grounding. I hated how it calmed me.

"Perfect," Richard chirped, snapping a photo with his phone. "America's sweetheart with her rugged cowboy. X will eat it up."

I gritted my teeth. "I'm not your dress-up doll."

Jake's voice rumbled low from behind me. "Could've fooled me."

I spun, ready to snap, but his eyes flicked to my outfit, then back to mine. He didn't smirk. He didn't tease. He just looked at me like I was someone who needed protecting, maybe from myself and it rattled me more than his sarcasm ever could.

"Places!" Richard clapped.

The front door swung open. Jake stepped closer, his hand closing firmly over mine. His palm was calloused, steady. Too steady. My stomach flipped.

"Smile," Richard hissed.

I pasted on my practiced grin, tilting my head just so, the way the tabloids loved. But Jake didn't smile. His stoic glare cut through the paparazzi like a surgeon's scalpel, his broad frame shielding me even as he dragged me into the spotlight. And the craziest part? For one traitorous moment, standing in his shadow felt safer than hiding behind all the neon bows in the world.

The second we stepped outside, the world erupted. Camera flashes burst like fireworks, reporters shoved microphones forward, and a mob of fans screamed my name. I'd lived this scene a hundred times, but this afternoon felt different, with Jake at my side, the energy tilted, sharper and heavier. I slipped into my trained performance mode: wide smile, practiced wave, glittery giggle. The flannel still clung to me, ridiculous against sequined heels, but the crowd lapped it up.

"Adorable opposites!" someone shouted.

Phones angled for selfies. I could imagine the hashtags already buzzing like neon signs above their heads.

Beside me, Jake didn't play along. No fake grin. No carefully man-ufactured charm. Just a wall of six-foot-three cowboy in boots and hat, hazel eyes analyzing the press like they were enemy combatants. He wasn't posing. He was calculating. His hand stayed locked around mine, solid and immovable, like he was daring anyone to try to pull me away or was ready to snatch me back in a heartbeat.

Reporters screamed their nonsense. "Isla Dove's mystery cowboy!" "Her new man?" "Still innocent, Isla?" Questions flew like daggers. I answered with chirpy soundbites, but my pulse kept tripping on the way his body hovered just behind mine, close enough that I could feel his heat more than the California sun.

For once, even in front, I wasn't center stage. He was. And the audience loved him. His rough edges, his quiet defiance, the way he looked ready to deck anyone who came too close. It all played perfectly into the narrative of a pop princess tamed by a real cowboy.

I should've hated it. Hated him stealing my spotlight. But standing in front of a hundred lenses, I realized I didn't mind his tall presence behind me. For the first time in years, I didn't feel like I was in a cage. It felt like cover, a safe hiding place.

Then we were closing the front and out the back, heading to rehearsal. Once inside the venue, I yanked off the flannel and shoved it at Jake's chest. "I'm not your dress-up doll."

He caught it easily, folding it once before slinging it over his arm. No apology, no smirk. Just that steady stare, the one that made my stomach dip even as irritation spiked hotter.

Fans online would already be squealing about the photo ops. Pop Princess Isla Dove wrapped in her cowboy's shirt, walking hand-in-hand like some fairytale cliché. My manager probably thought it was genius branding. But to me, it felt like another layer of suffocating costume, one more mask in a life already buried under neon curls and fake innocence.

And yet...

The truth was, Jake's shirt hadn't just smelled like laundry soap and cedar. It had smelled like him, warm skin, leather, grit. When reporters shouted questions, it had wrapped around me like armor. I hated myself for noticing. I hated that something as simple as flannel and his hand had made me feel steadier than sequins and glitter ever did. I was used to standing on my own two feet. Always had.

It wasn't attraction, I told myself. It was combat. A standoff. His rules versus my rebellion. Except when his gaze lingered a heartbeat too long, heat flared low in my stomach, and I realized maybe it wasn't just me feeling the burn.

I turned away, forcing a bright smile for the crew bustling past. But inside, the image lingered: me in his flannel, his scent clinging to my skin. And I wasn't sure if I wanted to forget it.

"Your bow's crooked." Lily warned, ushering me into my dressing room.

I let her herd me into my chair where she fixed whatever had become imperfect from the brief trip from the house to here. She sang quietly as she worked, and I realized it was one of my songs. She was using the same squeaky, little girl voice I did, mimicking me perfectly.

"Maybe I'll just send you out there." I said, not looking forward to anything today.

Lily giggled shyly and waved the lip gloss at me to get me to open my mouth.

I left my dressing room and cornered Jake near the stage door, the flannel still slung over his arm like a trophy. My blood was humming with irritation. At least that's what I was naming it.

"I'm not your responsibility," I shot at him.

"You're exactly my responsibility, princess." His voice dropped to gravel, the weight of it thrumming straight through me. He wasn't shouting, wasn't posturing. Just raw certainty, and somehow that shook me more than if he'd barked orders.

For a moment, the hallway noise dimmed. Crew voices blurred, footsteps faded, until it was just the two of us locked in a silent stand-off. My pulse drummed hard, not from fear, not from anger, at least, not only those.

His gaze dipped, briefly, to my mouth. Then back to my eyes, hard and unreadable. Heat licked under my skin, sharp and terrifying, because I knew exactly what that flicker meant.

"Careful, princess," he murmured, so low I barely caught it. "You keep poking the bear, you may not like how it ends."

I swallowed hard, but I didn't back down. I tilted my head, lashes low, daring him. "Maybe I would."

The tension between us snapped taut, humming like a live wire. My heart hammered against my ribs, wild and reckless, and for one dizzy second, I thought he might actually close the distance, crowd me against the wall and prove me right. I wasn't sure if I was wildly terrified or something else.

But a stagehand bustled past, breaking the moment. Jake pushed off the wall, shoulders rigid, leaving me breathless and furious with myself.

Because for all my defiance, part of me had wanted him to.

By the time I got back to the stage, my cheeks were still hot, my pulse uneven. Jake lingered a few steps behind me, arms crossed. He hadn't touched me, hadn't even raised his voice, but somehow, he'd managed to burn his presence into my skin.

I was desperate for a distraction, any distraction, when one of the stage assistants handed me a box. Small, pink, tied up with a glittery bow that would have made my stylist swoon.

"Fan mail," she chirped before flitting away.

Fan mail. Right. I should've been used to it. Flowers, stuffed animals, handwritten letters begging for my love. It was all part of the brand. Still, something about the careful wrapping set my nerves prickling. Probably still reacting to cowboy drama.

I slid my thumb under the tape, tearing the paper. The lid came free. Inside, nestled on white tissue, lay a single rose.

Or what was left of one.

Its petals were shriveled, edges black, the stem bent at an unnatural angle. The smell hit me a second later, sweet and rotten all at once, like death disguised in perfume. My stomach lurched.

Jake was already at my side, big hand closing over the box before I could drop it. He lifted it like it was a ticking bomb, eyes narrowing, scanning the corners of the room like the sender might still be watching.

I forced a laugh, but it came out shaky. "Guess somebody skipped the florist this time."

He didn't smile. His gaze flicked to mine, hard and unyielding. "This isn't a joke."

The staff around us kept moving, oblivious. I stared at the wilted rose, bile rising in my throat. If it wasn't a gift, was it a warning? And the worst part? I couldn't tell if it was meant for Isla Dove, pop princess...or me.

Jake shifted the tissue paper, and something fluttered loose from beneath the dead rose. A small white card, the kind that usually came tucked in with bouquets. For one brief, foolish second, I thought maybe this really was just a botched fan gift.

Then I read the words.

You're old and wilted too.

My skin went cold. By the time I hit the last word, my breath was gone. The handwriting was jagged, uneven, like it had been scratched out with more anger than ink.

I felt Jake's presence before I even registered, he'd stepped closer. His arm brushed my shoulder as he studied the note, and for once I didn't move away. My body wanted the barrier. My pounding pulse wanted to deny how much I needed it.

"Where did this come from?" His voice was low, controlled, but there was an edge under it that made the air buzz.

"One of the assistants dropped it off," I whispered, suddenly aware of how empty the area had gotten. Everyone else had drifted back to rehearsal prep, leaving just me and the cowboy, the rose between us like a corpse.

Jake slipped the card into his pocket with a precision that felt military. Saving evidence, not sentiment. His jaw ticked as his eyes swept the high corners of the room, like he expected to see the sender watching.

I wrapped my arms around myself. His scent was still stubbornly there. For the first time, the ridiculous bow in my hair felt like a target painted on my skull.

He turned back to me, expression hard enough to cut steel. "You're not walking out of my sight again."

And for once, I didn't argue.

Chapter 4
Under the Lights

I took up position at the back of the rehearsal hall, where the shadows pooled thickest. It wasn't habit; it was survival. You learn quick in the Army that the safest place isn't where the light shines, it's where you can see everything without being seen yourself.

The place was chaos. Techs shouted across catwalks, cords snaked underfoot, and spotlights swung erratic beams that made the whole stage look like a funhouse. Isla's voice carried through it all, bright, sugary, too polished to be natural. The kind of voice that made fans swoon and predators' circle.

I cataloged threats the way other men made grocery lists. Exits: four, only two staffed. Catwalks: unsecured, one kid up there texting instead of checking rigging. Crowd control: nonexistent, crew wandering in and out unchecked. Every sloppy detail raised the hairs on my neck.

Then there was Isla.

She spun through choreography in a skirt too short for the stage, curls bouncing neon pink, green and blue under the lights. Everyone else saw a pop goddess. All I saw was how easy it would be to take her down: one loose wire, one unstable light, one obsessed fan slipping past an unstaffed door. Any rifle in the darkened auditorium and it would be over before I could blink. I hated it.

She laughed when she missed a step, flashing a smile big enough to light Los Angeles. The crowd of backup singers, dancers and techs laughed with her, charmed. I didn't. I scanned again, hand near the small of my back where my Glock rested. This wasn't a rehearsal. This was a battlefield painted in glitter. And I was the only soldier on watch.

Then the next song hit me. High-pitched, sweet, so damned innocent it could rot teeth. The ballad that made her famous. The one the fans still screamed for. My shoulders went rigid before I could stop them. That song had been my sister's favorite: *I'll Stand Tomorrow.* She used to play it on repeat, humming the chorus while she brushed her hair, back when the world still felt whole. Back before she was gone.

Hearing it here, coming from Isla's lips, didn't feel like nostalgia. It felt like a knife digging into my guts. Because what I saw onstage wasn't the girl who had once given my sister hope. It was a woman forced into neon and bows, selling innocence like a product. Her voice cracked, her eyes flicked toward the ground, and for a moment I saw the truth. Exhaustion. Frustration. A cage lined with sequins.

She rallied fast, tossing her curls, flashing the smile the world paid to see. But I couldn't unsee that stumble, couldn't unhear the echo of my sister's laughter wrapped up in this lie.

My jaw clenched. Isla Dove wasn't protected by this brand. She was smothered by it and now her own mask was being used to paint a bullseye on her back. And if the song that once lit up my sister's world was now being twisted into bait, then this job wasn't just personal. It was damned near unbearable.

From the shadows, I watched Isla spin through the routine again, her curls bouncing like she didn't have a care in the world. Except I knew better. She hit a high note and faltered, her voice cracking on the end. No one else seemed to notice. The band kept hammering the chords, the backup dancers threw glitter smiles, and Richard clapped like a seal in the corner. But I noticed. The slip was quick, human, real shining out in this plastic world.

Isla pressed on, that practiced grin locked into place. I saw the tremor in her hand as she lifted one arm. Saw the flash of frustration when her heel caught in the tape marking center stage. For half a second, her mask cracked wide open, and I glimpsed the woman underneath. Not the pop princess. Not the neon poster child. Just a young woman drowning under a spotlight she couldn't escape.

It gutted me. I told myself I didn't care that it was just another liability to manage. But my chest tightened anyway. Because that look, raw, lost, desperate. It was too familiar. My sister had worn it too, the night before she left us for good. And that damn song was stripping away every barrier I had put in place to protect myself from the memories.

I forced myself to breathe, cataloging the weak points in the rigging instead of the weakness in her eyes. She wasn't mine to save, not in that way. I was here to stop bullets, not hold her up as the weight of fame dragged her down.

Still, I couldn't stop staring when she bit her lip and pushed harder into the song, as if defiance alone would keep her standing. Maybe it could. Maybe she didn't need me for that. But I knew she'd need me for what was coming.

The longer I stood at the back of that glitter-soaked room, the more out of place I felt. Steel-toed boots on a wooden stage, a sweat-stained Stetson under blinding lights, and a rifle-trained gaze cataloging threats while the rest of them laughed.

The dancers whispered to each other between takes, giggling and pointing toward me. I didn't catch every word, but I caught enough, cowboy, hick, out of his league. One even mimed tipping an imaginary hat before breaking into peals of laughter. Real professional.

Isla caught their performance and rolled her eyes like she was above it, but her smirk lingered. The kind that cut sharp. A silent "see what I have to put up with." Or maybe it was aimed squarely at me, at the way I stuck out like a raw edge in her polished world.

I wanted to tell them all that it didn't matter what I wore. That if someone pulled a gun or ran out of the darkness, I'd be the one pulling Isla out alive. Not them. Not Richard with his slick hands and trembling smiles. Me.

But I stayed still, arms crossed, every muscle tight. Let them laugh. I wasn't there to win points in the LA popularity contest. The only person who mattered was Isla. And no amount of mockery would shake that focus.

Still, I felt the heat crawl up my neck as the crew kept stealing glances. Back in the Army, I could silence a room with one look. Here, I was the punchline in boots.

I forced myself to breathe through the sting, eyes never leaving Isla. She was the mission. Everything else, every joke, every sneer, I let it roll off.

Because the moment I looked away, I knew the real threat would strike.

The hum of the stage blurred into white noise until a sound cut through it, a groan in the steel above the lights. My head snapped up. No one else noticed. Not the dancers preening in the mirrors, not the band fumbling through a riff, not Isla working through a half-hearted chorus in that sugary voice that made her sound younger than she was.

But I heard it. Felt it.

The rig above her trembled, bolts straining. Instinct shoved adrenaline through my veins. I was moving before my brain caught up, boots hammering across polished wood.

"Isla!" My shout was almost lost under the music, but my speed wasn't. She blinked at me, confusion flickering.

Then the spotlight cable shrieked. Metal tore. Gravity won. The rigging dropped fast, a black blur hurtling toward her head. I hit her low, arms locking around her waist, momentum carrying us both. We hit the boards hard. My shoulder slammed the floor, my hat skittered into the wings, but I didn't let go.

The crash behind us shook the hall, steel and wood shrieking as the spot shattered across the stage. Screams erupted. Dancers scrambled, crew shouted, instruments clattered to the ground with tortured sounds.

I rolled, covering Isla with my body as glass and debris scattered across the floor. Her breath rushed hot against my throat, her heart hammering like a trapped bird beneath me. For one suspended heartbeat, it wasn't danger I felt. It was something raw, magnetic, wrong in every professional sense and stronger than anything I'd fought in years. Her wide green eyes locked on mine. A question hung there, unspoken, pulling me closer before I yanked myself back to reality.

The rig's twisted mounting still groaned above us. Instinct had me up and shoving Isla toward the wings. She stumbled, and I caught her, pressing her back against the wall just as another piece of metal tore loose to fall to the floor. My arm bracketed her shoulder, my body still crowding hers, shielding her from the chaos.

For a moment, the world narrowed to the heat of her breath on my neck and the way her green eyes burned up at me. She wasn't the glitter-draped idol the cameras worshipped. She was a woman, scared but furious and alive, her pulse thudding so hard I could feel it through her ribs.

Her bow was tangled in my shirt buttons, neon ribbon pulling taut between us, glitter decorating my shirt. I swore under my breath, tugging it free, the ridiculous thing nearly strangling both of us. She let out a shaky laugh, breathless, and the sound went straight to places I had no business letting it go.

I should have stepped back. I should have checked the perimeter, shouted orders, done anything but linger. Instead, I froze there, every nerve alive with the pull between us. Her lips parted like she was about to say something or maybe kiss me.

The thought rocked me harder than the falling steel had.

I forced myself to break away, dragging in air that tasted like dust and her perfume. If I let myself lean in, even an inch, it wouldn't have stopped at a single kiss. And once that line was crossed, I wouldn't be able to guard her the way she needed.

Duty. Discipline. Distance.

I repeated the words like a mantra as I turned from her and faced the wreckage. But my heart was still slamming for reasons that had nothing to do with the danger. I pushed off the wall like it burned me, like she burned me, creating space where there hadn't been any. Isla stayed still for half a second, wide-eyed, her chest rising fast. Then her mouth curved, not into a smile, not quite, but something that made me wonder if she'd felt that same charge of heat.

She tried to cover it with bravado, brushing invisible dust off her sequined skirt. "Guess cowboys know how to make an entrance," she muttered, voice unsteady despite the jab.

I ignored the bait. My pulse was still hammering, and if I looked at her too long, I'd forget which of us had almost crossed a line. I crouched instead, sweeping the stage with my gaze, cataloging exits, shadows, potential threats. Anything but her.

But she didn't move away. When I looked back, she was still close, green eyes flicking from my mouth to my chest before she caught herself and glanced aside. That quick hitch in her breathing told me everything I shouldn't want to know.

I forced my voice steady. "You good?"

"Fine." Her answer came too fast. Too brittle. She tucked a strand of hair behind her ear, but her fingers trembled. She was rattled, and not just from the near miss.

Hell, so was I.

I'd been trained to face down bullets, blades, explosions. But nothing in my past had prepared me for the pull of one stubborn, glitter-covered pop star who made me forget discipline in the space of a heartbeat.

I clenched my fists, willing my body to remember what my brain already knew: she was a client. A job. Off-limits in every possible way. Still, when she finally walked past me, the brush of her arm against mine lingered like fire. And I hated myself for wanting to feel it again. I closed my eyes briefly, willing the forbidden away. It had to be that damned song, sanding me raw, bringing back too many memories and feelings. This wasn't me.

I hauled myself up onto the rigging, boots clanging against the metal. I crouched low, running a hand along the jagged edge of the bracket. My fingers brushed something smooth, too smooth. I turned on my phone's flashlight and angled it in close. The cut was sharp. Straight through the steel, no fray, no fatigue. It hadn't failed. It had been sawed. Deliberate. Precise. Someone had turned the spotlight into a weapon and aimed it squarely at Isla.

My stomach dropped, the taste of copper rising in my mouth. This was attempted murder, clean as a sniper's shot. I shoved the flashlight off, jaw clamped so hard it hurt. Down below, everyone was milling, trying to clean up the mess. They had no clue someone had tried to engineer Isla's death one careful cut at a time. I rose to my feet, pulse steady but rage burning hotter than it had in years. Whoever did this wanted a war? They just got one.

Sleep wasn't an option. I prowled Isla's property like I was back on patrol, senses keyed sharp enough to cut. Every creak of the trees, every hum of the security system, every shadow moving across the hedges put me on edge. The rig hadn't just "fallen." Somebody wanted her dead. And until I found who, she was my responsibility twenty-four seven.

That should have been the end of it. Duty, orders, protect the asset. But her face kept flashing in my head. The moment I had her pressed against the wall, her breath against my throat, the raw shock and heat in her eyes. I told myself I'd pulled back in time. That restraint still meant something. But truth was, the line between protecting her and wanting her blurred the second she looked at me like that.

My mind kept circling back to rehearsal, to the moment her voice carried that damn song through the cavernous hall. My sister's song. The one she used to play on repeat, curled on the couch, headphones too big for her face. Hearing it again, sung by Isla Dove under glittering lights, had punched the air right out of my lungs. I'd buried those memories deep, and now Isla's voice had dragged them to the surface, raw and bleeding.

As I rounded the back garden, a faint sound drifted from the open window above. Soft, unguarded. She was humming the same melody. No crowd. No bow. Just Isla, quiet and off-key in a way the world would never hear.

I stopped in the shadows, listening like a sinner. Her voice wrapped around grief and temptation both, threading them tighter until I couldn't breathe. My chest ached with memories I shouldn't resurrect and desires I couldn't allow. For one selfish moment, I wanted to walk upstairs, push open her door, and tell her what that song meant to me. Tell her what *she* was starting to mean to me.

Instead, I turned away, jaw locked, hands fisted. She didn't know she was haunting me with every note. Didn't know I was already losing the line between protecting her and wanting her.

Upstairs, her bedroom light glowed faint through the curtains. She was awake too. I could picture her pacing, maybe twisting that ridiculous bow in her hands. I told myself not to imagine more. Not to wonder if she was thinking about the way my body had caged hers. Not to think of her soft curves, her lips parted like she'd almost wanted me to close that distance.

I clenched my jaw until my teeth ached. Sierra Bravo trusted me to keep her breathing, not to get tangled in feelings I had no business touching. But when her light finally went dark, I didn't feel relief. I felt restless. Hungry. Haunted by the thought that maybe she wasn't sleeping at all. Maybe she was lying there, tangled in silk sheets, thinking about me the way I couldn't stop thinking about her.

And God help me, I wanted it to be true.

Chapter 5
Cowboy Rules, LA Problems

B y the time dawn hit the mansion, I'd already walked the grounds enough to know every inch, checked every lock, and reset the alarm system codes myself. The breach at rehearsal had been too clean, too close. Whoever was after Isla wasn't just bold. They were calculated. And if I didn't tighten control, she'd be in the ground before her upcoming concert.

I called her down to the kitchen. She shuffled in wearing satin shorts and a hoodie, hair piled in a messy bun, looking more like a stubborn college kid than a global superstar. She yawned and reached for the espresso machine, not a care in the world. My jaw tightened. I was about to ruin her morning. I laid it out plain: curfews, locked windows, no late-night wandering, and no public appearances unless I cleared them. My voice stayed calm, but steel underlined every word.

She froze mid-sip, then gave me a slow, disbelieving look over the rim of her mug. "You're joking."

"No. I'm keeping you alive."

"And who gave you that job, cowboy?"

"Listen. Our meeting was no accident. Your record company hired the outfit where I work. I was sent to protect you and find out who's behind the threats."

"I have bodyguards." She said uncertainly.

"Not like us from Sierra Bravo Security." I said firmly. "We don't lose clients. Ever."

Her laugh was sharp, almost musical. "So, you keep me alive, sure. But at what cost? You think locking me in a cage is living?" She waved a manicured hand toward the glass walls of the mansion, sunlight blazing off the Beverly Hills beyond. "This is my home, not your ... barracks."

I didn't flinch. I'd heard much worse from soldiers who hated the rules but loved walking away alive. "Better a gilded cage than a grave."

Her eyes narrowed. Fire sparked in those green depths. She hated the restrictions, hated me for laying them down, but beneath her defiance, I saw a flicker of fear she couldn't quite hide. That fear was all the permission I needed. She could rage all she wanted. I'd be the bastard prison guard if that's what it took to keep her breathing.

I forced Isla out to the backyard just after breakfast. The pool glittered under perfect LA sunshine, but I wasn't interested in her view or a swim. I wanted a clear patch of grass to drive my point home. She padded out behind me, still sulking, hair loose now, oversized sunglasses sliding down her nose. When she saw the rolled-up mats I'd pulled from my SUV, she groaned like I'd announced a root canal.

"You can't be serious," she said, arms crossed. "What is this, Cowboy Boot Camp?"

I didn't answer. I kicked my boots off, squared my stance, and gestured. "On the mat. Now."

She stomped forward in her ridiculous sparkly clogs, muttering under her breath. The moment she tried to mimic my stance, she wobbled. I shook my head. "Those shoes will get you killed."

"They're part of my brand," she shot back, chin tilting defiantly.

"Your brand won't matter if you can't run when someone's chasing you."

Her eyes flashed. "Ran just fine after my purse, didn't I? My brand pays for this house. And for you."

I didn't flinch. Instead, I moved in fast, taking her wrist and twisting her arm behind her back before she had time to squeal. Not enough to hurt, just enough to prove how easy it was to subdue her before she had time to get away.

She gasped, stumbling against my chest, hair brushing my jaw. Her pulse hammered against my fingers. For a moment, I felt the heat of her body pressed flush to mine, her breath shuddering out like I'd stolen it.

I released her too quickly, stepping back to put some needed space between us. "Lesson one," I said, voice rough. "Your enemy doesn't care about your brand. And neither do I."

Her cheeks flamed, but she didn't argue. Not with words. Just with the sharp, dangerous spark in her eyes. But she took me seriously and I taught her a few basic moves to break out of holds. I had no intention of her ever being far from my sight, but if she had the wit to struggle it might give me the edge to get to her in time to keep her alive. And with the fire in her eyes, it seemed like she had that will to fight back. She wasn't some damsel in distress about to faint waiting for a rescue. It gave me reason to catch a half breath of relief.

By mid-afternoon, I'd settled into my post at the front door, coffee in hand, eyes scanning the driveway like a hawk. Isla had been sulking upstairs since our little backyard lesson, slamming doors and blasting music loud enough to rattle the windows. I figured she'd wear herself out. I was wrong.

Isla floated down the stairs in a glittery miniskirt, curled hair, bow perched on her head like a crown, sparkly clogs. The full pop princess regalia.

"Going somewhere?" I asked, low.

Having not seen me, she jumped, then plastered on a smile that didn't reach her eyes. "Extra rehearsal. Richard texted. Getting ready for the big night."

I shifted, pulling out my keys. "Let's go."

Her lips parted, outrage sparking. "You're driving?"

"Or you don't go."

Her eyes narrowed, and for a second, she looked less like a pop star and more like a fighter sizing me up. She tried to sidestep. I shifted with her. She tried again the other way. Same result. The bow on her head trembled with the force of her huff.

"You're impossible," she snapped.

I leaned down just enough for her to hear me over the thump of her music still echoing upstairs. "Good. Stay angry. That means you're alive."

Her eyes flashed, green fire locked on mine, but there was no comeback this time. Just a sharp toss of her curls and a muttered, "I hate you."

The words shouldn't have stung, but they did. I swallowed it down, standing my ground. Better she hated me than for me to watch her end up on a slab because I didn't push hard enough. She got in my SUV but stayed silent the whole trip to the venue.

After Isla stomped to her dressing room, I finally got a little breathing room to do what else Sierra Bravo actually sent me here to do: dig. Richard had the cast spread out across half a dozen rehearsal rooms, but I started with the one that mattered: the backstage wing where the rigging had "accidentally" failed.

The air stank of sweat, hair spray, and burnt coffee. Crew hustled with cables, dancers practiced in clusters, but I had one person in mind. Jenna Marks. Ex–backup singer, now guitarist, sharp as glass, with eyes that never quite stopped cutting.

I found her leaning against a prop case, scrolling her phone like the world owed her a headline and it was in there somewhere. She looked up, expression twisting the second she saw me.

"The cowboy who saved Isla's purse," she drawled. "Shouldn't you be off polishing your spurs?"

I ignored her. "Where were you when that lighting rig went down?"

Her lips curved in a smirk that didn't reach her eyes. "Unlike some people, I was actually working. Playing guitar. You know, talent?"

I studied her, sweat slick on her collarbone, jaw tight, pupils sharp. Not guilt, exactly, but resentment. Maybe a woman simmering from years of being shoved into the background.

"You jealous of her?" I asked flatly.

Her smile cracked, replaced by almost a snarl. "Isla Dove is cheap bubblegum wrapped in glitter. I've got more voice in my pinkie finger. But no one cares when she bats her lashes and plays the virgin act."

I didn't blink. "Jealousy get you to saw bolts."

Her eyes flicked away, just for a second. That was enough. She had a chip on her shoulder big enough to sink a ship, but whether she wielded the saw herself or just wanted us to believe she had, that was the real question.

I didn't take Jenna's word for anything. People like her survived by spitting venom, hoping no one looked close enough to see the rot underneath. So, while she strutted back toward the stage, I ducked into the dressing room the band had been using.

The space reeked of different colognes and stale fast food. Sequined jackets and cheap jewelry were strewn across the counters, abandoned with extra drum sticks and guitar picks. But it was the trash can that caught my eye. It was overflowing with makeup wipes, crumpled notes, and torn sheet music. I pulled on gloves and started digging.

Halfway down, I found it. A glossy eight-by-ten of Isla, folded twice. It had been defaced. A thick red marker had been used to draw a bullseye across her face. Multiple circles tightened around Isla's green eyes until the paper had nearly torn. My gut went cold. This wasn't some random scribble. This was ritualistic. Maybe target practice.

I shoved the photo into an evidence pouch and kept digging, adrenaline sharpening every sense. More scraps, torn lyric sheets with Isla's name underlined in angry slashes. And on the mirror, faint but visible when I angled my flashlight, a smear of lipstick. Words were scrawled then wiped half away: *She's not forever.*

My jaw clenched so tight it hurt.

Either Jenna had crossed the line from bitter to dangerous, she was seriously mental, or someone wanted me to believe she was. Any option spelled trouble. In any case, even if she didn't commit any acts, she could be manipulated. I doubted anyone else in the band was responsible.

I straightened, scanning the room. My reflection in the mirror looked like a stranger, jaw hard, eyes burning. Protecting Isla wasn't just about blocking bullets or locking doors. I had to find who was after her. Someone in her world wanted her destroyed, and they were bold enough to leave messages in plain sight.

By the time I left Jenna's dressing room, my pulse hadn't slowed. That photo burned a hole in my pocket; the bullseye etched into my brain. I wanted to confront her right then, drag her under a spotlight until she broke. But instinct told me to wait. Predators made mistakes when you let them think you were blind.

So, I stuck closer to Isla than ever.

As rehearsal began, the pop spectacle train roared on as if the spotlight was merely a minor accident: dancers spinning, singers crooning, Isla twirling under lights that could kill her if someone so much as loosened a bolt. I had already walked the rigging and tugged at everything up there to make sure the bolts were tight. Then I kept to the wings, scanning every corner, hand never far from the Glock now closer at my side.

Isla noticed. Of course she did. She always noticed me, even when she pretended not to. Between songs she tossed a sarcastic glance my way, rolling her eyes like my scowl might ruin the boyfriend fantasy they were spinning.

"Sheriff," she mouthed with mock irritation, but her hand trembled at the next gesture. The gesture was small, quick. It was something the cameras missed. Not me.

I hated it. Hated how she wore glitter and bows like armor while fear leaked out through her fingers. Hated that her manager brushed it off as nerves.

I wasn't paid to care about her feelings, only her safety, but every time her eyes darted toward me, seeking reassurance she'd never admit to, I felt the line between us blur a little more.

So, I stood there, silent and immovable, a shadow at her back. I let her throw her little barbs, because if she was looking at me, she wasn't looking at the threats circling her. And if the stalkers were watching tonight, I wanted them to know she wasn't alone anymore.

Back at the mansion, the place felt too still, too polished. The security team Richard hired shuffled around like actors, more interested in looking important than doing the job. I didn't trust them. Hell, I didn't trust anyone but me.

So, I planted myself outside Isla's bedroom door, chair tipped against the wall, Glock resting on my thigh. I told myself it was protocol, that I was covering the weakest spot in the house. But the truth? I couldn't make myself walk away. Not after seeing her hand shake. Not after finding that bullseye photo in Jenna's trash.

Through the door, faint music bled out. Her voice floating over canned backing tracks. She sang the same bubblegum ballad the label had milked for years. Hearing it now made my chest clench, sharp as a shrapnel wound. I closed my eyes, swallowing it down. The past had no place here. Isla had enough ghosts without me dragging mine into the house.

Midnight ticked past. The music cut off. I heard movement, soft footsteps, a drawer sliding shut. Then silence. For a heartbeat, I imagined her curled just feet away, neon curls spilled across pillows, chest rising slow in sleep. I shoved the image back where it belonged. She wasn't mine to picture.

But the vow that burned in me wasn't professional anymore. It wasn't Sierra Bravo orders or a signed contract. It was personal. Whoever was hunting her had already stepped too close.

The hours crawled. My body knew exhaustion, but my mind stayed sharp, every creak of the mansion pulling me tighter. Around two a.m., the phone in my lap buzzed. No alerts from Sierra Bravo. No message from the security feed. Just an unknown number.

I thumbed it open.

The video started grainy, shaky, a shot apparently through glass. My gut clenched even before my brain caught up. Isla's bedroom. Her, curled on her side, one hand tucked beneath her cheek, breathing soft and even. Vulnerable. Oblivious.

I sat up so fast, the chair back smacked the wall.

The camera angle shifted, creeping closer like someone pressed it against the glass. For a second the lens lingered on her lips, parted in sleep. Then her curls. Then it tracked lower, down the slope of her body.

Rage detonated in my chest.

The video ended with the whisper of a laugh, distorted and low, before the screen went black.

I was already on my feet, gun in hand, storming down the hall toward the window in the hall. Curtains swayed faintly, the glass cool under my palm, but the night beyond was empty. Whoever had filmed her was gone, too quick, too careful.

Behind the door, I heard Isla stir, a muffled sigh reaching me through the wood. She had no idea how close danger had pressed. How far inside her life it had crawled.

My jaw locked, pulse hammering. This wasn't just a stalker with an obsession anymore. This was someone who wanted her terrified, violated, broken down piece by piece. And they were purposefully taunting me.

I sent the video to Sierra Bravo for analysis and to see if they could find out how someone had gotten my number.

I slid back into the chair, weapon steady, fury coiled tight in my chest. I was already cataloging what new security I would be installing come dawn: motion sensors, cameras, infrared alarms. Whoever crossed those boundaries next wouldn't be leaving upright.

And if they came through this hallway, they wouldn't walk out again.

Chapter 6
Forced
Handholding

I hated being paraded like a prize pony, but Richard insisted. He'd be right there in my earpiece if I needed him. Cameras were already waiting outside, and the only way to quiet the tabloids was to give them what they wanted: Isla Dove, pop princess, holding hands with her new cowboy boyfriend. My stomach churned at the thought.

Jake stood beside me in the green room, immovable in his boots and Stetson, radiating irritation and disapproval like a thundercloud. When Richard snapped at us to look "couple-like," Jake's large hand closed over mine before I could protest. His palm was rough, calloused, warm. I felt pinned in place by that grip, like he was branding me with possession.

I yanked against him once, testing him. He didn't even flinch. "You're choking me," I muttered, though my pulse betrayed me with its traitorous leap.

"Better choked than dragged off," he said without looking at me, voice low and hard.

I should have been furious. And I was. But a ripple of something hotter ran under the anger. I felt ... safe. It was sharp and unwanted.

The worst part was how my chest fluttered against my will, how my body responded as if it hadn't gotten the memo that this was all fake.

Richard beamed, oblivious to the battle raging between me and Jake. "Perfect," he chirped, ushering us toward the doors.

I plastered on my practiced smile, neon curls bouncing as I leaned into Jake's iron grip. The paparazzi roar from the audience hit like a wave, cameras flashing, voices shouting our names. My lips curled higher, my eyes sparkled, every move rehearsed. But under the lights, with Jake's hand anchoring mine, it felt less like a performance and more like a trap I couldn't escape.

The flashes were blinding, each snap like a firecracker against my nerves. Reporters shouted questions from behind the barricades, hungry for sound bites, for scandal, for any crack in the perfect façade. I tilted my head just right, giggled on cue, twirled a lock of my neon-streaked curls. Isla Dove, Forever Innocent™, always. But Jake? He didn't play the game.

He stood at my side, tall and immovable, his eyes watching the crowd like a Secret Service agent, no expression at all on his face. His hand never loosened around mine, steady as an anchor, but his body radiated disapproval. He wasn't smiling, wasn't pretending, wasn't feeding the beast.

"Smile, cowboy," I whispered through my glossy grin, lips barely moving. "The world's watching."

"Not here to smile," he muttered back, voice low enough only I heard. His hazel eyes never stopped sweeping the crowd, sharp and predatory, as though he was searching for threats while I looked for camera angles.

I turned toward him, lashes fluttering, my glitter mask firmly in place. "What's wrong, too country to fake it?"

He angled closer, his breath brushing my ear, sending a shiver I refused to acknowledge. "You sure you want to provoke me, princess?"

The word hit like a spark. I nearly tripped on my platform heels, covering the stumble with a flirty laugh. To the cameras, it looked like part of the act, me teasing my new boyfriend, him scowling like the stoic cowboy foil. They loved it.

Once indoors, my cheeks burned hotter than the lights. I hated that he could get to me with one word, one growl. Hated that my pulse leapt just from the rough scrape of his voice. I was supposed to be in control. But standing next to Jake Dalton, I wasn't sure who was handling whom.

Fans screamed from behind the ropes, some holding up handmade signs with glitter hearts and my name scrawled across them. We were a perfect pair of opposites: me in my ridiculous schoolgirl skirt and platform clogs, Jake looming behind me like some kind of old time outlaw dropped into Hollywood. We were straight out of a rom-com poster, and the paparazzi snapped away as if they'd struck gold.

"Give us a kiss!" one reporter yelled.

"Cowboy, smile for the camera!" another shouted, laughing.

"Still Innocent, Isla?"

Jake didn't move. His jaw stayed tight, shoulders squared, eyes on the crowd as if he were cataloging them for later. The more stone-faced he got, the louder the crowd squealed. They adored his silence, his cowboy scowl. It was meme-fodder in the making.

I forced a bubbly laugh, tossing my curls and tugging at his flannel sleeve for show. To anyone watching, it looked like I was the sunshine trying to melt his grumpy exterior. Inside, though? My pulse jumped for reasons I didn't dare admit.

His hand on mine never faltered. Warm. Firm. Protective in a way I didn't ask for but couldn't ignore. Every time his thumb shifted, just slightly, it grounded me, and I had to remind myself this was fake. All of it was fake. Just like me.

And yet, when the flashbulbs strobed and the shouts blurred together, I realized my smile had slipped into something softer, something real. For half a heartbeat, I wasn't posing for the cameras. I was leaning into the man beside me. I knew if there was a threat in that gaggle, he'd see it. He'd know what to do. I'd get yanked to safety in less than a blink. The idea of feeling that way terrified me more than any stalker. Because pretending was safe. But whatever I felt with Jake Dalton's hand wrapped around mine? That was dangerous. It wouldn't last.

The moment we slipped backstage between groups; I exhaled like I'd been holding my breath the whole time. My cheeks ached from smiling. My hand still tingled from where his had gripped it too tightly, too steady, like he owned it.

"You don't get to manhandle me like that," I said, spinning to face him.

Jake leaned against the wall, arms crossed, the picture of infuriating calm. I could see his eyes raking over me, cataloguing every weakness. "If I hadn't, you'd have been eaten alive out there," he replied, voice flat as a blade.

Heat crawled up my throat. "I've been doing this for years. I know how to survive a bunch of reporters and fans without your cowboy routine."

His mouth twitched, almost a smile, though it looked more like a warning. "Barely surviving isn't the same as staying safe."

The words struck deeper than I wanted to admit. I hated that my chest tightened instead of puffing up with defiance. I hated that some part of me wanted his hand back in mine, steadying me against the chaos of my life.

I tore my gaze away, desperate to reclaim control. "You're impossible," I muttered, grabbing a water bottle from the table. My reflection in the mirror showed a bow perched perfectly in my curls. It looked ridiculous now, like a child's costume instead of my brand.

Jake's voice dropped low, almost a growl. "Get used to it. I'm not here to please you, Isla. I'm here to keep you alive."

The room felt suddenly too small, his presence crowding every corner. I lifted my chin, pretending his words didn't dig under my skin. Pretending I wasn't rattled he'd called me by my name instead of princess. Because if he ever realized how much power he had over me already, I'd be completely undone.

Back on the carpet, the crowd pulsed like a living thing, shouting, reaching, pressing close. Flashes burned white spots into my eyes until the scene looked like a dreamscape. Jake stayed welded to my side, his hand firm around mine, his gaze warning back the crush. I should have hated it. I should have pushed him off or stepped to one side. Instead, my body betrayed me, holding onto the heat of his palm like it belonged there.

Then I saw him.

Brian. *The* fan. His face rose above the mob, pale and wide-eyed, a homemade sign clutched to his chest. Glitter hearts framed shaky block letters: *FOREVER INNOCENT.* His lips moved, forming the lyrics of the ballad, *I'll Stand Tomorrow,* that had made me a brand instead of a person. My stomach pitched.

The cameras and questions blurred to static. All I saw was Brian's unblinking stare. It wasn't devotion. It was primal ownership.

Jake noticed my flinch. His hand tightened slightly, protective, grounding. His eyes cut toward Brian, narrowing like a predator scenting fresh meat. That look steadied me, even as my knees wobbled.

Reporters screamed for sound bites, their words dissolving into white noise. A woman shoved a microphone in my face: "How does it feel, Isla, being America's virgin sweetheart?"

My throat closed. I pasted on my smile anyway, every muscle trembling with the effort. I tilted my head toward Jake, pretending to laugh at something he said, though my ears were ringing too loud to hear anything. The mob ate it up, flashes exploding harder. To them, it was cute banter. To me, it was survival, clinging to the cowboy shadow at my side while a stranger's obsession cut me open from across the crowd. And for the first time, I wondered if the mask I wore to keep me safe had turned into the very thing that would kill me.

The crowd's roar swelled, a storm I couldn't push back. My fake laugh faltered, my cheeks aching from the smile that wasn't real. I could still feel Brian's eyes boring into me, even though security had started to nudge him deeper into the sea of fans. His sign bobbed above the heads, the glitter catching light like broken glass. *Forever Innocent.* It made me want to scream.

Jake shifted his fingers around mine. Not showy. Not for the cameras. A grounding squeeze, subtle and deliberate. My lungs loosened as if he had reached inside me and turned a valve, I couldn't find myself.

"Eyes on me," he murmured, pitched low enough that only I heard. His hazel gaze cut through the chaos, sharp and steady. The noise faded for a moment, leaving just the two of us tethered in the glare of paparazzi strobes.

I should have pulled away. I should have reminded him and myself that this was fake. That he was paid to stand there. But instead, I let my fingers curl against his palm, greedy for the heat and steadiness that had nothing to do with the cameras. The illusion cracked when a reporter shouted a question about my upcoming CD. My smile slid back into place, too stiff, too bright. Jake didn't move, didn't soften. His glare swept the mob with a soldier's suspicion.

It struck me then. He wasn't just humoring the PR stunt. He wasn't here for show. Every muscle in his body was locked in defense, as if he'd take a bullet before he let me slip away into the chaos. For one dangerous heartbeat, I believed him. And I realized I wanted to.

Then my earpiece hissed.

At first, I thought it was just feedback, static from the sound crew. I lifted my chin, pretending I hadn't heard, and prepared to answer another question. But then a voice slithered through, distorted and low, crawling straight down my spine.

"Sing for me... or bleed."

The words hollowed me out. My knees nearly buckled, my breath locking in my chest. I clutched Jake's hand so hard my nails dug into his skin.

"What?" a reporter barked, mistaking my shock for hesitation. The crowd leaned closer, hungry for a headline. I swallowed hard, forcing out some glittery standard nothing about my CD. They ate it up like candy.

But Jake's eyes snapped to mine, sharp as a blade. He knew. He always knew.

The voice chuckled in my ear, a sound like glass cracking. *"Don't test me, princess. I'm closer than you think."*

I ripped the earpiece out, my hand shaking. The world tilted, lights and cameras and glitter signs smearing into one dizzying blur. I pasted on another grin, praying no one saw how close I was to crumbling. Except Jake. His body angled toward mine, his lips brushing my ear without ever moving his mouth for the cameras.

"What happened?" he asked, gravel low and steady.

My throat worked, but no words came. Because if I said it out loud, it would be real. And real meant someone wasn't just watching anymore. They were too close, in my head.

Jake's grip shifted, his thumb brushing over my knuckles as if he could steady the earthquake in my chest. I kept my smile plastered on for the flashing cameras, but inside I was shaking apart.

"Tell me," He murmured, so low only I could hear. His hazel eyes pinned me, unrelenting. There was no glitter, no bow, no pop-princess mask strong enough to hide from that stare.

"I..." My voice snagged. If I said the words, if I gave the terror shape, it would mean admitting the stalker wasn't just a shadow outside my world. They were here, inside, hijacking the very tools of my career. My pulse hammered so loud it drowned out the crowd.

Reporters shouted questions. Fans squealed. Phones tilted at every angle, capturing my forced smile. On the surface, I was Isla Dove, darling of pop purity. But my fingernails dug crescents into Jake's skin, and he didn't flinch.

Instead, he tightened his hold, pulling me an inch closer. The move looked loving, protective for the cameras. In truth, it was a vow. His body radiated heat, promise, steel.

"Whoever it is," he said, voice still low, "they just made the biggest mistake of their life."

The words should have comforted me, but instead they made the fear sharper and too real. Because the voice in my ear had sounded so close, so intimate, I could almost feel their breath.

I forced another smile, teeth aching, and leaned into Jake's arm so it looked like affection when the reality was it was all that was keeping me upright. My heart rattled against my ribs, my stomach flipped with dread. Jake was right beside me, strong and immovable. And yet for the first time I knew the truth.

The stalker wasn't circling anymore. They had a voice, and they were inside my skin.

Chapter 7
Shaking Off the Threat

B ack at the mansion, I cornered Isla in the entryway before she could scurry upstairs. She had her arms folded tight, chin up like she was ready for a fight, but her hands gave her away. They trembled, faint but steady enough that my stomach knotted. She could bluff the cameras, the fans, even her own damn manager. Not me.

"Tell me what happened in that earpiece," I said, my voice low. I stepped close leaving no room for evasion.

She flicked her hair over one shoulder, trying for sass, but her eyes betrayed her. "It was nothing. Some interference. Static."

"Bull." I stepped even closer, crowding her space until she had to tip her head back to meet my eyes. "Static doesn't say bleed." Because I had heard that word.

Her jaw tightened. For a second, I thought she'd snap back with some sharp-tongued retort. Instead, she looked away, shoulders sagging. "I don't want to make it real," she whispered.

The words hit me hard. She wasn't just scared. She was fighting to stay upright in a world that saw her as glitter and bows and perfect. Pretend long enough, and maybe you start to believe the mask too.

But the cracks were showing. You can't keep it up when people were literally whispering threats in your ear.

I wanted to reach for her, steady her, but I gripped the doorframe instead. "It's real," I told her. "And ignoring it won't keep you safe. Let me do my job."

Her eyes snapped back to mine then, green fire under glassy fear. "And what if your job ruins my life?"

Too late, I thought. It wasn't me. Whoever was out there had already done that. I swallowed the truth and gave her the only thing I could. "If it comes down to it, I'll give up my life before I let them take yours."

She froze. No quip. No smile. Just silence thick with all the things neither of us dared say. And then she whispered the words to me in a rush with large, frightened eyes.

"Sing for me... or bleed.

Don't test me, princess. I'm closer than you think."

"I will find this creep and make them regret every word." I promised.

What I wanted to say was decidedly more suited to an Army barracks, but she understood my intent. It sounded like her stalker was a deranged fan or focused on her upcoming concert. Without more research it was hard to know. They had the tech know-how to break into her earpiece frequency. That was another piece of the puzzle.

Isla took herself upstairs to blast music. I was getting the impression the decibels were her way of blocking off the outside world. I holed up in the mansion's security room with a laptop balanced on my knee, footage looping across the monitors.

I rewound the press event again. Isla, all glitter-bow perfection, smiling like nothing could touch her. Except I knew better. I had been well aware of how she gripped my hand in desperation and after the earpiece message had leaned into me. I slowed the frame as the crowd pressed close, scanning faces. Jenna hovered in front near the restricted zone, eyes sharp, smirk curling like she was enjoying the chaos or knew what was going to happen. Richard was nowhere in sight, vanishing just before Isla's earpiece spat its toxic message. And Brian, that super fan, stared straight into the camera with that unsettling devotion, lips moving like he was praying to her or singing one of her songs only he could hear.

Every path looked suspicious, every shadow sharpened my instincts. I replayed the moment Isla faltered onstage during the rehearsal, her voice catching, eyes searching. I remembered what I'd told her: breathe, eyes on me. She steadied then, pretending to glare but finding her rhythm again. My chest tightened. She thought it was just reassurance. For me, it was proof: even wrapped in bows and neon lies, she trusted me to hold her steady.

I went slowly through another angle, fingers tight on the mouse. The threats weren't random. They mirrored her schedule, her songs, the brand that painted her as "Forever Innocent." Whoever was behind this wasn't just watching. They were using her image like bait and the songs could be a cue. I just couldn't decipher the code yet.

The bile in my throat tasted like war. Richard's debts, Jenna's jealousy, Brian's obsession. It could be any of them. Or all of them. But until I nailed it down, Isla was still the bullseye.

By the time I left the security room, I'd already mapped out the next steps. Isla was curled on the couch in her glitter heels, scrolling through her phone like nothing had happened. But I'd seen the tremor in her hands earlier, the way her voice cracked when that earpiece spat poison. She wasn't fooling me.

"We're tightening things up," I said flatly. "From now on, you don't take calls alone. No wandering the house without me. No late-night rehearsals unless I clear the staff first."

Her head snapped up, green eyes flashing. "You're joking. You can't seriously think I'm going to live like a prisoner in my own home."

"It's not a home; it's a target," I shot back. "You want to keep breathing? You follow my rules."

She pushed to her feet, chin high, curls bouncing like she was stepping onto a stage. "You think barking orders makes you in charge of me? Newsflash, cowboy—you work for me."

Her defiance hit like a gut punch, mostly because it stoked something I shouldn't have felt. Fire. Life. The spark that made her more dangerous to me than any stalker.

I stepped closer, close enough to catch her perfume under the glitter. "I work for Sierra Bravo," I corrected, voice low. "Which means I work for your survival. Hate me all you want, princess. I'd rather see you angry than dead."

For a heartbeat, neither of us moved. Her chest rose and fell, rapid, furious. Mine felt like a loaded gun ready to go off. Then she spun away with a sharp laugh, pretending she didn't care. But I'd seen the crack, the fear under the fight. She could scream all she wanted about freedom. I wasn't giving her an inch.

The next night, rehearsal was supposed to be routine. Supposed to be safe. I'd walked the perimeter twice before we even set foot inside, checked IDs, confirmed crew logs. Still, my gut itched the second Isla stepped onto the stage.

She shimmered under the lights, bow perched on her head, sequins catching every spotlight. It wasn't a dress rehearsal. This was just how

Isla showed up. To the crowd of staff and dancers, she was a star. To me, she was a neon target begging for a bullet.

From the wings, I scanned every face. A grip lingering too long near the lighting board. A backup dancer whispering, eyes darting toward Isla. Even the sound tech overhead, hands fidgeting at the console. Too many people, too many moving parts. And over it all, the steady thrum in my chest that told me someone was watching her with intent.

I shifted closer to the stage, hand brushing the grip of my concealed weapon. The music thundered, dancers twirled, Isla belted out bubblegum lyrics. But my eyes weren't on the show. They were on the shadows beyond the stage lights, where the air seemed heavier, wrong.

Something scraped above, too faint to make out but too loud for the music to mask completely. My head jerked up, tracking the catwalks. Nothing but silhouettes against steel beams. Still, the hair on my neck rose.

Her voice cracked on a high note. Just a stumble, nothing that the casual ear would notice, but I'd been studying her rhythms long enough to catch it. Isla's shoulders stiffened, bow wobbling as she faltered. The dancers glanced around, irritated, but I knew the truth. It wasn't fatigue. It was fear.

The music ended. Crew applause filled the hall. And all I could think about was how her strength was tangled up in me and how that tether could get us both killed.

The moment rehearsal wrapped, Richard shoved her toward the back exit like she was late for another show. I caught the flicker of annoyance in her eyes, but before she could voice it, the double doors flew open. A swarm of paparazzi poured through, shouting her name, cameras flashing like lightning. I swore. No one had cleared this with me.

I jumped in front, shoulder braced, carving a path with my body. Isla tried to hold her practiced smile, but the edges cracked. The crowd pressed closer, voices sharp, questions seeming ugly. My hand lifted instinctively, a barrier against the sea of hands and lenses.

Then I felt it, her grip latching onto my arm. Not dainty. Not staged. Desperate. Her nails bit through my sleeve, and for the first time tonight, she wasn't the pop princess smiling on command. She was just a woman, frightened and clinging to the only thing between her and chaos.

I should have shaken her loose, reminded her this was an act, that none of it meant anything outside the assignment. But I didn't. I kept moving, forcing a path through to the SUV, letting her fingers stay tangled in my shirt. Her head pressed close to my shoulder, her perfume ghosting through the acrid sweat and camera flashes.

She whispered it then, so low I almost missed it. "I hate needing you."

The words should've been a slap. Instead, they cut deeper. Because no matter how much anger she tried to lace into that admission, she didn't let go. Not until I had her inside, the doors slammed, the roar of the crowd muffled to a distant storm.

Her hand slid away then, leaving my arm cold. But the imprint of her touch burned like a brand I couldn't scrub off.

The ride back was quiet, too quiet. Isla always played music but not now. Isla sat angled toward the window, neon curls brushing her cheek, her phone limp in her lap. She didn't say a word, but I could feel the tension rolling off her like static. My own pulse hadn't slowed. I kept replaying her grip on my arm, the whisper she thought I'd forget. *I hate needing you.* She might hate it, but the truth was, she did.

When we pulled into her driveway, every instinct in me went sharp. The house looked normal from the outside, gates closed, lights glowing soft in the windows. But normal was a lie I never trusted.

I stepped out first, scanning the hedges, the roofline, the shadows. My boots crunched against the stone walk as I circled to the front door. That's when I saw it.

A sheet of paper, taped dead center on the polished wood. My jaw tightened as I peeled it free. The handwriting was jagged, pressed hard enough to tear the page in spots.

She's safer with me.

I stood there, knuckles whitening, the note trembling just once in my grip before I shoved it into my jacket. A message left at her front door meant someone had walked right up to her home, close enough to touch the walls.

Behind me, Isla's heels clicked as she joined me. "What is it?" Her voice was lighter than she meant it to be, false brightness cracking at the edges.

I turned, keeping my face stone-hard. "Nothing you need to see tonight."

But her eyes caught mine, wide and searching. She knew I was lying. Inside, my gut burned. The stalker wasn't circling anymore. He'd drawn blood without lifting a blade.

I walked her inside, every sense sharp, every muscle wired tight. Isla trailed behind me, silent, the click of her heels echoing through the wide, empty foyer. I locked the door, then the deadbolt, then the chain, then set the security system on. Still didn't feel like enough.

She lingered in the middle of the room, arms wrapped around herself, green eyes flicking to me. "You're not going to tell me, are you?" she asked softly.

I didn't answer. Couldn't. Not when the words on that paper were seared into my brain and aimed straight at me. *She's safer with me.*

I shoved the note deeper into my pocket and met her gaze. "Go upstairs. Rest. I'll be right here." My voice was calm, but inside I was fire and steel. She hesitated, searching me like she wanted to crack my armor. Then she nodded, slow, and slipped up the staircase.

I waited until she disappeared around the landing before pulling the note back out. My thumb dragged across the torn edge. The handwriting was erratic, desperate, but the message was clear. This wasn't a warning anymore. This was a claim. A flat out statement that I wasn't enough.

I crumpled the paper in my fist until it cut into my palm. Whoever wrote this had already walked too close, already gotten under her skin, already dared to believe she belonged to him. I'd scan the note and send it to Sierra Bravo for handwriting analysis, but I doubted they'd come up with anything.

I moved to the window, staring out at the night beyond the glass. My reflection glared back—cowboy hat, hard eyes, jaw clenched tight.

Whoever left that note and disabled the front camera just made this personal.

Chapter 8
Rebellion Brewing

I was sick of being handled. Sick of rules, drills, and Jake's constant shadow. I couldn't live under this constant threat shadow on top of the stress of the upcoming concert and tour. I needed a break. So, when morning sunlight spilled through the Beverly Hills windows, I took one look in the mirror at the dark circles under my eyes and decided enough was enough. I yanked on jeans, shoved my neon streaks under a hat, and left the glitter heels in the closet. No bow. No costume. Just me. Isla Donovan was making a prison break.

When I came downstairs, Jake was already waiting, arms crossed, boots planted wide. Always the sentinel. His hazel eyes narrowed as soon as he saw me. "Where are you going?"

"Out," I said, grabbing my sunglasses from the table. I didn't owe him more than that.

His jaw ticked. "Not without me."

"Fine," I shot back, smirking. "But you're coming on my turf this time."

The corner of his mouth twitched like he wanted to argue. Instead, he followed me out to the SUV, silent as ever, radiating disapproval. That was fine. I'd wipe it off his face soon enough.

The moment he realized where we were headed, his scowl deepened. The neon-green sign of *Leaf & Love Vegan Burgers* glowed cheerfully over the sidewalk. A chalkboard menu promised hemp milkshakes and beet sliders. Jake muttered something that sounded suspiciously like a prayer.

"Relax, cowboy," I teased, sliding out of the car. "It won't kill you to eat a plant once in your life."

He gave me a look that could've curdled soy milk and a two-word condemnation. "Rabbit food."

I laughed, the sound bubbling out more freely than it had in weeks. For once, I wasn't Isla Dove, Pop Princess. I was Isla Donovan, dragging a grumpy soldier into my favorite hole-in-the-wall diner, determined to prove I still had control over something in my life. And maybe, just maybe, to see if the cowboy still looked at me when the glitter was gone.

Jake sat across from me like he was bracing for combat, elbows on the table, shoulders tight. The laminated menu quivered in his big hands as his eyes scanned it like it was written in a foreign language. I bit my lip to keep from laughing.

"Chickpea sliders? Quinoa wrap?" His brows slammed together. "What the hell is a tempeh taco?"

I leaned back, enjoying every second. "Protein-packed soybeans fermented into a delicious, sustainable patty."

He lowered the menu, staring at me like I'd just threatened national security. "Princess, people ferment grapes. For wine. Not beans."

I grinned, victorious. "Relax. I ordered for both of us already. Two house special veggie burgers, one hemp shake, and kale fries. You're welcome."

His jaw clenched. "Isn't hemp marijuana?"

The waitress appeared, setting down two sweating mason jars filled with creamy green milkshakes. Jake eyed his like it might detonate. When he finally took a sip, his expression didn't change, but I caught the tiniest twitch at the corner of his mouth.

"It's not poison, right?" I teased.

He set the jar down carefully, like admitting anything would hand me the win. "Cold. Sweet. Strange."

I clapped my hands together. "Translation: you like it."

He glared, but the flush creeping up his neck betrayed him. For the first time since I met him, the impenetrable cowboy shield cracked, just a little. He was out of place, out of control, and it was glorious.

I leaned across the table, lowering my voice so only he could hear. "You can survive bullets and bombs, Private Dalton, but can you survive kale?"

His eyes narrowed, the muscle in his jaw ticking again. "It was Sargeant and we'll see."

And suddenly, lunch felt like a battle I desperately wanted to win.

The waitress reappeared, balancing two plates stacked with towering veggie burgers and a tray of sweet potato fries. Jake gave the burger a long, suspicious stare, like it might sprout legs and run off.

"Where's the beef?" he muttered.

"Buried under flavor," I shot back, taking a giant bite. The bun was warm, the patty smoky. I hummed exaggeratedly, just to needle him. "Mmm. Heavenly."

He rolled his eyes but finally lifted his burger. His hands dwarfed the bun, and when he bit in, juice dribbled down his wrist. He froze, clearly hating the mess. I nearly doubled over laughing.

"Don't tell me the big bad cowboy can't handle a veggie burger."

His glare should have singed me, but his ears were red. "It's... edible."

"Edible?" I snorted. "That's high praise coming from you."

He took another bite. Then another. By the time he set it down, the tiniest smile tugged at his mouth. My chest did a stupid flutter.

"Admit it," I teased, leaning across the sticky table. "It's not terrible."

He grunted, swallowing a bite with deliberate effort. "It's food. Suppose it beats a MRE." But the corner of his mouth twitched. Just a little. A victory.

The noise of the diner faded into a comfortable hum around our booth. The frantic energy of the week, the constant strain of being 'on' for the cameras, began to leach away, leaving me feeling soft and unguarded.

"Richard wants me to close the charity gala with "I'll Stand Tomorrow" next week," I found myself saying, tracing a pattern in the condensation on my glass. "The press loves it. That song... it's like my own personal brand of kryptonite."

Jake went very still. It was a different stillness than his usual alert vigilance. This was heavier, turned inward.

"That one of yours?" he asked, his voice low and gravelly.

"Yeah. The one that started it all. The big breakout ballad." I rolled my eyes, a practiced gesture of disdain. "The song that built the 'Forever Innocent' prison."

He was silent for a long moment, his gaze fixed on a point somewhere past my shoulder, seeing something I couldn't. "My sister," he said heavily, and the words seemed to cost him. "She loved that song. Played it on repeat. Drove me crazy with it."

My breath hitched. The air rushed out of the moment. My flippant words felt cheap and ugly now. I had no idea he had a sister, that someone real, not just an anonymous fan, loved that song. "Oh," was all I could manage.

"She's gone," he continued, the words flat, final. "Car accident. Almost ten years ago."

The confession hung between us, raw and devastating. This gruff, unbreakable cowboy had a crack in his armor, and it was shaped like a loss I couldn't even fathom. And my voice, my stupid, manufactured brand, was tangled up in his grief. That song had to be a fiery poker into his heart. And I had been singing it at every rehearsal. Shame washed over me, hot and immediate.

"Jake, I... I'm so sorry." I reached a hand across the table, stopping just short of touching his. "I didn't know."

He finally looked at me, and the pain in his hazel eyes was so stark it made my chest ache. "Why would you?"

The need to explain, to justify myself, to be seen as more than the product that had inadvertently hurt him, rose up in a sudden, uncontrollable wave.

"I wrote that song after... after a bad thing happened," I whispered, the words tumbling out before my internal censor could stop them. I stared at my half-eaten burger, unable to meet his gaze. "In high school. A guy... I wrote it because I felt broken. The full title is *I'll Stand Tomorrow-I Can't Today*. It's not meant as a song about a stupid teenage breakup. It was about not being able to face the day after what happened. And then Richard and the label, they took that feeling, that pain, and they... they packaged it into a pop anthem about losing love and teenagers rebelling against responsibility. They sold my trauma as a virtue. They built this 'virgin idol' brand on top of it, and now I'm trapped inside it. It's not innocence, Jake. It's a cage. It's a choice I made because I was scared, and now I can't get out."

I risked a glance at him. I expected pity, or worse, dismissal at thinking my song drama could compare to the loss of his sister. But his eyes held none of that. They were steady, clear, and focused entirely on me. He wasn't looking at Isla Dove, the pop princess. He was looking at Isla, the woman who was sharing a shattered piece of her soul.

He gave a slow, single nod. "They used you."

It wasn't a question. It was a statement of fact. And in those three words, I felt a validation I hadn't realized I'd been starving for.

"Yeah," I breathed, my shoulders slumping in relief. "They did."

The silence that fell between us then wasn't awkward or heavy. It was spacious. It was real. In the warm, greasy glow of the diner, surrounded by the clatter of plates and the murmur of other people's lives, I felt, for the first time in years, truly seen.

When the waitress returned, she carried two small mason jars layered with something decadent-looking, chocolate, whipped topping, and a cherry on top. Jake perked up. "Now that looks like dessert."

The waitress winked. "Sugar-free, gluten-free, vegan chocolate mousse."

Jake's smile died on the spot. "You're kidding."

I burst out laughing so hard the couple at the next table glanced over. "Don't worry," I gasped. "It won't kill you. At least not quickly."

He dipped his spoon in, tried it, then scowled. "Tastes like dirt pretending to be chocolate."

I licked mine clean off the spoon, slow and dramatic. "Tastes like victory to me."

For once, his laughter slipped free, low, rough, real. The sound shot through me, sparking in places I didn't want to acknowledge in public. And suddenly, this didn't feel like some battle anymore. It felt like a date between two real people.

By the time the mousse jars were scraped clean, Jake had quit glaring at the food and started studying me instead. Which, honestly, was progress.

"You enjoy making me look like an idiot, don't you?" he asked, leaning back in the booth. I could see the corners of his mouth fighting another smile.

"Not an idiot," I said, twirling my straw. "Just... adaptable."

"Pretty word for fool."

I tilted my head. "Maybe you needed to be knocked down a peg. You stomp around like the world owes you obedience."

That earned me a grunt. "And you flit around like nothing can touch you."

I hoped the words hit harder than he meant them to. It wasn't true. I felt everything. I stared into my glass, ice clinking. "That's the point. Nobody wants to see what's under the glitter."

He went still. For once, no comeback. Just silence, heavy and uncomfortable. I finally glanced up. His gaze had softened, stripped of its usual steel.

He shook his head. "My sister thought you were brave."

My eyes felt damp. Maybe his sister had listened to the words of my song. And for the first time in a very long time, I wished I was. The diner buzzed with clattering plates and low conversation, but I couldn't hear any of it. Only the echo of his words. His sister thought I was brave. If only she knew. If only he knew. I suddenly wanted to tell him the whole truth behind the song.

Then my phone buzzed on the table. The vibration broke the spell like a slap.

Jake pulled back first, all business again, scanning the screen like it might hold a bullet. I grabbed it before he could, hoping for a distraction. Something normal to reset my world. A rehearsal update, a text from my assistant Lily, even one of Richard's frantic reminders about hair or makeup.

Instead, the words flashing across my lock screen made my blood run cold.

Your home security has been disabled.

I stared at the notification, willing it to vanish. Maybe it was a glitch or a system update from some other time. But the timestamp said otherwise. Two minutes ago.

Jake saw my face pale and snatched the phone out of my hand. His eyes narrowed as he read the alert. He didn't swear, didn't shout. He just went very still and cold. Then he threw cash on the table and stood.

"Let's go," he said, already moving toward the door.

My chair screeched as I scrambled after him, stomach twisting. The warmth I'd felt only seconds ago vanished, replaced by a coil of fear. Jake pushed me into the passenger seat of the SUV, his movements sharp and fast, and the engine roared to life. His jaw was stone, his eyes scanning every car, every pedestrian like they were suspects. I clutched the phone in my lap, staring at the words again, my heart hammering. Someone had been inside my home. Inside my life. And Jake was driving like hell itself was already waiting there.

The city blurred by in streaks of neon and shadow, my seatbelt biting into my shoulder as Jake pushed the SUV harder than I thought possible. His hands gripped the wheel, knuckles white, every muscle taut with a focus that made my pulse trip faster than the speedometer climbing past eighty.

"Jake," I whispered, my throat raw. "What if they're still there?"

"They won't be when I'm done," he said, voice flat. It was the tone of a man who'd seen war, and suddenly I hated how much safer it made me feel.

I stared down at the glowing phone in my lap, that one line still burning across the screen: *Your home security has been disabled.* My house. My sanctuary. The place where I'd hidden jewelry in safes, sung lyrics into mirrors, dreamed in secret. Violated.

The thought of strangers in my room made bile rise in my throat. I wrapped my arms around myself, shivering, not from the air conditioning but from the invisible hands I swore I could feel rifling through my life.

Jake didn't look at me, but his voice cut through the silence like a knife. "Stay in the car when we get there. No arguments."

I wanted to argue. To remind him that I wasn't some medieval damsel in distress, that I'd chased down my own purse in a crowd full of cameras. But the words died. My lips parted, then closed again, because some part of me already knew the truth: I wasn't ready for whatever waited there.

The SUV screeched around the last corner, gravel spitting as we tore up the drive. The mansion loomed in the dark, all the lights dead. The front door stood ajar like an open wound betraying any last hope that this was some accident.

Jake braked hard, throwing the car into park. He glanced at me once, sharp and sure. Then he was out, gun in his hand, vanishing into the dark mouth of my violated home.

Chapter 9
The Silent
Approach

T he night pressed in heavy as I killed the engine. No crickets, no rustle of palm leaves, not even the faint hum of the mansion's security lights. Just darkness and silence. Too much silence. My boots hit the driveway gravel, every step deliberate, measured. I drew my Glock, muscle memory sliding into place like it had a hundred times in a war zone. Only this wasn't a battle front, and the target wasn't some insurgent. This was Los Angeles, and the person they wanted was sitting terrified inside my SUV.

I signaled Isla with two fingers, sharp and quick—*stay down, don't move.* She nodded, wide green eyes glinting under the glow of the dashboard. For once she didn't argue.

The front door gaped open, a dark maw against white stucco walls. The hairs at the back of my neck lifted. Entry was forced, but it wasn't sloppy. Whoever did it knew how to move fast and clean. They had disabled the security system-not triggered it as an intruder. That meant skill or insider knowledge.

I pressed my shoulder to the wall and slid inside. The air was wrong, cold and stale like the house had been holding its breath. My eyes swept over the foyer: vase knocked over, rug bunched, but no obvious looting or vandalism. That told me enough. This wasn't about valuables. This was about her.

Every creak of the floor echoed loud in my ears, each corner cleared with the kind of precision drilled into me years ago. Living room clear. Dining room clear. My pulse ticked in time with the sweep of my barrel.

Kitchen, faint glass crunched. A window. Broken. Just a petty act of vandalism but I was sure that was not the objective. Everything else was too clean. Behind me, the front door hinges squeaked. Isla. I growled. She hadn't stayed put.

The stairs smelled like smashed glass and cold air. Each step up I took, the house seemed to fold inward, quieter, as if someone had sucked the life out of it and left only echoes. I moved with a slow, deliberate precision, clearing rooms the way I'd been taught: sweep, announce, hold.

Isla's bedroom door hung open a sliver. I pushed it the rest of the way with my boot and stopped. Clothes lay scattered like they'd been tossed in a hurry. A lamp lay on its side, shade ripped, small chaos. It looked messy but it was too careful to be random. Then I saw the safe, its door yawning open. The hinge still had metal shavings clinging to it. Whoever had done this knew where things were kept. They had an insider's map.

My eyes snagged on the empty jewelry tray and then on the bed. Sheets rumpled, her pillow dented. Someone had been here recently, not hours ago. The air carried the faintest hint of perfume and cigarette smoke, a nasty contrast to the strawberry scrub she usually carried. My gut went cold.

I checked the closet, the en suite, the windows. One pane was spiderwebbed with a clean impact. Someone had hit it in anger or frustration and left it. The panic room door was locked tight, exactly like it should be. Whoever breached the house had avoided it or didn't have time. That told me they were efficient and had a destination in mind.

A crumpled scrap on the vanity caught my eye. A smear of dark ink across a torn page. I palmed it, reading the scrawl: *She's safer with me.* Same damn message. I ground my teeth. This wasn't random trespass. It was a message from her stalker left where we both had to see it.

She stood in the doorway like someone who'd been stripped of armor and left raw. Neon curls mussed, makeup running, eyes wide and glassy. For a second I didn't register the details, only the fact she looked broken in a way rehearsals and headlines had never shown.

"Isla," I said, voice low and steady, but she didn't move.

Her hands fluttered at her sides like she couldn't remember what to do with them. The house had been violation turned physical, her bedroom rifled, her life rummaged through. That look in her eyes told me her trust had been stripped away.

She bolted toward the bed and went to her safe like a drowning person searching for air. When she pulled it open, her hand dove inside and came out clutching empty space. Her shoulders sagged and she let out a sound that wasn't a sob so much as a small animal's surrender.

"My locket," she whispered, like saying it any louder would make it gone forever.

My blood went cold. That locket was more than jewelry. It was memory. It was a hinge into things she buried and kept locked up. Somebody had reached in and touched the parts of her that mattered most.

I moved until I was in front of her, close enough she felt my breath.

"Who took it?" I demanded, not shouting but the words were edged steel.

Her eyes flicked to me, and for the first time she didn't look at me like I was a prop or an employee. She looked at me like she needed someone to be furious for her, to save her from this.

Instead of answering she folded into me the way only the exhausted do, clutching my shirt, arms tight. I let her, because whatever line we had been keeping between us shattered as she trembled against my chest. For a long beat I held her and let the control I'd trained into muscle and bone fall away. The man who monitored radios and cleared entries wanted to break the throat of whoever dared touch what belonged to her.

Then my phone buzzed. New footage from the security cameras had come through. I thumbed it open and froze. The camera showed a figure in a staff security jacket leaving her room tucking something small inside his or her coat. They wore a hoodie to disguise their gender. Someone on the inside had hands on her life. My jaw clenched until the taste of metal was in my mouth. I didn't care who it was. I only cared that they had her locket.

The safe was small, bolted under her bed frame, painted white to blend with the baseboards. It should have held her most valuable things, contracts, jewelry, whatever pop stars locked away. But what gutted her wasn't cash or credit cards. It was the empty velvet slot where one little trinket should have rested.

Her voice cracked when she said it again. "My mother's locket."

I crouched beside the open box, scanning the contents with a soldier's eye. Her passport was still there, stacks of cash untouched, a few rings glittering under the flashlight beam. None of it mattered to whoever had broken in. They had bypassed the valuables to take the one item tied to her heart.

That made it worse.

This wasn't a robbery. This was personal. A message.

"Tell me about it," I said. My tone was flat, but my pulse was hammering.

She hugged her arms around herself. "It was hers. My mom's. I wore it to every concert until Richard made me lock it away. Said it didn't match the brand." Her laugh came out strangled. "Guess the stalker disagreed."

I wanted to punch a hole through the wall. She wasn't merchandise to be packaged and stolen from. She was a woman being hunted by someone who knew exactly how to hurt her.

I slid the safe shut and rose. "They weren't after money. They wanted you to know they'd been here."

Her eyes filled again, wide and glassy, and I almost reached for her cheek before I caught myself. She didn't need comfort. She needed the truth.

"Whoever did this doesn't just want your career, Isla. They want pieces of you. They have to know you, be close to you." I holstered my weapon, forcing calm into my voice. "And I'll find out who."

She stood in the wreckage of her room like a porcelain doll about to crack. Neon streaks still tainted her curls, glitter dusting her lashes, but none of it mattered. The mask had slipped. What I saw was a woman shaking in the aftermath of being violated.

Her breaths came shallow, lips trembling as she clutched at the hem of her skirt. Then she reached for me, sudden and desperate, fists knotting into my shirt. "I feel dirty. Like he was here, touching everything. Touching me."

The words gutted me. I'd spent years training to neutralize enemies, to plan tactical strikes, to defend perimeters. None of that prepared me for a trembling woman in glitter shoes who just wanted to feel safe again.

I cupped the back of her head. My palm fit the shape of her skull, grounding us both. Her forehead pressed to my chest, her small frame shaking against me. For a breathless second, everything inside me burned to close the distance, my mouth to her hair, my hands lower, my body a shield not just from bullets but from the loneliness she carried like a second skin.

I stopped myself by brute force. She wasn't a conquest. She wasn't one more mission to win. She was Isla, and she was looking at me like I was the only thing keeping her from falling apart.

"I've got you," I said, voice low, steady. The vow tasted like steel.

Her grip tightened. She whispered something into my shirt I couldn't make out, but I didn't need the words. I felt it in the way she held on, like maybe I was the first anchor she'd trusted in a long time.

Her breath hitched, warm through my shirt, and for one reckless heartbeat I let myself feel it, the way her body fit against mine, the way her pulse thundered in time with my own.

She tilted her head back, green eyes shining wet under the bedroom's wrecked lamplight. We were so close, her lips trembled just shy of mine. My chest tightened, every instinct screaming to close that last inch, to take what I'd wanted since the first day she smart-mouthed me in the plaza.

I bent forward before I knew I was moving. Her eyes widened, lashes fluttering. Time slowed. Then I stopped, every muscle locking. If I kissed her now, it would be for me. It would be about need, not about giving her the safety she deserved.

My hands dropped from her hair to her shoulders, steadying her without pulling her closer. "You're safe now," I said, voice rougher than I intended.

She searched my face, lips parted, like she could hear everything I wasn't saying. For a moment I thought she'd push anyway, increase the small space I'd put between us. Instead, she pressed her cheek back to my chest, breath shaky but more controlled, her hands still fisted in my shirt.

I let out the air I hadn't realized I'd been holding. Discipline had kept me alive through warzones, hostage rescues, too many nights of rage and grief. Tonight, it kept me from breaking the only line that mattered, hers. Still, the echo of that almost-kiss lingered, electric and sharp. My heart wouldn't stop pounding, and my body wouldn't cool from the heat of her pressed against me.

Protect her. That was the mission. But as I held her trembling frame, I couldn't ignore the truth any longer. She wasn't just the job. She was already under my skin.

I forced myself to ease her back, though every instinct wanted to keep her anchored against me. "Stay here," I said, tone sharp enough that she didn't argue. My pulse was still hammering when I crouched by the gutted security panel.

The keypad was dark, wires stripped clean. I knew this kind of work. Military precision, quick and quiet. Not some random junkie breaking through a window for kicks. This was someone who'd studied the layout, someone with time and inside access.

I pulled the housing open wider, tracing the cuts with my flashlight. Clean slices. No jagged edges. Whoever did this knew their way around circuits. My gut twisted tighter.

Behind me, Isla shifted on the bed. "What are you seeing?"

I didn't answer right away. Telling her the truth meant admitting she wasn't safe here, not even behind locked doors. When I finally spoke, my voice came out flat. "It wasn't forced. They bypassed the system from inside."

Silence. Then a sharp intake of breath. "You mean—"

"Yeah." I stood, scanning the room again. "This wasn't an outsider guessing codes. Someone close to you gave them a way in."

She hugged her arms around herself. Her trademark bow lay on the carpet. Her eyes were wide with something deeper than fear. Betrayal. She'd built her whole career surrounded by handlers, assistants, managers. Any one of them could be the leak.

I was grinding my teeth hard to keep from swearing. I'd served long enough to know the kind of damage insiders caused. Friendly uniforms could kill faster than any enemy in camo. The brand had painted a target on her back. But it was her inner circle that was tightening the noose. And until I ripped the traitor out by the roots, I couldn't promise her safety.

Behind me, Isla whispered, "Jake?"

I forced the words out steady. "They're not just watching you anymore. They've been inside this house. In your room."

Her breath caught, sharp and shallow.

This wasn't some outsider with a crush gone wrong. This was personal. Calculated. Someone who knew her schedule, who knew what mattered.

I'd hunted enemies overseas, but this was different. Closer. Dirtier. And it had just crossed a line I wouldn't allow.

I looked at her, pale in the wreck of her room, bow tossed aside like the lie it was. My voice came out low, lethal.

"They're already inside your world, Isla. And I'm going to drag them out."

Chapter 10

Panic Room Orders

I wanted to argue. God, I wanted to scream that I was done hiding, done being caged like some fragile bird with painted wings. But Jake's face left no room for debate. His hazel eyes were flat steel, his shoulders a wall of muscle as he steered me down the hallway toward the panic room.

"You're not sleeping in that bedroom," he said. His voice carried the same weight as the locked steel door. "Not until I know every inch of this house is clean."

"I'm not going to be a prisoner," I shot back, heels clicking angrily on the tile. The adrenaline from the break-in still coursed through me, making my hands shake even as I balled them into fists. "I'm not crawling into some metal box while you play cowboy commando."

Jake didn't even flinch. "You're not a prisoner. You're a target. There's a difference."

He pressed the keys on the hidden keypad, the reinforced door sliding open with a mechanical hum. Cold air rushed out. It smelled sterile, metallic, unwelcoming. I glared at the steel walls and narrow cots inside, bile rising. This wasn't safety. It was suffocation.

Jake gestured me in. "It's this, or I stand in your bedroom all night with a gun in my hand. Pick one."

I crossed my arms, chin high, refusing to move. "You can't just shove me into a box and expect me to—"

Then I caught the flicker in his eyes. Not annoyance. Not stubbornness. Fear. Raw and unmasked for a heartbeat before he buried it. My chest tightened. The man wasn't doing this to control me. He was doing it because he'd rather lock me in steel than risk finding my body in the morning. My bravado cracked. If I was in that much danger, he would be too. Because I knew, he would stand in front of anything trying to get to me. I couldn't do that to him, risk him or worry him into standing guard over me all night. Without another word, I stepped inside.

The door sealed with a heavy clank that echoed in my chest like a verdict. I stood in the middle of the panic room, arms wrapped tight around myself, glaring at the walls as if I could will them and the threat to vanish. The fluorescent lights buzzed faintly, too bright, too cold, and too close. I hated everything about it.

Jake leaned against the steel door like he was carved from it, arms folded, gaze steady. He didn't speak, didn't move, just watched me. I could feel his eyes on me, hot and unyielding.

"Don't look at me like that."

"Like what?"

"Like you're seeing something I don't want you to."

He shifted slightly, one boot scraping against the floor, but he didn't answer. The silence between us thickened, seemingly charged like a show about to start. I hated how naked I felt without the bow. Without the armor of it and glitter, I was just... me. A woman with too many scars and too many fears, locked in a room with a man who could break me apart without even trying if he knew. The thought should have terrified me. Instead, it made my pulse trip faster, an ache spreading low and insistent.

Jake tilted his head, studying me. "You'll be safe here," he said finally. His voice was softer now, almost gentle.

I wasn't sure if that was a comfort or a threat.

The panic room hummed like a held breath. I should have hated the closeness, the forced quiet, the way every sound bounced off metal and made the world smaller. Instead, my mouth moved before my head caught up.

"I'm tired of pretending," I said, voice thin. The words tasted like rust and relief. "I'm tired of the bows and the squeaky girlish voice they make me use."

Jake's jaw tightened. He didn't look surprised. He looked like a man who'd been waiting for me to cross the line and now watched with a sharpshooter's patience.

"It started because of him," I blurted collapsing onto one of the cots.

His name was lodged so deep I'd kept it wrapped in silence for years. Talking about it felt dangerous, like handing a loaded gun to someone else. Then the panic room lights dimmed to a dull nighttime glow as if to help me dump my secrets into the dark.

My voice cracked, but I pushed through in a whisper staring at the metal floor. "I had never, you know, been with a guy before but a boy I dated in high school decided *no* didn't matter. I swore no one would ever take that from me again. So, I built a wall out of the only thing I had control over, my body, my image. I declared I was a virgin and it became my shield. My curse. My brand. Forever Innocent."

Saying it out loud felt like peeling back skin. I braced for pity, or worse, judgment. Glancing at Jake, he hadn't flinched. He didn't look away. His jaw worked, his hazel eyes deep and unreadable, but there was no disgust in them. No pity. Only a quiet, burning respect that made me ache.

"You held on to something when the world wanted to rip it away," he said, voice low, almost reverent. "That isn't weakness. That's strength."

My breath stuttered. No one had ever said that to me. Not my manager. Not fans. Not even myself. For the first time in years, I felt seen. Not as Isla Dove, not as Forever Innocent™, just Isla. Me. And it terrified me. Because if he could see me this clearly, he could hurt the real me without even trying.

And when the words left my mouth, Jake's face changed. The easy pull at his jaw became a hard line. For a second he looked like a soldier remembering a war, every muscle coiled and ready.

"I want his name," he said quietly, like he was listing chores. The tone was casual and lethal at the same time. My stomach flipped. What I heard under the sentence wasn't paperwork. It was a promise that had teeth.

I wanted to give it to him. I wanted him to march across this city and make it right like in a movie, to hand me justice on a silver tray. Instead, I swallowed the name down, because saying it out loud felt like giving over the last piece of me. The brand had taken everything else. I couldn't give him that.

Jake's hand found mine across the narrow space between the cots, large and warm as he sat across from me. He didn't press me for it. He didn't need the name. He already knew the truth. The anger in his eyes softened into something else, fierce and protective and unbearably private.

"You don't have to tell me now," he said. "When you're ready." His thumb stroked the back of my hand in a slow, steady circle. The motion was small, but it struck like an arrow.

I wanted to push away, to insist on independence and strength, but his touch folded something shut inside me that had been raw for years. Heat moved through my chest, slow and dangerous, like embers catching on dry grass.

My voice came out thin and honest. "I don't know if I ever will be ready."

He lowered his voice and leaned closer, until his breath ghosted my face. "Then let me be ready for both of us."

The words landed and broke me open. For the first time I let the pretense slip. I wasn't even Isla Donovan. I was just me. We stayed there, hands linked, the panic room noise fading until it was just the two of us and the raw, terrifying possibility that either of us might save the other.

The moment lingered. Jake's hand on mine, the way his eyes softened in that hard-lined face, making me forget the world outside. For once, it wasn't bodyguard and client, cowboy and pop princess. It was just Jake and Isla, no cameras, no brand. And his warm hand in mine.

Silence answered me first, heavy and full. Then Jake's voice came, low and careful. "You don't have to make yourself small for them anymore." He said it like a command and a plea, like he was begging the world to stop stealing pieces of me.

I laughed, but it sounded broken. "You don't get it. The managers, the record execs, turned my pain into product. They sold me as innocent because it made money. They built a cage and called it protection. I wanted to burn it down, but I was trapped. And now— Who will want a former innocent pop princess?" My hands shook, and the sentence thinned out.

He didn't ask for more. He didn't push. He just reached up, tucked a loose curl behind my ear with a thumb that was rough and careful at once. The gesture stole the breath out of me.

"You're not that lie," he said, voice raw. "You're not merchandise. You're a person. I won't let them use you anymore."

I wanted to believe him so badly my throat hurt. The panic room felt less like a prison and more like a promise for a second. The lights flickered, dropping us into the dim orange glow of the emergency strips. Shadows crawled over the steel walls, making the panic room feel smaller, closer, intimate. My breath came shallow, too loud. I wrapped my arms around myself, nails biting through silk.

"I can't keep doing this," I whispered. My voice sounded alien in the hollow space. "I can't keep playing the doll while someone out there sharpens knives with my name on them."

Jake didn't answer. He looked at the door briefly, weapon on one side of him, his hat on the other. His eyes, though, God, his eyes never left me. Steady, watchful, too full of truths I wasn't ready to hold.

Something inside me cracked. "I've never..." I swallowed, but the words came anyway, jagged and sharp. "Not since high school. Not since that night. I swore no one would ever get close again." My chest rose and fell in quick, ugly jerks. "And the world turned it into a brand. Into Forever Innocent. Do you know what it feels like to see the worst night of your life sold on a billboard? To hear it on the radio and sing it at every damn concert?"

Jake's face hardened, then softened all at once.

"I know what it feels like to lose and know it's your fault," he said, voice rough. "My sister. I was supposed to drive her that night, but I stayed out with my friends and she drove herself. Couldn't handle the snow and ice. I thought rules would keep me from ever failing again." He shook his head. "Turns out rules don't protect anyone. People do."

Something hot pricked behind my eyes. The silence between us felt different now, less prison, more battlefield truce. Two broken people trading scars in the dark while an unknown threat lurked somewhere just outside.

He sat forward, forearms braced on his thighs, gaze fixed on the floor as if the steel could answer questions neither of us wanted to ask.

"I wasn't supposed to tell you that," he muttered, almost to himself. His voice was low, gravel threaded with something raw. "Sierra Bravo doesn't hire men who bleed out their ghosts on the job. But I felt you should know who's standing between you and the monster outside."

I sat opposite him and tucked my knees against my chest, chin resting there, waiting. For once I didn't fill the silence with sarcasm or sass. I wanted the truth, and Jake Dalton didn't seem like a man who gave it easily.

"When my sister died, it was because I wasn't there," he said finally, eyes lifting just enough to pin me. "I told myself the rules would save anyone else if I just followed them and they did too. Curfews. Locks. Routines. Orders. But maybe rules wouldn't have saved her. And they won't save you." His throat worked as he swallowed hard. "What will save you is me not stopping until I've put myself between you and every damn threat out there."

I had never seen him like this. No cowboy swagger, no soldier steel. Just a man cracking open the armor he lived inside. For me.

The bow usually in my hair felt like a cruel joke. The brand wanted me flawless, untouchable. Yet here was a man laying his scars at my feet, offering them as proof of his devotion to saving me. Even though I had shown him behind the glitter, he was still holding to his vow. He still believed in the Isla behind the brand.

I whispered, "And who saves you, Jake?"

His mouth curved, not a smile but something sadder. "No one. Not until tonight."

The words stole my breath.

Silence pressed in after his confession, heavier than the reinforced walls around us. I lay back on my cot, though my eyes stayed fixed on him, on the tension winding through his broad frame. He looked ready to spring at shadows, yet his jaw flexed like he was fighting something closer, something harder to face.

"Why'd you become a soldier?" I whispered.

"I needed to run away. After my sister ... I couldn't face seeing her empty saddle in the barn anymore and the recruiter's office was right opposite the high school. I just walked across the street and signed up. Left the day after graduation."

"So, the hat isn't something they told you to wear to make you look different next to me? You're actually a cowboy?" I asked, really surprised.

"I'm the real deal." Jake said, his lips twitching slightly in almost a smile, "My parents owned a small ranch in southern Colorado until they sold it while I was overseas. Don't think they could stand that empty bedroom either."

"I'm sorry." I said, about a lot of things. About his sister. For thinking he was pretending like I did when he was the realest person I'd ever met. For fighting things inside that I didn't know what to do with or how to fix.

"Everyone's got something." He said quietly.

I shifted onto my side, the thin blanket slipping down my shoulder. He noticed, of course he did. His gaze flickered, catching the bare line of skin before he snapped it back to the far wall. That one glance set fire beneath my skin.

"Jake," I whispered. The sound of his name in the dark felt like crossing a line I couldn't uncross.

He turned his head slowly, eyes shadowed, unreadable. Our cots were close, too close, barely a foot between them. I could almost feel the heat of his body seeping into mine across the narrow gap. Every shallow breath made me aware of how much I wanted to close it. The air vibrated with tension. His fingers twitched against his thigh, and I imagined them sliding over me, steady and rough, anchoring me the way his voice had earlier.

"Don't," he said softly, as if I'd already reached for him.

"I didn't," I shot back, though my heart pounded loud enough to give me away.

His mouth curved in a ghost of a smile, the kind that both punished and tempted. "You were about to."

I clenched the blanket tighter, cursing myself because he was right. The need thrummed in me like a second pulse, and the steel walls felt too small to contain it. For the first time, I wanted to break every rule I lived by.

The cot creaked when he shifted, the sound loud in the hush of the panic room. My pulse stuttered as his hand slid, just a fraction, across the mattress. His knuckles brushed mine. Barely a touch, yet it lit a spark that raced up my arm and stole my breath.

I froze, not daring to move, terrified he would pull away. Terrified he wouldn't. Not having any idea which I really wanted.

His eyes found mine in the dim glow of the emergency light. No bravado, no armor, just Jake, raw and unguarded. I saw everything he tried to bury there: grief, guilt, hunger. It called to the same broken pieces inside me, the parts that had longed for someone to see me, not the costume, not the mask. Just me.

I turned my hand slowly, pressing my palm against his. Heat radiated between us, searing and steady. His breath caught, and I felt it, the shift in the air. One more inch, one more heartbeat, and our mouths would close the distance.

I wanted it, God, I did want it. To feel his lips, his strength, to know what it was to be wanted by a man who wasn't taking but giving. My chest rose, trembling, lips parting as if I could draw him in by sheer will.

He leaned closer, his jaw tightening, breath feathering against my cheek. My heart slammed against my ribs, wild and certain. This was it.

And then, just as suddenly, he pulled back. His hand slipped from mine, leaving a cold ache in its place.

"Not like this," he said, voice low and rough, as if dragging the words from somewhere deep.

I swallowed the sting, nodding even though my body screamed against it. Almost. We had almost crossed the line.

The silence stretched, heavy as a chain, both of us caught in the aftershock of that almost. I tucked my hand under the thin blanket, hiding the tremor, wishing I could bury the ache with it. Jake sat rigid on his cot, back against the wall, eyes fixed on some point beyond me. He had built his walls back up, stone by stone, in the space of a heartbeat.

I wanted to scream at him. To demand why he kept wanting me with one hand and pushing me away with the other. But before I could gather the courage, the intercom above the steel door crackled to life.

Static hissed, loud and jagged, making me jump. Jake was on his feet in an instant, gun raised toward the speaker as if he could shoot through the sound to the person on the other side.

Then the voice came. Distorted, metallic, yet intimate enough to crawl across my skin.

"Jake can't save you."

The words oozed into the room, curling around me like a snake. My stomach dropped, breath catching hard. For weeks, the stalker had lurked in the shadows, hidden behind notes, gifts and whispers. Now he was in our sanctuary, his voice seeping through steel meant to keep us safe.

Jake's jaw locked, his silhouette massive in the dim light. Fury rolled off him in waves. "Show yourself, you coward," he growled, but the intercom only hissed, then died.

The silence after was worse.

I hugged my knees to my chest, nails biting into my skin. If the panic room wasn't safe, nowhere was. Not my mansion, not the stage, not even in Jake's arms.

But when I looked at him, standing like a fortress with murder in his eyes, I clung to the only truth I had left: if anyone could drag me out of this nightmare, it was him.

Chapter 11

Suspicions & Taunts

A major issue with being close protection for a public figure was being the only person watching when they were in public. Basically, there was no way to clear rooms and simultaneously watch everyone near the client while escorting them. It was the classic ducks, wolves, grain and the boat only holding two of the three trying to cross the river and I was the boat. Of course, the best option was to prohibit the client from being in public. That always went over well. And in this situation? Forget it. It defeated the whole purpose of my being here. She was supposed to be protected so she could launch her new CD starting with this huge, sold out mega-hall concert. And that concert meant rehearsals, advance publicity appearances, photo shoots and endless meetings.

All this while trying to discover who it was that was stalking her. If I had been prone to stomach issues, I would have been in the hospital. Instead, I was nearly mainlining coffee trying to be hypervigilant while researching the potential threats. A couple more escalations and I was calling in backup. I wasn't risking Isla on my ego. Same logic as to why the Secret Service always had a team guarding their targets. You couldn't watch your own back, let alone your client's.

Sierra Bravo respected that fact. I wouldn't get any flack from them. I'd been sending in daily reports. They knew what was happening on the ground. If I called for support, it'd be answered with no problem. They had nearly a full squad of SWAT-level operatives on standby and a helicopter ready for emergency evac if the need arose. Ordinarily, they didn't have a full court press a hotline away but with Isla's international reputation, she was too big of a target to go with anything less.

In the meantime, I was keeping Isla on a very short leash. That put her in a foul mood with me and everyone around her. Too bad. I could take that better than a funeral. She simply had to get used to seeing me at her side at all times when she wasn't in bed or in the bathroom. And we were living in that panic room until after the concert.

So, we arrived at the venue for yet another rehearsal after a long grumpy, pouty Isla car ride. When I asked Isla how many of these things they needed, she'd scowled and told me they would be hitting it every day until the actual concert. Apparently, this being the kickoff of not only the CD but an entire concert tour, there were new dancers, backup singers, band members, lighting techs, sound techs, stage hands, dressers, costume changes and I couldn't even keep track as she went on and on through what sounded to me like enough people to make a full-length movie. The pyrotechnics technicians did get my attention because I hadn't interviewed them yet and explosives on the stage seemed like a very, very bad idea. I had requested a list of everyone involved in this circus because I was sending that on to Sierra Bravo for background screening.

With the high-profile nature of this case, I wasn't too surprised to hear that Connor Wilson was managing the tech support from home base. He was Sierra Bravo's genius when it came to understanding the electronic world. Background checks would be beneath him but figuring out who was hacking into my phone, Isla's earpiece and the panic room's intercom and how they were doing it was right in his wheelhouse. If anyone could nail down a name, he and his team could and I was more than ready to knock down someone's door for a very pointed conversation.

I pulled into a parking space at the concert hall for today's rehearsal.

"Stay right behind me." I told her, "No wandering or stopping to talk. We are heading directly to your dressing room. Once you're secure there I will clear the rest of the hall."

It was about the best I'd been able to come up with aside from having her hand in my back pocket as I cleared every inch of the place. That had some appeal but while I was bent over checking under every seat or climbing into the scaffolding, she'd be an open target. Having her locked down in her dressing room that I'd already cleared was marginally safer. Another escalation and I was calling in a second Sierra Bravo bodyguard to tag team me.

"Ok." She said with no comment.

The home invasion had accomplished that concession. She was listening to me. I wasn't sure how long it might last but I'd take what I could get. Her eyes behind the glitter eyeshadow and sparkly lashes were serious now. Ever since we'd had that exchange of panic room secrets, she'd dropped some of the plastic between us. On the one hand it felt good, like it would be easier to protect her but on the other, it was hitting places that wanted more. To know her, to touch her, to do a lot of things I had no business thinking about. And I had to lock those down under reinforced concrete. I had a job to do here. And that should have been my only focus. Not on helping Isla escape her brand box and definitely not on wanting the woman behind the glitter. Which if I was being honest, I did.

We walked straight from the stage door to Isla's dressing room door. I could hear her heels behind me as she greeted people she passed but she didn't stop.

"Good afternoon, Isla." Lily sang out joining our parade, "I put your gifts on your side table just where you like them."

"Thanks, Lily. Don't know what I'd do without you organizing everything." Isla said, stopping at the door to her room as I entered.

"What's up?" Lily asked.

"Jake just wants to check everything out." Isla said brightly, "You know how these overprotective boyfriend types are." She added with a giggle as if sharing a joke.

I ignored her. The giggle sounded false to me, but Lily didn't comment on it. I was looking for threatening notes or worse. Then I looked under her chair, through her costumes and that gift table for anything suspicious that could be explosive or toxic. Her water bottles were sealed as were a stack of protein bars. I had noticed that Isla ate almost as much as I did but I had watched her stage routines. She moved and danced nearly nonstop. She needed the calories.

"Clear." I said, "All right. You will stay in here until I come back. I don't care who calls or if the building explodes. Got it?"

Isla rolled her eyes at Lily as if to say 'see what I have to put up with' but when she moved into the room, she reached over and squeezed my fingers for the briefest of seconds. It felt like her way of acknowledging my rules as justified instead of unnecessary. At least that's what I hoped. I needed her to work with me.

"All right, cowboy. Got it. Sit. Stay. I'll just write thank yous or something safe." Isla giggled, "I'll yell if I get a paper cut."

I shook my head and left the room to clear the rest of the hall. There were a lot of dressing rooms, recital areas, a few offices, the massive hall itself with all those seats to check, the sound booth up above the auditorium and ...

"Jake!"

The cry was tortured, pleading and clearly Isla's.

I ran back to her dressing room. It only took less than a minute, but it felt too long as my mind played horrible scenes on what might have happened for Isla to produce that sound. I slid into her dressing room, gun drawn, prepared for anything but Isla standing in the far corner. She was trembling and pointing toward her mirror like the ghost of Christmas Future, her eyes wide and fearful.

I stared for a full thirty seconds before I tracked on what had stricken her. Then I stumbled forward kicking myself. This had to have been here when I had cleared the room, and I had missed it. It was her mother's locket. Draped over one corner of the mirror. It was nearly invisible among the pictures and other jewelry hanging or taped everywhere. I holstered the gun and lifted the necklace. I opened the locket. There was nothing inside other than pictures I was guessing were Isla's mother and a baby that was probably her. The clasp was damaged but I didn't know if it had been that way before.

Its owner was not fine. I turned to Isla, and she dove into my arms, sobbing.

"They were here." She wailed. "How did they get in here?"

I sighed. For all my efforts, the venue was not secure or ever would be. Ignoring all the people on staff, there were delivery drivers, temporary staff coming in to make repairs, managers, supervisors, assistants to those people, record company staff, reporters, venue staff, security for several organizations and probably more I hadn't identified. This job was impossible. I vowed right then. I was calling in Sierra Bravo. Even rookies could help lock this place down. We had three days of rehearsals and then the big concert. I was splitting my focus now to find the culprit and to protect Isla. Watching what felt like hundreds of random people in this huge venue was clearly beyond me.

And right this minute, my entire body was reacting to the feeling of a very warm body pressed against mine. A body I fervently desired but I had to resist. Because she deserved better than a broken excuse of a man chased by his sister's ghost singing Isla's song. She'd had one horrible experience in high school. She didn't need anyone this tortured.

Maybe I should just get Sierra Bravo to send in someone else entirely.

"Don't leave me, Jake." Isla whispered as if reading his mind.

"I'm here." I said, seeing Lily staring and frowning at us as she twisted Isla's bow in her hand.

She must have been worried about Isla and had no idea what to do. I wanted to tell her to join the club.

Chapter 12
Rehearsal Pressure

Backstage smelled like hairspray and burned coffee, a false kind of intimacy that made my stomach twist. I hated walking in here feeling like a target wrapped in glitter. The crew moved with energy, but their eyes flicked at me like I was a fragile exhibit behind glass. I felt every stare like a prickle along my spine.

Jenna tuned her guitar in the corner, jaw set, eyes darting away when mine found hers. For years she'd been the shadow at my shoulder, the voice in the backup harmony who never quite made it as a solo. Now she moved like a woman who'd swallowed a grudge, and it was sitting heavy. My chest tightened. If anyone had motive to be dangerous, it was her.

Richard hovered nearby, phone glued to his palm, smile too wide. His laugh sounded brittle. He was my manager. I was supposed to trust him. But could I? He was the one who packaged me like whitening toothpaste and sold me everywhere he could. The taste of that trust was growing sour on my tongue. Maybe I was just getting paranoid.

I walked in with my bow too tight and my voice too loud because if I didn't act like I was happily in charge, everyone would smell weakness. The rehearsal would crash and burn into a messy pile of arguments, missed cues and sour notes. The date was coming up fast. We didn't have time for any of that.

"Who screwed up the sound cues last time?" I snapped, not bothering to cloak my anger, my frustration. And then, out of nowhere, the real issue just exploded out of me. "Who thought it'd be funny to nearly kill me onstage?"

Heads swiveled. Jenna's hand paused on a tuning peg as if she'd been struck. "I didn't—" she began, voice sharp, but I cut her off.

"Awfully quick with a denial. You either know more than you're saying, or you're hiding something," I said, stepping closer until the whole band felt like an audience to my accusation.

The words burned in my throat before I even realized I was shouting. "Don't you dare pretend you're innocent, Jenna!" My voice cracked against the walls, bouncing off amps and drum kits, ricocheting like it belonged in a courtroom instead of at a rehearsal. "You've been glaring at me for years, wishing it was you onstage, and now suddenly things start falling apart the second you're back on payroll? Convenient, isn't it?"

Gasps rippled through the crew, people shuffling their feet, pretending to adjust lights, anything to avoid watching me rip into the woman who once sang backup harmonies at my side. But I couldn't stop. The anger clawed out of me, raw and jagged, fueled by fear I hadn't admitted to anyone, not even Jake.

Jenna's eyes snapped up, cold and cutting, and her lips twisted into a smirk that made my blood boil. "You think you're untouchable because of the stupid bow and the fans screaming your name," she shot back, voice dripping poison. "Newsflash, princess. Every glitter-smeared lie Richard sells is the only reason you're still standing here. Without it, you're nothing."

I flinched. The words found cracks in my armor and slid straight through. Because I'd whispered them to myself on nights when I couldn't sleep, when I wondered if I was only the costume and the mask, if my songs and voice meant nothing without the heavy marketing.

My fists curled at my sides. I wanted to hit her. I wanted to claw the smirk off her face until she couldn't use it as a weapon anymore. Instead, I stepped closer, chest heaving.

"If you had an ounce of talent, you'd know what it feels like to have everyone depending on you," I spat. "But you don't. You never did. That's why you're still bitter in the shadows."

Jake loomed at my side then, simply his presence solid enough to yank me back from swinging. His silence pressed against my rage like a wall. I was shaking, breathing hard, knowing I'd gone too far but unable to stop the wildfire burning in my chest. I knew it was fueled by fear, but I couldn't stop myself.

Jenna lunged a step closer, her perfume sharp and bitter as old wine. "Spoiled little princess," she hissed, her voice just loud enough to draw everyone tighter into the circle. "Handed everything because you look cute in pigtails and sing about first kisses. You don't deserve half of what you've got."

Something inside me snapped. All the fear of the last few weeks, the notes, the broken spotlight, the invasion of my home, ignited the flames into uncontrollable rage. "Don't you dare," I snarled, shoving at her shoulder. Gasps echoed across the stage.

Jenna didn't stumble. She shoved me right back, hard enough that my heel skidded across the polished floor. For a split second, I thought about letting it go. Walking away. Proving her wrong. But my pride roared louder.

I grabbed a mic stand and swung it up like a shield, not to hit her, but to keep her away. "Try me again," I warned, my voice shaking, "and you'll see I'm no princess."

Her eyes blazed, and she swiped the stand out of my hands, metal clattering across the floor. Crew members scrambled to get between us, but the damage was done. Everyone had seen it, the pop princess clawing at her former backup singer like a cat in an alley. Jake had moved in to grab the mic stand before Jenna could swing it.

Jenna leaned in, flushed with triumph and whispered so only I could hear. "Keep pretending, Isla. You know the truth. You're terrified they'll all see what I see. That without the bow and the bubblegum act, you're nothing."

The words were worse than her shove. For a moment, all I could do was stand there, chest heaving, hands trembling, trying not to let her see how deep the claws had struck. Fighting back tears of rage and pain.

My pulse pounded, anger, fear, exhaustion braided together. I wanted answers. I wanted someone to be honest. Jake was at my side before I could start up again, his presence a physical thing that crowded everyone else away. He didn't speak. He didn't need to. The way he looked at Jenna said everything he had stored in those weeks of watching and waiting. Protection radiated off him, not performance. For a moment I felt less like a showpiece and more like a person someone would fight for.

"Enough," Jake's voice cut through, clean and cold, and everyone simply stopped.

He stepped between us, one hand lifted, the other firm around my waist and steady. Heat and humiliation rushed my face, but his grip anchored me against the spin inside. Jenna hissed something ugly, still straining, and the crew muttered like startled birds around us. Jake did not raise his voice again; he looked at her, unblinking, lethal and still. She shut up first, which felt like winning and losing at the same time tonight. He turned to me, not gentler, but careful, like he was handling broken glass.

Jake shifted, placing me behind him, his body a wall, his voice a locked door against chaos. He told the crew to take five, then told Jenna to clear the floor. Now. She started to fling a last dig, but his stare wiped it off her tongue to nothing. My pulse still skittered; adrenaline tasted metallic, like pennies held in my mouth too long. He moved me to the wings, not touching more than necessary, still holding authority carefully.

"You are done shouting," he said quietly, and somehow it landed like a verdict.

The words should have enraged me; instead, my lungs remembered how to pull in air again. He asked if I was hurt, and I heard the fear under iron control there.

"I am fine," I lied, while my hands shook and glitter rained from my hair.

He passed me a water bottle, then faced the stage again, already scanning people and exits. With his back to me, I finally breathed and hated how safe I felt in his presence.

Jenna's laugh cracked sharp across the room, bitter as vinegar. She leaned against a prop trunk, mascara smudged and sneered at me like I was the punch line to a private joke.

"Ask your manager where the real danger comes from," she said, voice full of venom. "Richard's been drowning in debts for years. Selling favors is the only thing he does well since he loses at poker."

The words sliced cleaner than anything she'd thrown in our fight. My mouth opened to snap back, but nothing came out. Around us everyone froze, trading glances, whispers rolling like low thunder. Jake's eyes narrowed, a flicker of calculation passing over his face.

I shook my head hard. "You're lying. You always hated me. This is just another dig."

Even to my own ears it sounded thin, desperate. Jenna's smirk only widened.

She shoved off the trunk and stalked toward the door, muttering loud enough for everyone to hear. "Check his books, princess. You'll find out who's really pulling the strings."

Jake's hand hovered at the small of my back, steady, grounding. I stiffened at the touch but didn't move away. I couldn't. My heart banged against my ribs too loud, drowning everything else out.

The stage lights dimmed as techs went through lighting cues, but the air felt brighter, harsher, exposing cracks I had worked so hard to hide. Was Richard really capable of selling me out? The thought slithered deep, burrowing under skin already raw.

Jenna's heels clicked down the hall until the sound vanished. The silence left in her wake felt heavier than the shouting had. I wanted to believe she was just jealous, just cruel, but the certainty in her tone clung to me. For the first time, I wondered if my prison bow had been built by the man who tied it.

I stood in the wings long after Jenna's voice faded, the bow in my hair suddenly feeling like a choke chain. My reflection shimmered in a darkened mirror at the edge of the hall. The wide-eyed doll staring back didn't look like me at all. Richard had built her. He had polished her, pitched her, sold her. He had promised safety in sequins and innocence, said the brand would protect me. And I had believed him.

But Jenna's words burrowed deeper with every breath. Gambling debts? Selling favors? If even half of it was true, then the image I hated so much wasn't a shield. It was a leash he tightened whenever he needed more money.

Jake lingered beside me, arms folded, scanning the shadows as if expecting the stalker to step out. His silence pressed heavier than his orders ever did. He didn't try to argue Jenna's claims. That alone set my stomach twisting.

I pulled the bow free and crushed it in my hand, the plastic bending with a faint crack. For a heartbeat I felt lighter, like I had torn away something false. But then I remembered Richard's voice in a hundred interviews, promising the world that Isla Dove was pure forever. That lie had bought houses, cars, and contracts. It had made him rich too. What if it had also painted the bullseye on my back?

The thought clawed at me until my throat tightened. I wanted to scream at Jake, demand he tell me Jenna was wrong.

Instead, I whispered, "Do you think she's lying?"

His jaw flexed but he didn't answer. The silence was its own confession. Doubt festered inside me, sharper than any threat note. If Richard had betrayed me, then every bow I had ever worn was just another link in my chain.

I found Jake later in the stylists' room, laptop open on the battered table where stylists usually dumped curling irons and spray cans. The glow lit his face, sharpening the lines around his eyes. He was scrolling fast, jaw set, his shoulders coiled tight. I lingered at the door, arms wrapped around myself.

"Looking for cat videos?" My voice sounded brittle, like glass cracking.

He didn't glance up. "Financial records," he muttered, low and even. "Richard's."

My stomach dropped. The word alone made me queasy. Richard had always bragged about deals, about investors, about how he kept the brand alive. Now Jake's silence felt louder than Jenna's accusation. I edged closer, my heels clicking too loud on the tile. Numbers scrolled across the screen, lines of deposits and withdrawals that blurred together. I caught just enough to see the totals weren't small. Six figures. Seven. More money than I had ever signed off on.

"Where did that come from?" My whisper scraped my throat.

Jake finally looked up. His eyes were hard, unreadable, like the soldier he used to be had replaced the cowboy. "Working on it."

He angled the screen away from me. A subtle move, but I saw it. He didn't want me to see more. The rejection stung, sharper than if he had shouted.

"You think I can't handle it?"

He said nothing. Just closed the lid with quiet finality. His fist rested on the cover like he could crush the secrets inside. The silence between us swelled. I wanted to shake him, to demand every ugly truth he was hiding. Instead, I wrapped my arms tighter, nails biting my skin. Because a part of me already knew. Richard had built my cage out of neon and bows. And Jake had just found the key.

The room felt suddenly too small, like the walls were inching closer with every breath. Jake's silence pressed harder than a hand on my throat. He had answers, and he wasn't giving them. My pulse hammered as I stepped closer to the table. His phone buzzed, the sound sharp in the quiet. He grabbed for it, fast, but not fast enough. I snatched it from the table, my hand moving on instinct.

"Isla—" His warning came too late.

The screen glowed in my grip. Bank statements. Rows of payments, heavy and dark, flooding into Richard's accounts. Each transfer date lined up with the worst nights, the threats, the sabotage, the break-in. My chest caved, air refusing to come.

Jake reached for me, but I staggered back, the phone clutched tight. "You knew." My voice cracked, raw. "You've been looking at this, and you didn't tell me."

His mouth opened, but no words came. The soldier who always had a plan looked cornered now, caught between truth and protection. The numbers blurred as tears welled. Richard. The man who discovered me. The one who said he believed in me when no one else would. The one who told me glitter bows and bubblegum songs were my ticket. My prison guard in designer suits. Betrayal settled in my stomach like broken glass. Every bow, every staged smile, every syrupy lyric, sold, traded, weaponized.

The phone slipped from my fingers and hit the floor with a hollow clatter. I pressed a hand to my chest, as if I could hold myself together with sheer will. Jake finally said my name, voice low and wrecked.

But it was too late. The truth was out, and it was poison.

My whole world had been bought and sold, and I was the product.

Chapter 13
Pattern of Spectacle

We sat in her dressing room silent. I knew Isla was furious, probably thinking I had deliberately kept things from her. The room was quiet except for Isla's playlist buzzing through the speakers. All bubblegum beats and sugar-coated lyrics, the kind of noise Richard loved to package as innocence. My jaws ground in rhythm. I had no idea what to say to fix this. I had only learned most of this a few hours ago and it wasn't clear yet. I couldn't offer her explanations or proof. She sat glaring into the mirror, finishing her eye makeup angrily, hair curled into neon streaks, a bow perched like a crown, skirt glittering under the room's light.

It made me furious. Not at her. At the way the industry had carved her into something she wasn't. Twenty-five years old, treated like a child in costume. I wanted to rip the bow out and toss it onto the floor, wanted to see her in jeans and bare feet, the woman I glimpsed at that veggie restaurant when she left the mask behind.

She caught me staring. "What, cowboy? Never seen a pop princess put on her makeup before?" Her smile was brittle, sharp enough to cut.

She turned back to the mirror, but her reflection showed more than she wanted. Her eyes shimmered, not glitter, not stage lights. Fear.

Respect kept me from reaching over, from pulling the bow off myself, from telling her she was worth more than the lie wrapped around her shoulders. Respect and restraint were the only things holding me together.

Because the moment I let myself touch her outside the mission, I wouldn't stop. And this was already dangerous enough.

The concert hall swallowed me the second we stepped inside. Spotlights blazed down, hot and sharp, painting Isla in a glow that turned her into something otherworldly. She twirled onto the stage, skirts swishing, curls bouncing. The crew clapped along, fans squealed from the handful of seats filled for rehearsal. It had the appearance of a celebration. To me, it looked like a kill box.

I stayed in the wings, arms folded, eyes scanning everything that moved. Rigging overhead. Cables at my feet. Every shadow behind a curtain. I had walked into ambushes before, and this reeked of one.

Isla's voice lilted sugar-sweet over the speakers. She giggled on cue, winked like she had been taught. The audience swooned. They saw the doll, the fantasy. But I saw the truth hiding under the glitter. Her smile trembled when she thought no one noticed. Her shoulders sagged between spins. She was exhausted, running on fumes, and no one cared as long as the bow stayed upright.

Richard stood offstage, clapping too hard, eyes on the money not the woman. My jaw locked. I wanted to tie him to a chair for a lengthy interrogation.

I murmured into the comm at my collar, a low growl only she could hear. "Eyes on me."

Her head turned, green eyes locking with mine across the glare. For a heartbeat the act slipped, the mask cracked. Her voice steadied, real and raw for the first time all night. The crew thought she had found her groove. I knew she had just found me.

Heat stirred in my chest, dangerous and unwanted. I shoved it down, focusing on the exits again. Because if my gut was right, tonight wasn't just rehearsal. Tonight was bait on a hook, and Isla was standing right at the end of the line.

Halfway through the second number, Isla's smile faltered. It was quick, a hairline crack, but I caught it. Her voice slipped, the bubblegum tone breaking into something raw before she pulled it back together. The crew laughed like it was nothing. Richard made a note on his clipboard. Nobody saw the truth but me.

She wasn't losing her pitch. She was losing the mask.

I shifted closer to the stage, boots thudding against the wood. Her eyes darted toward me, wide and unguarded, like she had been waiting for me to see through it. I didn't look away. Couldn't.

I pressed the comm again. "Breathe. Eyes on me."

Her chest rose on a shaky inhale, then her voice steadied. Not sugary. Not fake. Her own. The note carried across the hall like glass ringing. For a second, the whole room hushed, drawn in by the real Isla. And then she spun again, giggling on cue, forcing the mask back into place.

My fists tightened. I wanted to drag her offstage, tell them all she wasn't their doll. But that would paint a bigger target than she already carried. Still, the way she had looked at me gnawed at something deep. It wasn't just fear. It was defiance. It was trust.

I stepped back into the shadows, jaw tight. This job was supposed to be simple: guard the girl, catch the stalker, go home. But now every bow in her hair felt like a noose around my own neck. And every time her mask cracked, I wanted to be the one who caught her before she broke completely.

Halfway through the second act after the costume change, I saw it. A pinprick of red glowing across her chest, steady as a heartbeat. The crowd didn't notice. The crew didn't notice. But I had seen that mark too many times in sand and jungle. My blood iced.

"Down," I barked into the comm, already in motion. Isla spun mid-step, confusion flashing across her face. Then she caught sight of the dot and froze, eyes wide.

I launched onto the stage and slammed into her, driving her low behind the monitors. Her mic screeched, dancers scattered, and the rehearsal hall erupted in shouts. She gasped under me, trembling, clutching the sequins on her skirt as if they could stop a bullet.

"Stay still," I hissed, scanning the rafters, the balconies, anywhere a shooter could nest. My heart hammered so loud, it drowned the noise.

Security scrambled, crew shouted, but the laser didn't move. It just hovered like a predator's smile now aimed at the back of the stage.

I bolted from cover, sprinting up the aisle. Rows of folded seats blurred as I hunted the source. My instincts screamed sniper. My gut told me something was off.

And then I saw it. Back row. A phone taped to the seat, a laser pointer app aimed straight at the stage. A cruel toy. A fake threat dressed up like the real thing.

I ripped it free, jaw clenched and crushed it in my fist until plastic cracked. Rage surged hot through my veins. Whoever planted this knew exactly what they were doing, testing me, testing her, showing us how easy it was to mark Isla like prey.

When I turned back, she was still crouched on the stage, eyes locked on me. Not the crowd. Not Richard. Me. And all I could think was that next time, that dot might not be fake.

I strode back down the aisle, the crushed phone biting into my palm. I knew there wouldn't be prints or anything useful in a burner phone. And smashing it released some of my rage before I let the anger fly at anyone in my path. The crew swarmed the stage, chattering about cables and cues, blind to the fact that Isla had been branded as a corpse in front of them.

She crouched behind a speaker, hugging her knees, curls falling out of their clips. The bow drooped sideways, ridiculous against the terror etched across her face. My chest tightened. She wasn't the idol right now. She was just a woman who had seen her own death painted in red on her chest.

I climbed onto the stage and knelt beside her. "It was fake," I told her, voice low. "Just a phone rigged with a laser app."

Her eyes snapped up to mine, wet but fierce. "*Just?*" she whispered, shaking. "That dot was on me."

I wanted to lie, to tell her it was nothing. Instead, I opened my hand, showing her the broken shards of plastic. "It was a message. Meant to scare you."

Her fingers brushed mine as she reached for the pieces, trembling. I closed my hand before she could take them. "Don't. Let me carry this."

For a long moment we stayed there, the noise of the hall fading to a hum. She leaned toward me, closer than she should, closer than I had any right to allow. Her perfume was laced with fear, her breath warm on my cheek. I could have taken her into my arms and kissed her then. God, I wanted to, simply to try to reassure her that she was alive, that I was here, watching over her.

Instead, I forced the space back between us, pushing to my feet. "We're done here," I said, sharper than I meant. "Get your things."

Her chin lifted, pride flashing, but I caught the way her hands shook as she smoothed her skirt.

The stalker had turned rehearsal into a battlefield. And I had let myself want her in the middle of it.

The hall emptied fast, crew scattering with excuses and halfhearted promises to check equipment. Richard barked at everyone, his voice high and shaky, but nobody listened. The smell of hot bulbs and sweat hung heavy in the air. Isla stood off to the side, bow limp in her hand, glitter shoes planted but unsteady.

I crouched near the control board, picking up the severed wire that had triggered a short blackout earlier in the day. Clean cut. No fray, no accident. The same precision I had seen in the bolt on the rig weeks ago. Different tactic, same message. Someone had planned this rehearsal like a sniper lays out his field of fire. It was probably when the phone had been planted. After I had checked the hall.

Richard rushed up, sweating through his suit. "She's fine, see? Just a scare. We can spin this."

I turned on him, holding up the cut wire in his face. "This wasn't a scare. It was a message. That they can get to her." My voice dropped to a growl. "And it's not the first time."

His face drained of color. He stammered something about jealous rivals, about Jenna, about fans sneaking in. I didn't buy a word.

Behind me, Isla whispered, "Jake."

I looked back. Her eyes were on me, wide and raw. She didn't need to say more. She knew. This wasn't random. It was a pattern, and she was the centerpiece.

I pocketed the wire with the phone pieces and scanned the rafters again. The phantom dot still burned in my head, bright as blood. This was more than obsession. It was strategy.

Whoever was pulling the strings had just made one thing clear. They weren't done. Not by a long shot. They were escalating.

And I was damn tired of being one step behind.

Chapter 14
Glitter and Blood

The dressing room smelled like some battlefield dressing for a wedding, like hairspray and adrenaline. I had glitter in places I could not name and the taste of copper at the back of my throat from where I'd sucked in breath too fast. Lily kept fussing with my curls as if tidying would fix the fact that someone had rehearsed killing me onstage. A crew kid handed me a towel and then backed away like I was a bomb set to explode. Confetti stuck to my skin and to the adhesive on my cheek. My hand came away petal pink and warm. I blinked and realized the warmth was blood.

Someone yelped. I felt the room spin. Hands were suddenly on me, voices rising in a broken chorus. Lily, who used to pull my scarves into perfect bows, stood frozen with mascara tracks like war paint. Richard hovered at the doorway, face the wrong color for a man who could manufacture headlines. He kept trying to smile but the smile kept cracking.

Jake was at my side before the panic in the room could settle into hysteria. He touched my elbow like I might break if he held me wrong. His fingers were steady when they found the split on my lip, steady when he wiped glitter away with the corner of a towel. I hated that he could make me feel both exposed and somehow safer in the same breath.

"You okay?" he asked, voice flat but not unkind. The question was stupid and perfect.

I opened my mouth to say 'of course' but the truth tumbled out anyway. "I feel like I am falling apart, and they still expect me to smile."

He said nothing. He just gathered me close, careful, like I was fragile china he'd carry through any storm. I knew the cameras would spit out the stage story tonight. The fans would paint me in martyr colors. But under the mirror lights, with blood drying in the hollow of my throat, I realized the brand was not just broken. It had turned into something violent.

Jake's jaw tightened. His hand closed on mine until I felt the warning there. Whoever had done this had not just tried to scare us. They had aimed to hurt me where it mattered, on stage. And hurting me had a price I was suddenly not willing to pay. Because there was now someone else in the crosshairs, Jake.

Jake tried to brush me off, like the blood running down his arm was nothing more than sweat but his arm must have snagged on a monitor bracket when he tackled me, and he was still bleeding. He stood there stubborn and unmovable, shirt-torn, muscle flexing as he reached for the door like he was already headed back out into the chaos.

"Don't," I snapped, grabbing his wrist. His skin was hot, slick with blood that kept soaking through the cotton. He tried to shake me off, but I clung harder, nails digging. "You're hurt."

"I've been hurt worse," he muttered. That quiet growl, so certain, so dismissive, lit a fuse in me.

I shoved at his chest, anger swallowing fear. "You think I care about your macho soldier routine? Sit down before you pass out."

For a second I thought he'd push back, thought he'd storm out and leave me choking on adrenaline and fear, alone in my room. Instead, his gaze locked with mine, stormy and unreadable. He let me tug him backward, step by step, until I had him inside the dressing room. I slammed the door closed with trembling fingers leaving everyone else in the hall calling after me.

The roar of voices outside faded to a dull hum. In here it was just us. Me with bloody towels. Him bleeding all over the floor and looking at me like I was more dangerous than the man who had put a laser in a seat to scare me.

I forced him into the chair, heart pounding. The nearness of him, the size of him, the sheer heat rolling off his body made me dizzy. My hands shook as I tore open the first aid kit, but when I pressed gauze to his arm, something steadied. His eyes never left mine, hazel burning deep, a promise and a warning at the same time.

For once it wasn't the pop princess sassing the cowboy. It was me caring for him. And God help me, I liked the way he let me. I liked my hands on him.

His shirt clung to his skin, shredded across the bicep, the fabric dark with blood. I peeled it back carefully, my fingers brushing hard muscle as I worked the cloth free. He flinched but didn't pull away, jaw set tight like he could will the pain into silence.

I dabbed at the wound with antiseptic, my hands trembling until they found his heat, his solidity. Then, somehow, I calmed. Every time I pressed the gauze, his breath hissed sharp through his teeth, a sound that slid straight through me.

"You're supposed to be protecting me," I whispered, my voice thinner than I meant. "Not bleeding all over my floor."

His eyes lifted, hazel darkened to molten gold. "It's nothing. I can take it."

That was the problem. He took everything. The weight, the blame, the cut from something as he'd tackled me to the floor. And now the silence stretched thick between us, charged with something neither of us were naming. My fingers lingered too long against his arm, tracing the line of his vein, the ridge of muscle.

"Hold still," I muttered, though I was the one unsteady. My pulse hammered, loud in my ears, louder than the commotion beyond the locked door.

His gaze dropped to my mouth. I saw it. Felt it. A jolt snapped through me so strong my knees weakened. I leaned closer without meaning to, close enough to feel the heat of his breath fan my lips.

For a single, reckless heartbeat, I forgot the cameras, the brand, the threats. There was only me, him, and the dizzy truth that I wanted him more than I feared anything else. His hand twitched like he might reach for me. Then he went still, every muscle locked in restraint. But his eyes never wavered.

And in that silence, I burned.

The scent of antiseptic faded, but the heat in the room only grew. Jake sat there with his shirt half torn away, chest rising slow and heavy, eyes locked on me like I was something dangerous. I pressed the bandage down harder than I needed to, not out of cruelty, but because I needed to feel him flinch, needed proof I wasn't the only one unraveling.

"I can't keep doing this," I blurted. The words scraped my throat raw, but once they were out, I couldn't stop. "I can't keep pretending I'm a wind up they shove onto a stage. I hate the bows, I hate the songs, I hate the lie."

Jake didn't move. His jaw ticked, his gaze steady, piercing. He didn't offer comfort or argue. He just watched me like I'd peeled off my own skin.

My fingers shook as I tossed the bloody gauze aside. "Do you know what it's like to smile while you're dying inside? To sell innocence when you feel like a fraud every time you open your mouth?" My chest heaved, the glitter on my skin catching the lights like broken glass.

His eyes softened, the edges of steel melting into something hotter, deeper. It made my knees weak. It made me furious. "Say something," I demanded, because silence was too much.

"You're not a lie," he said at last, voice low, rough. "Not when you look at me like that."

I froze, heart slamming. No one had ever said it. No one had ever looked at me and seen anything past the costume. The mask I had worn for years cracked wide open, and I wasn't sure if I could ever put it back on again.

His words still echoed in me, louder than the cheers of any stadium crowd. *You're not a lie.* I wanted to believe him. I wanted to drown in the way he looked at me, like I was a woman and not a brand. My pulse beat hard in my throat as I shifted closer, unable to stop myself.

Jake didn't move away. His eyes dropped to my mouth, and the room shrank to the space between us. My fingers curled into the arm of his chair, knuckles white, because if I touched him now, I wouldn't let go.

I leaned in, slow, my breath hitching. He was heat and strength and danger wrapped into one man, and I had never wanted anything more. His scent, sweat, leather, something raw, wrapped around me. The whole world narrowed to the millimeter of air left between us.

His lips brushed mine. Just a ghost of contact, a whisper of what could be. My heart slammed, my body trembling with need. It was nothing and it was everything. I tipped forward, desperate to close the gap, to finally claim something that was mine, not theirs.

And then he broke it. Jake jerked back, a curse under his breath. His hand fisted on his thigh, like he was chaining himself down.

"Not like this," he said, voice hoarse, ragged.

The rejection sliced through me even as my lips still tingled from the almost. Shame and want tangled until I could barely breathe. "Why not?" I whispered, hating the crack in my voice.

His gaze met mine, molten and tortured. "Because if I start, Isla, I won't stop."

And in that moment, I knew he was right. But I didn't care.

The space he left between us felt like a chasm, but the heat still pulsed in the air, thick and undeniable. My lips tingled, my chest heaved, and my hands trembled like I'd touched fire and wanted to reach back for more.

He sat rigid, every muscle locked, jaw set like a soldier under orders. "Not like this," he'd said, as if discipline could erase what was burning between us.

I couldn't stand it. Couldn't stand the silence, the distance, the weight of wanting.

"I'm falling for you," I blurted, the words cracking loose before I could shove them back down. They hung in the air, raw and dangerous, more terrifying than any threat note taped to my door.

Jake's eyes snapped to mine. Hazel, storm-dark, unreadable. For a moment, I thought he would deny me, push me away, retreat behind the walls he built from duty and guilt. My stomach twisted.

Then his face shifted, the hardness breaking, his breath shuddering out like he'd been holding it for days. "You're under my skin," he admitted, voice rough, low. The sound of it crawled over my body, igniting everything the almost-kiss had left smoldering.

Relief flooded me so hard it hurt. I wasn't being rejected. Not really. My throat tightened, my heart clawed against my ribs, but I still managed to whisper, "Then stop fighting it."

His hand lifted, like he wanted to touch me, to close that damn chasm. His fingers hovered near my cheek, trembling with restraint. He didn't close the distance. But the look in his eyes said enough.

For the first time, it wasn't Isla Dove the idol, or Isla the product, or Isla the victim. It was just me. Isla Donovan, a woman falling headlong into danger, into him, and not caring about the crash.

His hand hovered so close I swore I could feel the heat radiating from his skin. One more inch and I would have been his. My pulse thundered, every nerve begging him to close the gap.

Then the door banged open.

"Isla, we need to—oh."

Lily froze in the doorway, clipboard clutched to her chest, eyes flicking from me to Jake. I jolted back, blood rushing hot to my cheeks, shame and fury colliding inside me. Jake straightened like a soldier caught off his post, his face shuttering into stone.

Lily's wide eyes took everything in, the bandages, the closeness, the air still sparking between us. Then she pasted on a smile, syrup-sweet, pretending to have seen nothing.

"Your hair's a mess," she chirped, already bustling forward with a fresh bow clutched in her hand.

The sight of it snapped something inside me. Plastic pink with glitter, ridiculous, everything I hated about the brand that had become my cage. She held it out like armor, like shackles, like proof that I wasn't allowed to be a woman bleeding for something real. I was supposed to be the pop princess with perfect curls and a bow glued to her head.

"I don't want it," I snapped, voice sharp.

Lily blinked, confused, as if she couldn't comprehend the words. Behind her, Richard's voice carried down the hall, barking about spin and press. The walls closed in, glitter and lies pressing against my chest until I could barely breathe.

Jake said nothing, but I felt his eyes on me, steady and molten, like he could see the war raging inside. His silence was louder than all of Richard's shouts.

The bow slipped from Lily's fingers and landed on the floor between us.

And for the first time, I didn't reach to pick it up.

The bow lay there between us, cheap plastic, ribbon and glitter catching the fluorescent light. For years I had let people tie it to me like a leash. Now it sat on the floor like a symbol of a bygone era. I wanted to grind it under my heel, to feel it crack into pieces.

Before I could move, my phone buzzed on the counter. The sound sliced through the room, sharp as glass. I grabbed it, half expecting Richard with another demand, half hoping it was nothing.

A voicemail waited. One new message. My thumb hovered, pulse skittering. Jake stepped closer, his presence crowding the space, his body taut as a bowstring. "Play it," he ordered softly.

I hit the speaker.

Static hissed, then a distorted voice slithered through.

"You bleed, he bleeds. Next time, it's for real."

My breath snagged. The words echoed in the room, hanging heavy over the glitter and gauze. The bow at my feet might as well have been a landmine.

Jake's hand closed over mine, steady, grounding, but I felt the tremor in his grip. His jaw flexed, eyes burning like wildfire as the message ended with a click.

Silence pressed in. Lily shifted in the corner, clutching her clipboard too tight, her smile cracking at the edges. I stared down at the bow, that bright scrap of plastic glowing obscenely against the linoleum. It no longer looked like something innocent. It looked like a bullseye painted by someone who wanted me destroyed.

My knees threatened to buckle, but Jake tightened his grip until I steadied. His voice was low, fierce. "They won't win."

But the truth cut sharper than his promise. The game wasn't over. It was only getting bloodier.

Chapter 15
The Threat Replayed

I played the voicemail again. The warped voice filled the room, crawling under my skin like barbed wire. *You bleed, he bleeds. Next time, it's for real.* The words were a blade pressed to her throat and mine at the same time.

My grip on the phone tightened until plastic creaked. I wanted to smash it against the wall, but I forced myself to hold still. Losing control wouldn't help Isla.

She stood a few feet away, pale under the stage makeup, curls sliding from their pins. She looked small, shaken, like the bow on the floor had stripped the armor away. My chest ached for her, but I shoved the feeling down where it couldn't get in the way.

This wasn't about me. It was about keeping her alive.

I saved the message to my secure folder and shoved the phone into my pocket. I would forward it to Connor's team later. My fists itched for a fight, for something real to hit, but all I had was static and shadows.

"They're not bluffing anymore," I said, my voice gravel.

Isla flinched, then straightened, chin tilting like she refused to show fear. God, she was brave. Braver than she knew.

"I can't do this, Jake," she whispered. Her eyes were glassy, her shoulders trembling. "I can't keep waiting for the next attack."

I crossed the room and stopped inches from her, close enough to feel her breath. "You won't face it alone," I said, low, steady, iron in my voice. "Not while I'm breathing."

Her lip trembled, but she nodded, trusting me. That trust was a heavier weight than body armor. I couldn't fail Isla. I wouldn't.

I spread every file I had on the kitchen table like a crime scene. Photos, timelines, rigging reports, the log I kept of threats. Patterns showed up like blood on white cloth if you stared long enough. Every escalation clustered around rehearsals, every sabotage timed to make the spotlight the danger zone. Whoever wanted her dead understood spectacle.

The bank records I'd pulled from Richard painted a picture so ugly my gut turned cold. Large transfers in and out of anonymous accounts, payments to event crews that had no reason to exist, invoices for equipment that was never delivered. It read like a money trail with a purpose. Someone bought access and then brought chaos.

I traced dates with my finger until the ink blurred. The laser phone was placed two weeks after a payment cleared one of Richard's accounts. The cut wire matched the same tool marks I'd seen on the bolt from the earlier incident. Same hand, same level of craft. This was not a jealous fan lashing out. This was organized.

I called for Sierra Bravo expertise. They worked their network of contacts. Badge logs were pulled. Crew lists were cross-referenced. I was fed names that smelled of hands greased, money passed and a lot of nerve. A producer who liked quick returns. A supplier who took cash under the table. Pieces slid into place, and the image that formed was a set of hands shaping a hit list around a brand.

When I looked up, Isla was watching me, stripped of performance, watching how I held her life in the palms of my hands. She didn't ask for details. She didn't try to rate the danger. She simply let me work.

I felt the map of her danger like heat through gloves. There was a thread tying the attacks together, and it led back to people who could move a stage as easily as they moved money. Follow the thread, and we might find the man who thought he owned her. I was ready to unravel the whole sweater.

We went to Richard's office before dawn. I figured men who sold betrayal probably did not sleep well. Worst case, we would be his first appointments for the day. The receptionist hadn't arrived yet, but I doubt by the look on my face she would have dared to call security. I pushed the door open without knocking. He was at his desk, coffee gone cold, suit rumpled the way not having made it home looked. He definitely had the appearance of a man whose world was rocking. I intended to tear it down.

I put the bank statements on his blotter like a verdict. He stared as if the numbers were alien. Until I pointed out the transfers, anonymous accounts, and payments clearing the same days rehearsals had gone wrong. My jaw worked around the taste of bile.

"Why don't you explain these," I said, flat and patient in a way that meant I had no patience left.

He tried to charm, to call it investor noise, to frame it as protecting the brand. I watched him script excuses that would play well to cameras but not to anyone with a conscience. I gave him a four-letter description of my opinion.

"I thought I was helping her," he said. The words sounded small, a man trying to trade guilt for applause.

I didn't let him shape the narrative. I pushed dates at him, signatures, vendor names. I didn't allow him an inch of deniability. His face creased. The man who built her image had also sold access. He kept calling it opportunity. I called it theft.

When he finally spluttered a name that kept coming up in the logs that I had already run badges on, I felt the thread tighten. He had drawn a line he could not unpaint. Then Isla walked in, an Isla devoid of glitter, wearing regular clothing.

"Now. Explain yourself to her." I snarled.

"I never wanted it to go this far," he said, voice raw. "I thought I was protecting you. I thought I could manage it." His language tried to bleach responsibility. "There were payments. I took them. I thought I could control who came close."

"You need to come clean. Tell the police everything." Isla said, though her eyes were hollow with his confession of betrayal.

He said he would but he sounded unconvincing.

We left him in that cheap office with his apologies like unpaid receipts. His empire smelled like numbers and old perfume. I had what I needed to pull the next knot loose.

We headed back to the mansion and Isla collapsed onto the couch as if someone had pressed pause on her. Her hair hung loose and wrong in the best way. For once no one had fussed with her to make the world like her better. She looked tired in a way performance could not fix.

I sat down beside her without asking. The silence between us was not empty. It held the shape of what I'd found.

"You knew?" was the only question she needed to ask. It came out small. Her hands kept folding the thin blanket on her knees. I took them and held them like I could anchor her to the floor.

"Didn't put all the pieces together until last night," I said. "But enough."

She let the news settle like someone hearing a name for the last time.

"Everything is a product to him," she murmured.

The betrayal had a new texture. It was not just business. It was personal theft. I felt anger coil through me the way muscle anticipates a fight. I promised her we would cut the thread. Promises were cheap in this life, but I meant mine. I tightened my fingers around hers and told her we would get answers while I kept her safe. The mask between her and the world had cracked. There was no fitting it back easily.

Back at my rigged command table I replayed footage with a thin coffee and less patience. The old ballad bothered me in a way that had nothing to do with charts. My sister had loved that song until she could not sing anymore. It hurt to hear it used by men using Isla as a plastic brand.

I cross-checked rehearsal lists, payments, and the times of interference. A pattern glowed like a bruise. The same set list, the same lyric turned into a taunt, the same vendor names floating across invoices. A concert promoter's name kept showing up where it should not and the name behind him, I had met. Lucas DeWitt.

I called back into Sierra Bravo to get supplier invoices, any overlap between Lucas's crews and the nights that went wrong. They came back with the kind of neat solution you could follow like a flare. Lucas booked the venues. His supplier showed up on the budget entries that matched the sabotage.

The song was the trigger. Someone had weaponized the one thing that once comforted my sister and used it to order violence. The thread ran from Richard's accounts into Lucas's calendar. The knot now had a leader. I felt the cold certainty of a hunter who had just found the trail.

"Ready for the next link of the chain?" I asked as I walked into the living room.

"Probably not." Isla said, standing up.

We walked out to the SUV to head to Lucas's office.

We never made it.

A tiny red dot burned on the SUV glass. It moved with a focused patience and settled like a curse on her chest. My brain unclipped from deliberation and slammed into action. I threw her down beside the car, my body a shield as the night exhaled glass.

A rifle crack rang out somewhere ahead, distant and obscene. I saw a muzzle flash in the direction across the street. The shooter had not been subtle.

I had to get Isla out of here before he took his next shot.

Chapter 16
Red Dot Freeze

The red dot landed on my chest like a tiny fatal spotlight. It was an obscene pin of light, steady and cruel, and for a second the world narrowed to that one bloody point. I felt Jake moving like a storm before I heard him.

"Down," he shouted, voice ripping through the music in my ears. He was on me in one breath, pushing me low beside the car. I smelled grass and him and the metallic tang of my own fear.

Glass exploded less than a heartbeat later. A window shattered above my head, tiny shards skittering like teeth on the concrete. For a second everything was chaos and sound and the beat of my heart punching in my throat. Jake's arms folded around me like a cage and a refuge at once. He pressed me flat, his chest a living wall over mine, breath hot against my ear.

"Keep your head down," he hissed.

I could feel the tremor in his hands. I could hear the soldier behind the cowboy, calculating what to do, where to go, tallying threats. I shoved my glitter shoes off and scrambled as he pulled me up, bare feet slapping on the concrete as we ran. Jake dragged me through the house and straight toward the panic room like it was the only place in the world that still made sense. Maybe it was.

The door slammed and the steel thudded in my chest like a second heartbeat. He hit the lock, then folded me against the wall. The room smelled of cool metal and canned relief. For a wild, guilty second, I wanted to laugh, to tell him I had never felt more alive, then the reality settled like ice. I had been seconds from dead.

He whispered my name like a prayer and then, fiercer, like a promise. "I'm not letting them have you."

The words were a lifeline and a threat all at once. I caught my breath as Jake hammered some code into his phone. I clung to his arm like it was a lifeline. The adrenaline burned behind my ribs and made my hands shake. I kept thinking about the tiny red dot and how small it had seemed until the rest of the world had exploded. How close I had been to being roadkill in my own driveway. Except for Jake, I would have been just tomorrow's headline, then gone.

I watched his face as he scanned the small metal room like he was mapping exits even here. I felt small and held, like a secret no one else had the right to touch.

The panic room smelled like cold metal and the kind of safety they sell to people who believe security is a product. The walls were thick, the air conditioned into an aseptic chill. I paced once, twice, like a caged animal testing the distance. The light above hummed with a steady clinical patience that made me think of hospitals and things you put away into permanent storage.

Jake moved with a rhythm I recognized from too many of his training drills. He checked the lock, the vent, the hard lines of the room as if each seam might be a lie. He set up a small lamp on the low table, only enough to see without painting our faces for anyone outside monitoring a camera. He balanced between war and tenderness. He made room for me on a cot like he was dividing something equally and fairly.

The silence had weight, like we were waiting for something. It held the shape of what had happened and what might come next. I wanted to cry because everything about me felt fragile and ridiculous. My hair was a mess. My make up smeared in the corners. The woman named Isla Dove on the magazine covers could not have been farther from me.

I tried to breathe without sounding like a siren, without panicking. Jake whispered instructions, practical things no one had ever spoken to me before. How to check locks. Where to listen for the softest footsteps. He moved through the room like a man who had lost people before and learned how to stop it from happening around him again.

At some point my hand found the cool steel of the wall and I pressed my forehead to it. It felt both safe and like another cage. I hated that everything that made me 'me' had been boxed into armor and protocols. I hated that I liked the safety of this tiny box, too.

"Talk to me," he said low, like a doctor in this war zone. "Tell me anything that matters."

I wanted to tell him everything and nothing at once. Where do you start when your life has been packaged for sale and was now being used for target practice?

The darkness and the hum made honesty feel possible, like the room's smallness had given me permission to say what I hid behind glitter. I pushed my palms between my knees until the ache went through to somewhere calmer.

"Jake," I said, voice small. "I am not who they sell."

The words were light but true. The confession had been lurking under my tongue for years, swollen with resentment. To say it aloud in the safe thin light felt like unclipping a choke chain.

He watched me, every line on his face softening. "Say it," he urged as he sat beside me.

I let the knot of it spill out. I told him I had never wanted the bow. I told him I had let people decide what to sing and when to smile because I was too scared to fight them, too afraid no one would like the real Isla.

"In high school, that guy I dated, the one who ignored me when I said 'no'. He was bigger than me. Hit me when I tried to fight. He raped me. When I got home, I wrote I'll Stand Tomorrow and then I swore I'd never to let anyone touch me again. I took on the image of the Forever Innocent Isla." I whispered.

The memory tasted bitter. He held the shape of the words with steady hands. He did not flinch. He listened the way you listen to someone who you know will be a person in your life after the sound has gone. When I told him I feared I had been sold and that my life had only been a ledger entry, something quiet and fierce lit behind his eyes.

"You did not sign up to be a product," he said. His voice was soft but iron. "None of that was theirs to take anymore than that boy's in high school."

I wanted to believe him. I wanted to stitch the pieces back together with that sound. The truth had no pretty edges. It was jagged and hot and real. But saying it out loud made some of the weight move, made some of the shame unhook from my ribs. For the first time I felt like the person in the room cared not about the brand, but about the woman who hated it.

He switched from comfort to business without ceremony. One moment he was the man holding me while I trembled; the next he was the soldier who read maps in the dark. He must have been mapping the house on the inside of his skull because he listed exits and contingencies like memorized songs.

"Listen for the difference," he said. "Three dull taps means they are trying the door. Metallic scraping could mean tools. If you hear the snap of a bolt, head for the vent and remember where it empties out."

I think he spoke because speaking made danger a thing he could count, command. He moved around the room, cataloging the little practicalities I had never noticed. He said the vent led under a stairwell which went to a maintenance hatch and on to a crawl space to the outside. He marked them with the tip of his finger as if outlining the map of a battlefield. His hands were efficient. His eyes were quick.

I watched how he worked and felt a tug in my chest like relief and guilt braided together. He still had me in his charge. He set up a control that would sound if the outer door was breached. He made sure I knew how to turn it off if I had to move. He explained how to wedge something heavy behind a door and where spare phones were stored throughout the house.

There was precision in him I had not known before. The soldier inside the cowboy had not been erased by easy living. He took control like a man practicing a duty that had been carved into him. He had been organizing for just such an event the entire time he had been here. I wanted to crawl into his arms and hide there forever. I wanted to throw myself into the plan and feel useful.

When he sat across from me and told me to breathe, it was with the same calm he used to analyze the room. I trusted that calm more than any promise the industry had ever made.

The room shrank until it held only the two of us. Between plans and lists and the thin light, something real tightened like a thread. He had been my protector for more than a week, a wall of muscle and stubbornness. In the close quiet I realized he was also the man I wanted in the way people want oxygen when trapped.

He said something small and honest about my voice, about how it had steadied when I looked at him onstage. I lost whatever composure I had left. The way his mouth softened at the edges made the breath leave me.

I leaned closer, like a tide pulled by gravity. He did not move away. His eyes held me. For a moment the world outside the steel walls was an irrelevant rumor. I wanted to close the space and stop time and take what I had denied myself for so long.

His fingers hovered near my cheek as if testing whether touch was allowed. The almost kiss hovered between us, heavy and dangerous. The temptation was a live wire pulsing up my arm. I could have closed the distance. I could have chosen this place that had nothing to do with contracts or danger and everything to do with wanting.

He stopped it, the way someone puts a hand on a leash before it slips. He looked at me with an apology that was not spoken and said, "Not like this." The words were the same as before and they broke me open again.

I wanted to scream at him to stop being noble and to be human instead. Instead, I let my forehead rest against his chest and listened to his heart beat like a drum. The sound steadied me and also hurt in a way that made my fingers clench.

A sound from the other side of the door made us both freeze. It was the first real angry hit, the one that meant someone outside was not bluffing. Wood groaned, metal protested, and the room gave up the pretense of being safe.

Someone hammered at the door. A voice snarled from the other side, and it sounded closer than it had any right to be. Jake paled, jaw set, hands tightening around me until I could feel the lines of his knuckles.

"We're safe in here, right?" I whispered.

Jake didn't say anything. That was all the answer I needed. He moved without hesitation. He wedged a chair under the handle. He thumbed a small device and the room's light shifted to a low emergency glow. The intercom static snapped to life like a live wire. A voice hissed through the speaker, garbled but with a tone I recognized from the voicemails.

"Jake can't save you. No one can tonight," the voice said. The words were a taunt and a promise.

I heard the scraping of boots, heavy and measured. The hits against the door grew louder. Someone pounded as if hammers were designed to loosen bolts. The room felt like it was narrowing, like we were sinking under some weight. My knees trembled and I had to wedge my hands between my knees to stop the shaking. The panic became a choking thing in my throat.

Jake delivered quick commands in a voice that was both a lullaby and a line of fire. "If they get the door, head for the vent. Don't stop. Move when I say." His hands were on my shoulders, hard and steady.

All I could think was that Jake's broad shoulders would never fit through that vent. He expected me to leave him. I wanted to scream 'no'. I wanted to cry. But I just nodded, mutely as my heart pounded.

A thud higher up made dust fall from the ceiling seam. One of the outer walls shuddered. It became impossible to pretend the steel would hold forever. The noise from outside was urgent, a machine learning the exact tempo needed to get through.

My breath was shallow. They hit the door again and wood somewhere splintered. It sounded like bone. The hits turned into the sound of tools, then the weight of bodies. A voice outside bellowed talk about breaking and entry, about numbers and time.

The speaker spat another line of static and then the cruel whisper: "We're inside your world now."

Jake's jaw set and he moved like a machine. He wedged, kicked, and then pressed his shoulder against the door while he counted in a voice of steely calm. "Three, two, one." He shoved with everything he had and the chair on the handle held for a beat longer. The next impact splintered wood and a beam of bright light found a seam to pry into our world.

A shadow slid across the lip of the frame, a glint of metal. I smelled diesel and fear and something chemical that made my throat close. The air in the room felt thinner, as if oxygen was being rationed.

Then the handle ripped free with a sound like an animal dying. Someone screamed my name as the door gave way. I saw a silhouette with a hard face and hands that did not tremble. The room flooded with the shape of a man and the barrel of something metal.

Jake shoved me behind him as the first figure shoved through. The lights went wild and then cut to a low, red emergency flash. Splinters fell. I pressed my back to the steel wall and felt my own heartbeat fill my ears.

One of the intruders advanced with a grin like a disease. He pointed and said, loud enough for me to hear, "You're mine." The words landed like a death sentence.

Jake pushed me and hissed, "Not as long as I'm standing. Vent! Now!" He braced as bodies moved into the small room.

A gun went off. Blood flew in slow motion between me and the vent. Jake had been hit! But he was acting like it meant nothing, fighting like a machine. He had backed me up against the wall. I couldn't get to the vent or anywhere.

A blow landed so hard on Jake's chest, I jerked backwards, banging my head against the wall and seeing stars. The world narrowed to the sound of fists, grunts and the metallic taste of fear. I had never been so close to a man in my life and never so terrified he might not be enough. Or I might lose him.

Then a gunshot cracked in the hallway, followed by the howl of sirens growing distant and then near. The chaos swallowed everything else and left me with a single sharp thought: they had come inside the house. They had crossed the last line.

We fought. We ducked. I clung to Jake's shirt back like a tether, praying I would not be the one to let go.

Chapter 17
Smoke and Mirrors

The moment the door finally gave, everything turned loud and ugly. Guys in black filled the hallway like spilled ink, faces set, hands on weapons. They couldn't all crowd through the narrow opening at once. My brain clicked through tasks. Protect the asset. Anchor second. Move on threat. My gun was outside, fallen when I'd grabbed Isla to protect her from the sniper.

I shoved Isla back behind me, my body already answering before the fight did. One intruder lunged straight at me. His gun went off as I met him with a forearm, Fire exploded down my arm. I ignored it and executed a throw that put him down and out. Two more tried to come at different angles. The room smelled of adrenaline, cordite and the metallic tang of fear.

"Don't shoot! You'll hit her." One of them yelled after the first shot.

One of the bastards tried to reach around me for her. I did not let him. I wrapped an arm around his throat and drove him into the wall like I was pounding in a nail. There was no hesitation in my hands anymore. Only purpose.

Police sirens cut through the noise like knives. A neighbor must have heard the shots and called it in. Good. Bad. Both. Reinforcements meant help, but they also meant the fight would get more desperate before it got contained. I had hot lined Sierra Bravo when we entered the panic room but no telling when they'd arrive either. I knew this 'secure room' was only meant to slow down determined robbers. It would do nothing against anyone with experience or tools as evidenced by the attack we now faced.

I'd been backed up between the bunks, Isla behind me, wedged against the wall. The intruders now had control of the front half of the room; so, the vent option was out. I had to keep them back until backup arrived. Our only saving grace was they weren't just spraying lead into the room.

Isla stayed pressed to my back. Her breathing was fast and shallow. I felt every tremor in her body as if it were my own. The intruders had been organized enough to get inside, but sloppy enough in their execution to limit their own access. They were going to have to go through me to touch her. I didn't have time to evaluate odds or outcomes. I simply glued my feet to the floor and met every attacker with single minded fury.

And then, they exchanged angry glances and melted away. Something must have come over their comm units. I stayed in position for a full minute. Then I crept cautiously forward and pulled off the vent cover, motioning Isla in. As she knelt by it, a new figure appeared in the hall. I set my hand on her shoulder, stopping her. It was a uniformed SWAT officer, helmet on, eyes hard and unblinking. He barked into his shoulder radio. The chaos was over as quickly as it had started.

I let the professionals take over tasks I could not think through while Isla still needed me to be fierce and simple. I kept my hand on her back until they led her away for statements.

Sierra Bravo came in like a hammer on SWAT's heels. Black armor, helmets, faces shadowed, boots pounding. Trained movements. No theatrics. The lead shouted into a radio, and the rest answered like it had been rehearsed for a production.

I fell into their perimeter like I belonged to the plan. They ran a sweep, and I watched the methodical way they mapped the rooms. We made division of labor an art. One team went for rooftop access. Another took the perimeters. Breach teams checked chokepoints.

They asked me questions in quick bursts as a medic treated my arm, the kind that wanted nothing but facts. Who was in the house. Where had we come from. Who had seen what. I told them everything that mattered. I pointed to the seam in the front door where the pry marks told that story. I explained the rehearsal laser test, the staged attempts. Every detail I gave them made their scope tighter. SWAT was taking notes.

They found remnants in the yard that matched tools used on the door. A scope lens. A length of wire. When the SWAT leader told me they were also pulling camera footage from neighbors, I felt some of the pressure lift. Not because I trusted systems, but because the heat around the case was growing.

Isla watched from the kitchen doorway, face hollowed but determined. Her eyes met mine and I offered the only thing I could without giving her false hope. A nod. She gave one back and then stepped away to work with detectives. It was the smallest gesture and the only armor we had left: the world was now officially on notice.

They found Jenna in the basement, mascara streaked like a confession and mouth full of excuses. She looked like she had been turned inside out. Seeing her hauled through the front door in cuffs shook something loose in the room.

She screamed and wailed and said the things people say when cornered: 'I loved you. They told me I was supposed to get my break. I was jealous.' It was messy and terrible and human in the usual way.

The officers read her rights, and the world processed it as closure. The cameras out front would probably eat it like candy.

She kept insisting she had no part in the sniper plans, that she wanted only the spotlight, not violence. Her voice broke on that one. The detectives believed her story. They believed the jealous angle because it was neat, tidy and within the margins. It was an LA kind of solution.

The Sierra team leader and I exchanged looks. We had to be careful not to offend any local police, but this scene felt like someone had handed us a partial hand-drawn paper map of a minefield. Jenna's tears were loud and raw but not necessarily truthful about everything. She had motive for some mean things, but motive was not the same as skilled execution. The rifle found at the perimeter did not look like something a backup singer had brought along. It looked like professional work.

I watched Jenna's hands clench when an officer mentioned the bolt cutters found outside. She went silent and then looked frightened. That fear was a component too. But the team and I kept our eyes on the pattern. Jenna might have been hungry and dangerous in a small way, but someone else had orchestrated the real machine.

SWAT laid the rifle out on the kitchen table with the clinical care of morticians. The scope was polished, but the work on the mount was sloppy in a way that screamed of someone in a hurry. Not hurried by incompetence but hurried by someone who knew they had to move and move now.

What mattered was the photograph taped to the stock. It was Isla, from six years earlier, blonde and different but unmistakably her. Someone had glued it like a calling card. That was not a random stalker, not Jenna. That was a pro with a target.

Forensics would pull prints and fibers and chemical residue if any existed. The serial number had been sanded but not perfectly. Someone had wanted deniability. Someone had also underestimated the amount of work it takes to scrub a weapon clean. A Sierra Bravo tech called my name and handed me a print match on a glove found near the panic room. It was not Jenna's. It was not a name in the long lists of people I had sent in to be checked. A new name. It belonged to someone tied to one of Lucas DeWitt's contractors. The kind of contractor you called when you wanted results and no questions, one with a long record.

I felt the thread go from suspicion to proof. Someone with access, someone paid, someone on call had helped arm the play. The rifle was probably not a separate act. It was part of a team effort.

I went out to my SUV to retrieve my gun and thank the Sierra Bravo group who had answered my call. As they pulled away, my phone vibrated in my pocket like a small, impatient animal. I saw the message preview and felt my stomach fold.

Your deadline's up. Final concert. Final encore.

The words were simple. They were not a threat dressed up in flowers. They were the sentence of a man who had decided when the finale would fall. Whoever had orchestrated this had confidence and a time frame and now they had put us on notice without fearing we could do anything to alter the ending.

I did not answer. I would not give them the satisfaction of a reaction. Instead, I called Sierra Bravo. We made plans in terse sentences. The operation would be tactical. We would be methodical. We would make sure this sunlit city could not turn this into theater again with neat, tidy answers that didn't really solve the problem.

Chapter 18
False Alibis

They polished my face per usual, but I felt like an old relic. The makeup chair was my interrogation seat under bright lights while hands moved over me with practiced indifference. The bow on my head pinched at my scalp though I had largely forgotten what my head felt like without it. Stylist fingers tugged at neon curls, powder dusted my throat, and every touch felt like someone staging me for a funeral I had not agreed to.

I stared into the mirror at a stranger who had my eyes. It was definitely Isla Dove, pop idol in that mirror but I felt so different now. I had seen death painted on my chest, watched a safe room come unglued right in front of me and then waited for Jake to die as he stood firmly against men determined to destroy both of us without a thought. I hadn't been able to sleep thinking about all the what-ifs. And most of them kept circling back to what if Jake had ended up dead? How could I have dealt with his dying for me? How was any of this worth his life?

The production team laughed about lighting and camera angles. Lily fussed with my skirt and said things about "playing into the empathy" like it was a strategy and last night was not a crime, almost murder. I wanted to spit or puke. I wanted to tear it all off and run into the nearest diner and eat pancakes with Jake like a real person at this breakfast hour. Instead, I sat and let them make me a thing again.

Backstage I felt the weight of eyes I could not see. The bow felt heavier than plastic. It felt like the entire brand was closing around my throat. I thought about Jake's hands on my back the night before, how he had pressed me down not to humiliate but to protect, to keep a bullet from piercing my skin. I kept replaying Jake taking whatever came at him to keep those men away from me in the panic room. Not caring he was shot, hurt, bleeding, only that I was behind him. How did I rank that level of selflessness? I thought about Richard, hands that once promised safety and now seemed to have traded me for money. The costume felt like a superficial trap, like a slap in Jake's face for his real sacrifice.

Lily shepherded me onto the stage with the cheerful vigor of a woman who thought being onstage could fix anything. She reminded me of the release date and concert times to say in a happy voice and gave a thumbs-up like we were doing a commercial. I wanted to laugh hysterically and then slap her. Instead, I tilted my chin and went out because it was a live show. People were waiting. Hundreds of people's livelihoods depended on the success of my CD release and the tour.

When I stepped out under the lights, applause hit me like a hurricane force wind. I kept my mouth working. On set I said the scripted lines with the split-second timing I had rehearsed a thousand times. Smile. Wiggle. Giggle. The audience cooed on cue. Reporters scribbled, thirsty for a quote about bravery and resilience. Nobody asked what it felt like to be the target of someone who meant to kill you, to wonder if you were going to watch someone you cared about die protecting you.

Inside my chest a quieter sound was bubbling up. *Refusal.* The thing they bought and sold was not all of me. It was coming up like bad sushi and at some point, I wouldn't be able to stomach it anymore.

I would find a way to prove it without them realizing until it was too late for them to undo.

Jake stood in the wings like a monument. His hat shadowed his eyes, and his jaw was a hard line. He did not clap. He did not play a part. He had never succumbed to anyone's attempts to make him anything other than what he was. He looked at me like a man who wanted to reach inside to the real me. My heart yearned for him to do just that.

When I caught his eye, a flash of something passed through him. It looked like grief and like anger at the same time. He kept his posture neutral, professional. But I knew the small tells the way a musician knows a chord. He clenched his fist under his jacket, knuckles whitening. He mouthed nothing and yet the tension said everything.

On stage my smile felt like a lie I had rehearsed into muscle memory. I danced in time, lips moving on the chorus, the choreography a string of safe motions. Fans cheered because that is what they were trained to do. Cameras found angles that made me younger, purer, less like the woman who had been up late patching truths together with a man in boots for the police.

When the interviewer asked about strength on live TV, I gave them a neat, marketable line about resilience. It sounded like a press release, and we both knew it. In the audience, a sea of glittered posters and teenage faces ate it up. They needed my performance to be whole because their fantasies depended on it. What none of them could comprehend was the calculus of fear I balanced each time I stepped into the light. Waiting for another red dot. Looking for hostility. Wondering who would stab me this time. How the attack would look.

Between numbers I watched the crowd like someone learning a beast's movement. Faces blurred into signs, then into individuals, then back into a mass. My chest felt hollow and heavy at once. The brand that had been propped and polished by men who saw profit in purity had turned me into a performance that could be weaponized. I was the bait and the moral hazard and the product.

My breath hitched when I saw him. Brian had the smile of someone who thought ownership was a thing he could claim by chanting and holding up a sign. He stood mid-crowd with glitter on his cheek and a fan placard that read FOREVER PURE like it was a prayer.

Security moved those around him a little bit too slowly. By the time they pulled him, he had said something under his breath that crawled up my spine. He mouthed a phrase I recognized from "I'll Stand Tomorrow" but refashioned into ownership. He was saying 'I promise you a fairy tale'. The actual lyrics were 'You promised me a fairy tale - Then pulled the rug and watched me fail'. I felt nauseous that he was quoting a twisted line from my trauma song.

The crowd didn't understand the nuance. They only wanted drama. An assistant dragged him off with a show of muscle and mouthed apologies. The camera caught the flap of the moment and would probably cut to a segment about overzealous fans. They would turn the story into a clip and a headline and not a crime. He kept looking back at me like a man who had crossed a private line and expected it to be rewarded.

As I climbed the stairs to go offstage, I wanted to rip the costume and show them the real bruises under the glitter from being tackled to the ground to keep me alive. Instead, I let costume and makeup cover the reality, let the music whitewash the fear. For now, the performance would go on. But inside me a new script was writing itself. I would be the one to read it when the right mic came within reach.

Backstage at the venue felt like an animal trap. My dressing room was a wreck, not the usual stylized chaos but real ransacking. My vanity drawers yawned open. Makeup strewn across the floor. Jewelry, broken and smashed. A photo had been torn in half and slashed by lipstick, the red smear obscene across my smiling face. Reporters might call it a PR stunt. My skin crawled with how personal it seemed.

A security tech pulled me aside and handed me a photo that made my stomach flip. It was a Polaroid of me and Richard from years ago, a memory he used to frame as our "origin" story. The Polaroid was slashed, my side marked. Someone had written words across the torn edge in shaky handwriting that read like another threat: 'Your smile is just a lie'. It was another twisted version of lyrics from *I'll Stand Tomorrow*. It felt intimate in a way that made me sick.

I almost dropped to my knees. This was not about merchandise or a viral moment. This was about someone touching the parts of me that were private and making them public. Lily hovered and made noises about replacing hairpins.

Jake came in then, silent the way he was when he had found the phone with the laser. He no longer masked anger with professional calm. His face was a map of a man who had realized a friend had betrayed a family member. He gathered the Polaroid and filed it away. No doubt to add it to his collection of evidence. When he looked at me it was not pity. It was intent.

"Not one more," he said. He was seething.

The words were both plan and vow. I wanted to believe him with my whole heart, but I wasn't sure he could stop this insanity. I didn't think anyone could.

Richard called and his voice was different from the polished tone I had come to know. He started to apologize before he even got very many words out, as if he had been rehearsing and then found he could not sell his own lies anymore.

"I never wanted it to go this far," he said, voice raw. "I thought I was protecting you. I thought I could manage it." His language tried to bleach responsibility. "There were payments. I took them. I thought I could control who came close."

My hands tightened on the phone until the plastic creaked. The voice that had put glitter bows on my head and signed my contracts was asking for mercy as if I owed him something. I could hear papers rustling. I imagined a ledger under his hands like a confession.

I told him to come clean in terse monosyllables. I told him to tell the police everything. He said he would, and then he cried in a way that sounded unconvincing even to me. The call ended with a promise to meet me and Jake in person. I hung up and felt a cold that crawled under my skin.

I stood in the dressing room, phone warm in my palm, and watched the clock like a metronome counting down my life, my career. Richard had said he would meet us at his office tomorrow morning. He said he would bring proof and names. He sounded like a man who wanted absolution. I'd believe it when I saw it. I didn't trust anyone. Except Jake.

Chapter 19
Midnight Confessions

The place felt too quiet, like someone had turned off the world. I moved through it slow, boots muted on marble, checking doors and windows not out of habit but because my body had been rewired to expect danger. The trophies on the shelf looked ridiculous under the kitchen light. Posters and glossy proofs of a life I had only ever seen in fragments were every place I wasn't supposed to be. Platinum albums adorned the walls. It was a surreal world for a simple soldier turned bodyguard. I kept waiting for an alarm to scream or a shadow to move wrong.

When I found her on the bedroom dark balcony, she was a silhouette against the city, hair loose and the bow nowhere in sight. She held herself small, shoulders up like they were keeping something fragile from spilling out. The night air smelled like exhaust and jasmine, and she looked older than the girl on those billboards. Her eyes caught mine and I felt something in me go tight, like a wire pulled to full tension.

She did not run toward me. She did not preen for comfort. She was just there, honest and raw, and the sight of her like that hit harder than any threat had. The sound of the city took on the distance of a radio turned low. We did not need words right away. There was an ache behind her eyes I knew my hands could not fix, but I wanted to try anyway.

When she finally spoke, it came out small and jagged.

"I'm done," she said, her voice steady but raw, like she'd been holding those words in for far too long. Her tousled brown waves fell loose to her shoulders, the neon hardly visible in this light. They framed her face as she stepped closer. "No more 'forever innocent.' No more pretending. I'm tired of being sold as produce. Tired of promises that cost more than they pay."

Her voice almost broke. I let the silence hold us, and then I let my own defenses fall. I did not come up to her bedroom to play a boyfriend, to play a stunt. I came because she mattered.

"If I have to pull the world apart to keep you safe, I'll do it." I swore.

Maybe it was bravado. Maybe it was the truth. Either way, it was the only honest thing I had to offer.

She curled into herself like a woman who had learned to fold tightly to survive. The confession spilled out in fits between breaths. She talked about the bow, about the songs, about how every smile felt like someone else's script. She told me again about the night in high school that had closed something off inside her, and how that closure had been turned into a brand that ate her alive.

I listened. Learning the details felt like a betrayal I had a duty to repair. She said the words no publicist would ever allow on record, words about shame and wanting and being terrified to touch anyone. Her voice was small and then it was not. It grew teeth when she spoke about Richard and about how debts and deals had turned into threats with a pattern.

There, on the balcony with the whole city watching like it had the right, she let herself crumble. I wanted to take the pieces and put them back for her, not as a fixer but as a man who would hold the breaks together until she could find the glue herself. I kept my face even because anything else would have been selfish. She needed a steady thing, not another fracture, not a man with too many ghosts.

"I'm tired of being protected like I'm some valuable trophy." She said.

I nearly told her she had it wrong. I nearly said she deserved the protection, deserved to be shielded without feeling diminished. Instead, I said what she needed to hear: that her worth was not tied to what men paid for, that she was not inventory, that she was a woman who deserved to live for herself.

I had kept myself tight for weeks, practiced restraint like discipline. The line between job and want had been thin but defined. I had rules and I had kept them. But hearing her lay herself bare, seeing the way the city had chewed on her and spat out a girl I wanted to protect for reasons that had nothing to do with duty, something in me loosened.

It was not a sudden collapse. It had been a dangerous, slow erode. The soldier in me barked that this was a mission and boundaries were essential. The man in me, the one who had lost a sister and learned to move through grief without a map, recognized a familiar ache and wanted to fix it with more than tactics. That longing made my hands tremble.

She reached up and tucked a loose curl behind her ear. The gesture was small and intimate and made me want to close the distance like a man answering a command he could not refuse. I swallowed hard and kept the words locked behind the teeth: I need you, I want you, I cannot afford to let this turn us into more than this and I cannot afford to pretend I don't desire it like air.

I wanted to sign away all the rules. I wanted to hold her until the world made sense again. I wanted to press a claim on something that was nobody's right but mine. Instead, I steadied myself. I told myself the only way I would fail her is if I let my wanting blur my judgment. I would not be the weak link.

But restraint was fraying like a rope worn thin. The line between us had become a taut wire humming under the weight of two hearts. I did not know how long it would hold.

I felt my jaw tighten, my instincts kicking in. The bodyguard in me wanted to shield her, to keep her safe from whatever was driving her to this edge. But I wasn't exactly sure what she meant, and I wasn't about to start dancing into a potential minefield of possibilities.

"What do you mean, Isla?" I asked, softly.

"I mean." She said standing in front of me and reaching up to take my hat, "I am not a teenager. I am not their doll." She tossed my hat across the room toward her dresser. I paid no attention to where it ended up. "And if you say 'not like this' tonight, I swear I will tackle you and strip you naked. Got the message, cowboy?"

She wrapped her hands around my neck gazing up at me with daring in her eyes.

"Copy." I said, "But, Isla. Are you sure? Your brand and ..."

"Shut. Up!" she said, plastering her body against mine and sealing her mouth to my lips.

If I had any control left, I lost it. Between the sensation of her body pressed against mine, her perfume and the kiss I had craved, I had to force some semblance of sanity to keep from picking her up and throwing her onto the bed I wanted her so badly.

But I reminded myself, sternly, that Isla's past was trauma. I had to let her dictate the terms of surrender. I was bigger than her and the last thing I wanted was to remind her in any way of that high school bastard. So, though my usual bedroom technique was a bit aggressive, with Isla, I was going to have to let her take the driver's seat.

I pulled back, running my fingers through the curls along her cheeks, my gaze locking onto hers.

"No always means no to me, Isla. Doesn't matter when." I said, seriously.

She nodded, her breath quickening, blinking rapidly.

"And just like during rehearsals, you're the star. You set the pace and the direction. Ok?" I said resting my forehead against hers.

"You mean, I'm the boss of you for a change?" she said with a slow wicked smile.

"Eh, within reason." I said, "I'm not into some stuff."

"I don't know what I'm into." Isla laughed and then added breathily, "Except you."

Her fingers traced down my shirt buttons, and I had to groan. I already had a sizable erection pushing against my jeans and she was adding to the discomfort. But I'd told her she was in charge; so, I would just have to endure.

The heat that had been simmering between us all week only increased as she leaned into my touch, her body responding to my gentle touch. I cupped her face, my thumb tracing her lips, and she parted them, inviting me in.

Our kiss started soft, a tender exploration, but it quickly deepened, tongues tangling, hunger taking over. Isla's hands slid up my chest, gripping my shirt, pulling me closer, her perky breasts pressing against me. I groaned, my hands moving down her back, pulling her tighter. I'm sure she could feel my sex hardening against her thigh, but I tried not to move. I didn't want to give her any impression that I would attack her.

She broke the kiss, breathless, her eyes dark with desire. She took my hand and drew me to her bed. We tossed off shoes and laid down together. I stayed at first base, kissing her face, her jawline, up to her delicate ears. I sucked her earlobe making her giggle and trap one of my calves between her feet. Having one thigh that close to her crotch was torture. I wanted to shift slightly to offer stimulation but that would be jumping to third base. I had to remind myself that Isla was almost as much of a virgin as her brand declared. I had promised that she was in charge. I had to let her be. And thinking about her forced me to concentrate on her and not the increasing stress of holding back.

"I don't know why I'm feeling shy." Isla said, laughing slightly. "It's not like I'm not stripped nearly naked for every costume change in front of everybody."

"A bit different here." I said, playing with her hair and kissing her, "This is real."

"Yeah." She sighed, "Very."

Isla unbuttoned my shirt. I shrugged out of it and let it fall to the floor. Her hands slid up my chest, and I sucked in a breath to steady an overt need to clutch her tightly. I grabbed the sheet beside her head instead. I closed my eyes for a second, counting to a fast ten. Isla had fallen off the horse and not only not gotten back on, she had locked the barn and never looked at one again. I was not going to be a second bad experience, but she was driving me wild with desire.

"Like that?" she whispered.

"Yeah. Killing me by inches." I said, "But I'm tall. I can handle it."

She giggled and pulled her knit top over her head.

"Don't want you dead. Ever." She said and pulled my hand to her breast.

"Isla." I breathed and gently stroked her breast.

She bit her lower lip, and I bent back to kissing her with the added task now of stimulating her nipples. I could feel her breathing increase, her heartrate thrumming along her neck as I kissed her pulse point. She didn't say anything, simply pushed my head down. I got the signal, and I was more than willing to add second base to my kissing trajectory.

Now I could keep both breasts happy and by Isla's reaction, she was. She was breathing through open lips and had both hands on my shoulders, nails biting slightly into my skin. She arched slightly as I forced cool air against one wet nipple and then went to the other one.

"I want you." She breathed.

"I'm here. You're safe, Isla." I said, kissing her.

"I mean sexually. All the way. Now."

I didn't ask if she was sure. I didn't wait longer. I just peeled out of my tight jeans and underwear. When I turned back, she had tossed aside her shorts. I didn't move. I wanted her to still have the option of backing off. She could see all of me in the dim light through the windows and if she freaked out, I wanted her to be able to say 'no' without it being a big deal. It was still her show.

I just went in to kiss her again, letting her feel the fact that I was naked next to her. She wrapped her arms around me and pulled me in tight to her chest.

"I'm sure, Jake." She whispered, "Please."

No woman had ever said 'please' to me before and I was certainly not going to refuse Isla. Not when every fiber of me was crying out to be inside her. I made fast word of a condom and shifted slightly to put myself on top of her, making sure to hold my weight on my forearms. I sighed, feeling she was wet for me. I had been worried. I pushed, as gently as I could, entering her.

The rush was immediate and I groaned, freezing to keep from plunging all the way and possibly hurting Isla. She was hot and wet and damn, I wanted to but I held back, letting her adjust. She wiggled slightly and then relaxed with a deep sigh. She arched up to kiss me, driving her tongue into my mouth. I reciprocated and flexed my hips, pushing myself into her heat.

"God, Isla." I cried as I nearly reached my limit, having no idea she could accommodate me at all.

She shifted again and I did reach it. I could not stop myself from beginning to move. Her walls were gripping me like a vice. I stroked deliberately, deeply, and relentlessly. Isla's nails dug into my shoulders, her hips meeting my thrusts. She made little noises with each plunge, her eyes mostly closed. I leaned to my left and reached my right hand down between us to hit third base with my fingers. I wanted Isla's experience with me as positive as I could make it. I had read somewhere that some women responded more to direct stimulation than vaginal.

Isla reacted immediately. She nearly bucked off the bed, crying out. Maybe she had been going to anyway, but the combination was sending her there fast. That was good because the long foreplay after the week of heat between us was testing my endurance. Isla began panting, nearly drawing blood along my ribs, and making the best moaning noises I had ever heard.

"Let go, Isla." I whispered. "Let it out."

She arched a few times and then she screamed. I think the entirety of Beverly Hills probably heard her singer lung amplified cry. Her vaginal walls clamped down like a fist and I exploded. I cried out my own orgasm, catching myself before I collapsed on top of Isla. After all the frustration, the fighting, the fear, it was intense.

We remained tangled for a few minutes, catching breath and heart-beats. Then I fell over to her side. I pulled her close, my lips pressing to her forehead, my arms holding her tight. She fell asleep before I did and she slept like someone who had at last been given permission to dream. I watched her and felt like a selfish man and a grateful one at the same time. I had wanted this like I wanted a healing that would not arrive on order.

I wrapped an arm around her and whispered promises into the thin dark. She spoke back in the tiny syllables of sleep, and it felt like grace. We were not healed. We were not whole. But we had crossed a line together, and it was ours.

Chapter 20
Fatal Wreck

I woke to warmth and quiet, a rare kind of peace that didn't exist in my world. The morning light crept through the curtains, soft and golden, painting the room like a secret no one else was allowed to see. Jake's arm was heavy across my waist, the weight of it grounding me, protective even in sleep. For a long, dizzy moment I just lay there, listening to the slow rhythm of his breathing and the steady thump of his heart under my cheek.

The night before felt like a dream and a confession all at once, raw, beautiful, impossible. My body still hummed with the memory of his hands and the whisper of his voice when he'd said my name like it mattered more than the rest of the world. I should have been ashamed, maybe even terrified of what came next, but I wasn't. For the first time, I didn't feel like Isla Dove™, the "Forever Innocent" brand. I was just me, bare skin, tangled hair, bruised heart, and he still held on.

He stirred, eyes flickering open. Hazel, sharp and soft at the same time. "You okay?" he murmured, his voice gravel rough from sleep.

"I don't regret it," I whispered.

A slow smile ghosted his lips. "Good. 'Cause I'd do it all again."

Outside, a mockingbird seemed to try to sing *I'll Stand Tomorrow*. My song. The one that had built my cage. But today the melody sounded different, off-key, fragile, human. I almost smiled. Maybe the world was finally learning to hear it the way I meant it, not the way they sold it.

Then my phone buzzed on the nightstand. Once. Twice. The screen lit up with a single word that turned my blood to ice.

Richard.

For a heartbeat I thought I was still dreaming. The name on my phone didn't make sense. *Richard.* My manager. The man who'd built my career and lately, maybe the man who'd been tearing it apart.

I slid out of bed, the hardwood cold under my feet, and swiped open the message. A news alert filled the screen: **"Music Manager Richard Clark Dead in Late-Night Crash."**

The words blurred. "No," I whispered, shaking my head like it might change the letters. Behind me, Jake sat up fast. "What is it?"

I handed him the phone with numb fingers. He read, jaw tightening until I thought the bone might crack. "When?"

"Two a.m.," I said hoarsely. "They're saying single-car accident. Drunk driver."

But Richard didn't drink, at least not enough to kill himself on a canyon road. My stomach twisted. Guilt hit first, then confusion, then the faint taste of fear. Because if he was dead, all the lies he carried went with him. And maybe someone wanted it that way.

Jake swung his legs out of bed, already in soldier-mode: scanning the window, the corners, his discarded gun on the dresser.

"We're going to the hospital," he said, pulling on jeans. "Now."

I barely remembered dressing. My hands shook so hard I dropped my phone twice. The memory of Richard's nervous smiles, his half-truths, his promises of *"Just one more tour, sweetheart,"* looped through my mind like bad lyrics.

As Jake guided me out the door, the morning sun felt colder, harsher. I kept hearing my own voice from earlier, *I don't regret it.*

Now regret was all I could taste.

If Richard's death wasn't an accident, then we were already inside the final act. And the encore might just kill us both.

The emergency room smelled like bleach and burnt coffee, sterile, exhausted, wrong. Cameras already swarmed the parking lot, their flashes turning tragedy into clickbait. Jake parked at the curb, his hand brushing mine as if to say *stay behind me.* He didn't need to. I'd followed his lead since I accepted he was the only one standing between me and disaster and now wasn't the time to start pretending I could handle this alone.

Inside, chaos hummed behind curtained partitions. A nurse glanced up, recognized me, and froze. The same expression I'd seen a hundred times, shock, pity, morbid curiosity.

"I'm here about Richard Clark," I said, voice steady only because I'd forgotten how to cry.

Her eyes softened, but her answer gutted me. "He didn't make it, Miss Dove. I'm sorry."

Those words had no melody. No hook. Just silence afterward that swallowed everything else.

Jake asked the questions I couldn't. "Was anyone else in the car? Toxicology? Witnesses?"

The nurse shook her head. "Single vehicle. Speed and alcohol suspected. He was... unrecognizable."

My knees buckled. Jake's arm clamped around my waist before I hit the floor.

"Easy," he murmured, steering me to a chair.

But there was nothing easy about this. Recently I'd resented Richard, his control, his lies but I hadn't wanted him *dead.* Reporters shouted outside the automatic doors, their voices muffled by the glass.

Pop Star's Manager Dies in Fiery Crash. They'd turn his death into another headline about me before sunset.

Jake crouched in front of me, eyes fierce beneath his hat's shadow. "This doesn't smell right," he muttered. "I want to see his office, the car. Maybe the accident scene. Everything."

I nodded, unable to speak. My reflection in the lobby glass looked like a stranger again, painted, hollow, barely holding together. The pop princess everyone adored had just lost another piece of her world.

The police tape still fluttered across the door when we reached Richard's office, yellow against the sleek glass. Jake cut it with a pocketknife and stepped inside without hesitation.

"We don't have time to wait on red tape," he muttered. His voice carried that low, controlled fury that made me follow without question.

The air reeked of stale cologne and smoke. Papers littered the floor, drawers yanked open. Jake moved like a hunter, eyes cataloging every opened file, every scuff on the carpet. I lingered by Richard's desk, staring at the family photo still standing upright amid the wreckage. His arm around me at my first award show. His grin too wide. My smile too fake.

A soft ping from his computer made me jump. Jake crossed the room, crouched beside it.

"Looks like he left something running." He clicked through open tabs until a single document filled the screen, a scanned contract, pages signed in Richard's familiar flourish.

My stomach dropped as I read the names: **Jenna Harper – Lucas DeWitt Productions.**

"That's Jenna," I whispered. "And my producer."

Jake's jaw tightened. "Same tour dates. Same venues. Even the same stage designs."

It hit me all at once. They weren't just replacing me. They were *erasing* me.

Another file waited on the computer desktop: a voice memo labeled *Insurance.* Jake hit play.

Richard's voice, shaky and slurred. "Didn't... didn't mean for it to go this far. They said she'd be fine. I thought... I thought I was protecting the brand. Tell Isla... tell her I'm sorry."

The recording cut off with a sharp click. My throat closed. Protecting the brand. That was always the excuse.

Jake's eyes met mine, burning with a promise that felt like vengeance. "We're not done. Not by a damn mile."

Jake didn't say much as we left the office, but the silence between us wasn't peace anymore. It was pressure. The kind that builds before something explodes. He drove like the road owed him answers, his hands locked tight around the wheel, jaw grinding so hard I could hear it.

"They were replacing me," I said finally, voice thin against the hum of the engine. "Same venues. Same songs. Same everything."

"Same *brand*," he corrected. His tone was clipped, dangerous. "That's all you ever were to them. A voice they thought they could copy and repackage."

The words stung because they were true. I stared out the window at the city blurring by, glass towers and billboards plastered with my own smiling face. *Forever Innocent,* the caption read, mocking me. My throat tightened.

"Richard signed the contract, Jake. He's dead. Maybe that's punishment enough."

He glanced at me, eyes hard. "Punishment implies he was the one pulling the strings. I don't buy it. He was a middleman, a weak one. Someone else set the stage."

"Lucas," I whispered. The name tasted bitter.

Jake didn't deny it. His silence said everything.

I slumped back against the seat, guilt tangling with grief until I couldn't tell them apart. "If Richard thought he was protecting me—"

"He wasn't," Jake cut in. "He was protecting the image. There's a difference."

We hit a red light. For a second, he looked at me, not the idol, not the glitter-coated fantasy, but *me*.

"They don't get to trade your life for a brand," he said quietly. "Not while I'm breathing."

The light turned green. He pressed the accelerator; eyes locked on the road ahead like a man already planning the next war. And deep down, I knew he wasn't wrong.

Back at the house, the air felt heavier, as if the walls themselves knew too much. Jake moved through every room with the precision of a soldier sweeping hostile ground, checking locks and windows while I sat on the edge of the couch, Richard's phone trembling in my hands. The police had bagged it at the crash scene, but Jake had "borrowed" it before they finished paperwork.

He trusted his gut more than procedure, and his gut hadn't been wrong. The cracked screen flickered when I powered it on. Missed calls. Voicemails. One labeled only with a heart emoji. My chest tightened. Richard hadn't been the heart type.

Jake crouched beside me. "Play it."

A girl's voice filled the room, sweet, breathy, disturbingly familiar.

"Thanks for the chance, Richard," she giggled. "Pure Fire's gonna make me famous. Everyone says I'm younger, fresher. You were right.

Someone else is too old to play innocent anymore. And her cowboy boyfriend? He's just good press."

My stomach dropped.

The voice slipped into a childish singsong, quoting a lyric from *I'll Stand Tomorrow*—*I'll find my feet again, I'll have my say*. Then she laughed, high-pitched and off-key.

Jake's eyes met mine, cold fury simmering. "Who is that?"

I swallowed hard. "I... I don't know."

But I did. Not for certain, not enough to accuse, but something in the tone, the cadence, crawled under my skin. I was sure I'd heard that voice often. It wasn't Jenna. It was closer than a fan. But I couldn't quite nail it down.

Jake stood, pacing. "Whoever she is, she's inside your circle. This isn't a stalker, it's a takeover."

I gripped the phone tighter, bile rising. "She wants my life."

He stopped pacing, voice low and lethal. "Then she's about to find out what happens when she threatens it."

The message ended, but the sound of that laugh stayed in the room long after the phone went silent. It slithered under my skin like ice water. I dropped the device onto the coffee table, hands shaking so badly I nearly sent it skidding to the floor.

"She sounded so... happy," I whispered. "Like all this, death, fear, my career, was just a game."

Jake didn't answer right away. He stood with his back to me, shoulders broad and unyielding, staring out the window at the city lights like he could see the danger pulsing beneath them. His silence scared me more than his anger ever could.

"Jake," I said softly, "what if this is my fault?"

That snapped him around. "Don't." His voice was sharp, full of a heat I wasn't ready for. "Don't carry that."

I blinked through tears. "Everything that's happened started because of me. The brand. The songs. Richard. Now her." My throat burned. "You said it yourself. They're not after Isla Dove the woman. They're after the image. And who created it?"

He crossed the room in two strides and knelt in front of me, hands gripping my knees like he could anchor me to the earth. "You didn't make this. They did. They twisted it. You just survived it."

That broke me. The tears I'd been holding back since the hospital spilled over, ugly and hot. Jake pulled me against his chest without hesitation. His shirt was rough, his arms solid and warm, and I pressed my face there, breathing him in.

For once, I didn't hide the shaking. I didn't try to be strong or pretty or marketable. I just cried for everything I'd lost and for the one thing I was terrified I couldn't keep.

Because if this war took him too, I wasn't sure I'd survive it.

The tears dried, but the ache stayed. I didn't know how long we sat there, me in his arms, the world closing in around us, but when I finally pulled away, the sky outside had gone dark. The city glowed through the windows, all those glittering towers humming with a life that wasn't mine anymore.

Jake stood, rubbing a hand over his jaw. "We'll find her," he said. "Whoever's behind this. Before they get another move."

I nodded, but my gaze drifted to the phone on the table. The screen had gone black again, the reflection faintly catching the two of us, me, pale and tired; him, solid and steady, already halfway back into soldier mode. A part of me wanted to beg him to stay like this, just one more hour of quiet before the next blow. But peace wasn't an option for people like us. My phone this time.

I reached for my own phone to silence it and froze. A new notification pulsed across the lock screen.

TONIGHT'S EXTRA CONCERT: SOLD OUT.

My heart slammed against my ribs. I hadn't approved the event. I hadn't even confirmed the venue. Yet the public page had my name, my picture, my "Forever Innocent" logo, bright and polished, like nothing had happened.

Jake leaned over my shoulder, scanning the screen. "When was this posted?"

"An hour ago," I whispered. "And look. Same set list. Same backup lineup. Same everything."

His eyes narrowed. "Then the trap's already built."

I stared at the glowing image of myself in curls, bow and a plastic smile, a ghost version of the woman I'd become.

Jake's voice dropped to a growl that made the room feel smaller. "If they want a show, they're damn well gonna get one. But this time, we write the ending."

And for the first time, I wasn't sure either of us would make it to the curtain call.

Chapter 21
Dress Rehearsal Danger

T he concert hall was a cavern of echoing silence and potential threats. Twelve hours until showtime, and the air already tasted like adrenaline and fear. I moved through the gloom, my boots a soft counter-rhythm to the distant hum of traffic. My team from Sierra Bravo flanked me, a well-oiled machine sweeping every shadowed corner, every roped off access point, every air duct large enough to conceal a killer. My gut was a fist, clenched tighter than it had been on any IED-sweep in Kandahar.

Isla was a splash of defiant color against the monochrome dread, trailing our formation. Her team had already descended, stitching her into her costume, those neon-streaked pigtails, that skirt better suited for a doll than a woman who might need to run for her life. The "Forever Innocent" brand was a glaring beacon, painting a target on her back in glitter and gloss. Every click of her ridiculous heels on the hollow stage floor was a metronome counting down to chaos. She was the bait in a trap I was terrified I'd built myself. The stalker wanted a spectacle, and this hall, with its unsecured rigging and endless blind spots, was the perfect stage for a final, bloody encore.

The scent hit me first, a cloying wave of perfume-soaked roses that cut through the sterile air of backstage. A massive bouquet, wrapped in ostentatious pink foil, sat centered on Isla's dressing room vanity like a shrine. She saw it and her practiced, public smile flickered into place. It was a reflex so ingrained it was a kind of violence. She reached for the small card nestled among the blood-red blooms.

My hand shot out, closing over hers before she could touch it. "Don't."

Her eyes flashed with a flicker of irritation, but it was quickly drowned by the fear she was trying so hard to hide. I plucked the card free. The paper was thick, expensive. The message was typed in a deceptively simple font.

For Your Last Song.

Two words. That was all. But they landed like a hammer blow to my sternum, stealing my breath. This wasn't a fan's adoration or a critic's jab. This was a promise.

Isla's smile finally shattered. "What does it say?" Her voice was a thin thread.

I crumpled the card in my fist, the paper crackling like a dead leaf. "Nothing. Trash from a pathetic fan." The lie felt like ash in my mouth, but I wouldn't feed her fear. Not yet.

Her gaze dropped to my clenched fist, then back to the roses. "They're beautiful," she whispered, but her voice trembled. She wasn't seeing flowers anymore. She knew they weren't from any fan by my reaction. She was seeing a funeral arrangement. Her own.

My blood ran cold, a frigid certainty settling in my bones. The stalker wasn't just watching from the shadows anymore. They were in the wings, whispering from the rafters, leaving their calling card on her vanity. They weren't bluffing. They were setting the stage for her final bow, and every second that ticked by felt like we were marching in time to their countdown.

I found her standing at the edge of the stage, staring out at the thousands of empty seats that would soon be a roaring sea of faces. Her shoulders were set in a line of stubborn defiance, but I could see the fine tremor in her left hand where it hung at her side.

"We need to cancel the rehearsal," I said, my voice low so it wouldn't carry in the cavernous hall. "The full show. It's too big a risk. We're handing them a blueprint."

She didn't turn, her gaze fixed on some distant point in the balcony. "No."

"Isla, be reasonable. They sent a death threat in a bouquet. They've proven they can get past security, get into your dressing room. This isn't a game."

That got her to turn. The stage lights, set to a dim warm-up glow, caught the glitter in her hair and the fire in her eyes. "My entire career is dangling by a thread, Jake. Richard is dead. My manager was trying to replace me. If I cancel now, if I hide, the vultures will pick what's left of my name clean. They win." She took a step toward me, her glittery heels clicking decisively on the floor. "This is my stage. My life. I'm not handing it over to some... some ghost."

I wanted to shake her. I wanted to yell that her life was worth infinitely more than her career, that no album, no tour, no screaming fan was worth the price she might pay. But the words died in my throat. The stubborn set of her jaw, the raw, wounded pride blazing in her gaze, it wasn't just about the fame. It was about reclaiming the last shred of control in a world that had been systematically stripping it from her. She was drawing a line in the sand, and she was prepared to stand her ground, even if it meant standing alone in the crosshairs.

My job was to keep her alive, but in that moment, I realized part of keeping her alive was letting her fight.

The rehearsal was a controlled chaos of shrieking guitar amps and thumping bass lines that vibrated up through the soles of my boots. I kept to the wings, my gaze constantly scanning, dividing the crew into threats and non-threats. That's when I saw her: Jenna, Isla's ex-backup singer, a woman made of sharp angles and sharper resentment. She was loitering near the stage-left control board, a place she had no business being. Her access should have been revoked after the last incident.

As Isla launched into the bridge of a soaring power ballad, Jenna's hand darted out, not to adjust a fader, but to trace a finger along a row of unmarked switches. My body was moving before my mind fully processed the threat. I crossed the space in six long strides, my shadow falling over her.

I didn't touch her, just caged her against the console with my presence. "Looking for something?" My voice was a low growl, meant for her ears only.

She flinched, whirling around. The look in her eyes was a toxic mix of fear and venom. "I was just... checking the levels. Someone has to. Your little princess is flat."

"The only thing that's flat is your excuse. You're not crew. You're not welcome here." I leaned in, close enough to smell her cloying perfume. "Richard's dead. The games are over. You want to tell me what you were really doing by the lighting rig the night that spot fell?"

Her face paled, but her lips twisted into a sneer. "He got what he deserved. They all do. But I didn't kill him. I'm trying to prove it."

"Prove it by skulking around restricted areas?" I shot back, my patience fraying. Her words dripped with a bitterness that felt genuine, but there was a raw, desperate edge underneath that snagged on my instincts. A guilty person would lie better. A desperate one, however, was unpredictable and just as dangerous.

I used my earpiece to call over to a Sierra Bravo operative to escort Jenna out and then went back to my post in the wings to watch Isla. The lights, now at full performance intensity, painted her in a halo of gold and pink. She spun, she smiled, she hit her marks with a precision that was almost mechanical. The glitter on her cheeks caught the light, making her look like some ethereal goddess spun from sugar and dreams. But all I saw was a bullseye. Every sequin was a reflector, every neon curl a beacon. They had polished their asset until she shone, making her the perfect target in this shooting gallery of a concert hall.

The crew swarmed around me, a hive of practiced efficiency, but their glances were laced with a mocking curiosity. I heard the whispered words, "Yeehaw" and "Dude Ranch," snickered behind cupped hands. I was a fossil here, a relic of dust and grit in their world of gloss and illusion. My worn Stetson, my scuffed boots, the way I stood with my weight balanced ready for a fight, it was all a joke to them. I let them laugh. Their ridicule was just background noise, static to be filtered out. My entire world had narrowed to the woman in the spotlight, a radius of twenty feet that was my only mission, my only purpose. I'd never hated this city, this industry, more than today. It was a beast that fed on beauty and spat out tragedy, and it was holding Isla in its jaws, preparing for the slaughter.

The sheer artifice of it all was a physical ache. They'd built a fantasy around her, a fortress of bubblegum and bows, and called it protection. It was the flimsiest armor imaginable. I thought of my sister, of the real, unvarnished strength she'd had. This performance was the antithesis of that. It was a lesson in how to be weak, how to be prey. Every swish of that short skirt, every giggle piped through the massive speakers, was a lie that put her in greater danger. And she was the one who had to sell it, burying the fierce, resilient woman I knew under layers of marketable innocence. The weight of my sidearm under my jacket was a stark, cold reality against the fever-dream spectacle on stage. I was a man built for real threats, sandstorms, ambushes, tangible enemies. This, this was a war of perception, a fight against shadows that hid in plain sight, and I was terrified my kind of strength wouldn't be enough to save her from theirs.

The music was a physical force, a wall of sound that made the stage floor thrum. Isla hit a high note, her voice clear and strong, but my every sense was tuned to a different frequency, the silent one of threat. Then it came, a shift in the air pressure, a prickle at the nape of my neck that had nothing to do with the pyrotechnics cue. My eyes, constantly scanning, tracked upward, sweeping the metal latticework of the catwalks high above.

Movement. A flicker of denim and frantic motion.

My heart hammered against my ribs, a sudden, brutal drum. Brian. It was the fan, Brian, his face a mask of glassy-eyed devotion, clambering over the safety rail with the clumsy grace of the obsessed. He wasn't looking at where he was going; his gaze was locked on Isla, his lips moving, chanting her lyrics as she sang like a prayer.

Security radios crackled to life, voices sharp with alarm. But they were too slow, too far away. Brian ignored the shouts from the far end of the catwalk, his entire world narrowed to the glittering figure below. My instincts screamed, a raw, animal sound in my head.

Trap. This is the trap. He's the distraction.

Every muscle in my body coiled, ready to launch toward the nearest access ladder, to intercept. But in that frozen second of calculation, a different sound ripped through the hall, not a shout, but a choked, guttural cry from the stage. My head snapped back down. I saw Isla's eyes go wide, not with fear of the man above, but with horror at something happening right beside her.

The world pivoted. The threat from above was potential. The one on the stage was now.

I changed direction in a single, explosive motion, my charge toward the catwalks aborted. I sprang onto the stage, my focus laser-sharp on Isla. She was staring, paralyzed, at one of her backup singers who had collapsed a few feet away. The woman, a blonde named Chloe, was on the floor, her body seizing, back arching off the deck in a violent, unnatural spasm. A faint, acrid smell of burnt plastic, skin and ozone cut through the perfume and sweat.

"Get back!" I barked at Isla, shoving her behind me as I closed the distance. My training took over, pushing the adrenaline into a manageable channel. It wasn't a medical event. It was an attack. I dropped to my knees beside the twitching woman. The problem was immediately obvious: the delicate, flesh-colored chin mic she wore was sparking, a tiny, vicious flicker of electricity arcing from the wire to her skin, which was already blistering.

"Cut the power to this sector!" I roared toward the wings, but the sound crew was frozen, staring. Cursing, I yanked the band of my shirt cuff down over my hand, creating a makeshift barrier, and ripped the sparking mic from her face. It came away with a sickening sizzle, leaving an angry red blistering burn on her chin and neck.

Her body went limp, the seizures stopping. But she wasn't breathing. Her lips were tinged with blue.

"Medic! Now!" The shout ripped from my throat. I tilted her head back, my fingers finding her pulse. It was thready and far too fast. I locked my hands, one over the other, and started compressions on the center of her chest, the rhythm a brutal, familiar cadence trying to get hers to match it.

Stay with me. Come on.

Each thrust was a count against the bastard who had done this. The real threat hadn't been in the rafters. It had been in the props, in the costume, in the very tools of her performance. They weren't just trying to scare her anymore. They were executing the cast.

Above us, the chaos continued. Brian was still yelling, his voice a ragged scream that tore through the hall. "She belongs with me! You're all poisoning her! She needs to be PURE!" Security finally had him, two large men wrestling his thrashing form back from the edge, but the damage was done. The distraction had been perfect.

Beneath my palms, I felt a weak, shuddering breath from Chloe. A ragged inhale. Then another. She was breathing on her own. The medics finally swarmed the stage, pushing me aside as they took over, applying oxygen, preparing the gurney. I stood up, my hands tingling, my shirt sticking to my back with cold sweat.

My gaze found Isla. She was being held up by her bass player, her face as white as her current outfit, her green eyes huge with a terror that was no longer abstract. She was staring at Chloe, then at the discarded, sparking mic on the floor.

I looked from her, to the catwalks where Brian was being subdued, to the innocent-looking audio equipment. The pieces clicked into a horrifying picture. This was coordinated. The obsessed fan provided the spectacle, the panic, while the real attack was a silent, surgical strike. They had used the chaos they knew a "fan" would cause to mask an attempted murder. The mics were interchangeable. It could just as easily have been Isla being taken out on a gurney.

As the medics rushed Chloe away, the stage fell into a stunned, horrible silence. I strode over to the dropped chin mic. I didn't touch it, just crouched, examining the severed wire. It wasn't frayed. It had been cut clean, the wires inside deliberately stripped and crossed. Sabotage. Not an accident. A cold, calculated murder attempt.

I lifted my head, my eyes locking with Isla's across the ravaged stage. The message was clear: no one around you was safe. And we were running out of time.

Chapter 22
Dark Beneath the Lights

The silence after the medics wheeled Chloe away was heavier than any sound I'd ever known. It pressed down on me, thick and suffocating. The stage lights, still blazing at full intensity, felt like interrogation lamps. Every sequin on my costume, every strand of glitter in my hair, felt like it was weighing me down, pulling me under. I could still smell it, the faint, sickly sweet scent of burnt flesh mixed with Chloe's strawberry shampoo. My stomach roiled. The crew moved around me in slow motion, their faces pale masks of shock. This was supposed to be a final dress rehearsal, a polished run-through. Instead, it felt like a pre-funeral. My pre-funeral. The empty seats in the auditorium seemed to mock me, thousands of dark, judgmental eyes waiting for the main event: my complete and utter destruction. The "Forever Innocent" brand was a sick joke, a lie that was getting people hurt. I was a curse dressed in bubblegum pink.

My gaze, frantic and unmoored, swept the chaotic stage until it found him. Jake. He stood near the stage-left curtain, a stark, solid monument in a world that was crumbling into dust. He wasn't looking at the gurney or the panicked crew; his entire focus was on me. He was my physical tether in the storm. He gave a single, almost imperceptible nod. It wasn't a reassurance that everything was okay. It was a promise that he was still here, still fighting. I clung to that look, using it to steady my breathing, which was coming in short, sharp gasps. The compressions of his hands on Chloe's chest played on a loop behind my eyes. He'd fought for her life right here on this polished floor. He was my anchor, the only real thing in this house of mirrors and knives. As long as he was watching, I wasn't completely alone.

"They didn't find anything on him but a notebook," a stage manager muttered, passing by me with a clipboard held like a shield. "Just... lyrics. All your lyrics. Pages and pages of them."

The words washed over me, barely registering. Brian was gone, hauled away by security, his desperate screams of "She belongs to me!" still echoing in the hollows of the hall. He was a sad, obsessive fan. A symptom of the sickness my brand created, but not the disease itself. He was a pawn, a flashy diversion thrown onto the board to pull everyone's eyes upward while the real knife slid in from the side. The realization was a cold chill down my spine. The mastermind was smarter, cleaner. They used the Brians of the world as camouflage. They were still here, watching, maybe even feeling smug at how perfectly their distraction had worked.

A commotion near the backstage entrance snagged my attention. Jenna was there, her voice a shrill spike in the muted atmosphere. "I have every right to be here! I need to talk to Isla!" Security was firmly escorting her out, again. Her face was contorted, a mess of running mascara and genuine-looking fury. But as her eyes met mine across the distance, I didn't see the cold calculation of a killer. I saw the same hot, messy jealousy that had always been there. She wanted my spot, my fame, but this? The deliberate, cruel sabotage of a chin mic? The attempted murder of a colleague? It felt too clinical, too detached for Jenna's brand of fiery, personal vendetta. She was a red herring, another piece of misdirection in a game I never agreed to play. We were chasing shadows while the real monster walked among us, smiling.

Jake's hand was a firm, guiding pressure on the small of my back as he led me off the stage. The touch was supposed to be professional, but it sent a current of pure, undiluted safety through the paralyzing fear. We moved down the narrow, dimly lit hallway toward my dressing room, a path that now felt like a gauntlet. Just as we reached the door, a sliver of white caught my eye. Tucked into the frame, not quite hidden, was another note. My breath hitched. Jake saw it a second later, his body tensing, his hand moving to the weapon I knew was holstered under his jacket. He nudged me behind him and, using a pen from his pocket, carefully plucked the folded paper free. He opened it, his jaw hardening as he read. Then he turned it so I could see.

Three words, scrawled in the same jagged, frantic ink as the others: *I'm closer now.*

The blood in my veins turned to ice. This wasn't left during the chaos. This was left *after.* They'd walked this hallway, cool and calm, while we were dealing with the aftermath of their handiwork. They'd been right here, outside my door, while my friend was fighting for her life. The proximity was a violation, a whisper in the dark that proved the locks, the security, the panic room, none of it mattered. They were already inside.

The words seemed to pulse on the page, a malevolent heartbeat. *I'm closer now.* It wasn't just a threat; it was a boast. They were savoring this, the cat playing with a mouse that was already half-broken. The sterile hallway walls seemed to press in, the air growing thin. I could almost feel their breath on the back of my neck, their eyes on me from some hidden crack in my world. The carefully constructed fortress of my career had become a haunted house, and the ghost knew all my hiding places. My knees felt weak, the strength leaching from my bones. The composure I'd fought so hard to maintain finally began to crack, a hairline fracture that threatened to shatter me completely.

Back in the dressing room, the door locked securely behind us, I finally broke. The dam holding back the terror, the grief, the sheer exhaustion, gave way. A sob ripped from my throat, raw and ugly. I crumpled, my shoulders shaking, the glitter on my cheeks melting under the hot tears.

"I can't do this anymore, Jake," I choked out, the words muffled against my hands. "I can't wear these stupid bows that make me a target. I can't sing these songs that fuel some... some monster's fantasy. I can't be this product anymore. It's killing me. It's killing everyone around me."

I felt his arms go around me, not the hesitant touch of a bodyguard, but the solid, encompassing embrace of a man. He pulled me against his chest, and I buried my face in the rough cotton of his shirt, clinging to him like he was the only thing keeping me from being swept away.

"I know," he murmured, his voice a low, steady rumble against my ear. His hand moved in slow, firm circles on my back. "I know. But you're stronger than you think. You're still standing, Isla. That's what matters."

His words were an anchor, but the longing I saw in his eyes when I looked up, a reflection of my own desperate need, nearly undid me completely. In his arms, the line between protection and something more blurred into oblivion.

He didn't offer empty platitudes. He didn't tell me it would be okay. He just held me, letting the storm rage until I had nothing left. The frantic hammering of my heart began to slow, syncing with the steady, reassuring beat of his. In the quiet aftermath of my breakdown, with the scent of his skin, leather and soap and man, filling my senses, a terrifying, wonderful truth dawned on me. This was the only real safety I had ever known. Not the panic rooms, not the bodyguards, but this man's unwavering presence. And that realization was more frightening than any note slipped under a door. Because if he went, where would I be then?

The show, somehow, went on. Or at least, a hollowed-out, gutted version of it. My manager and the producers, in a display of breathtaking denial, insisted we continue the rehearsal.

"The show must go on, darling. Can't let the terrorists win," Richard's replacement had said, his voice dripping with a faux sympathy that made my skin crawl.

So, I went back out there. The lights felt hotter, the music louder, a brutal assault on my frayed nerves. I was halfway through the second act, my body moving on autopilot through a complex dance sequence, when it happened.

The world vanished.

One second, I was bathed in a blinding spotlight, the next, I was swallowed by an absolute, suffocating blackness.

The music died mid-note. The lights didn't dim; they were extinguished. A collective, startled gasp rippled through the cast on stage, followed by a beat of utter silence, and then panicked voices erupted everywhere. My chest seized, panic clawing its way up my throat, so visceral I could taste it, metallic and sharp. This was it. The trap had been sprung. In the pitch black, I was utterly blind, completely vulnerable. I couldn't see the threat coming. I could only wait for it.

The blackness was a physical entity, thick and heavy, pressing against my eyes, my skin. I stumbled, my glittery heels catching on a cable. I threw my hands out, grasping at nothing. The voices around me were distorted, directionless. I could hear the frantic scuffling of feet, the crash of falling equipment, but I had no idea if people were running from me or toward me. My breath came in ragged, shallow pants, my heart a frantic bird beating against the cage of my ribs. This was the stalker's element. The chaos, the fear, the isolation. They had plunged my world into nothingness, and in that void, I was completely, utterly theirs. I wanted Jake but I had no idea where to find him.

A hand closed around my wrist in the dark.

It was not Jake's. His grip was always firm, confident, grounding.

This was different. The fingers were smaller, sharper, digging into my flesh with a possessive, bruising strength. I tried to yank my arm back, but the grip was like iron. I was pulled off balance, stumbling forward into the oppressive black.

Then a voice, a hot, venomous whisper, hissed directly in my ear, so close I could feel the moisture of their breath.

"He can't save you."

The voice was distorted by a sibilant hiss, but underneath it, there was a haunting, terrible familiarity. It was a voice I was sure I heard every day. A voice I trusted.

My blood went from ice to fire in a single, terrifying second. I opened my mouth to scream, but the sound was strangled in my throat, swallowed whole by the consuming, absolute dark.

Chapter 23
Powerless

The blackout was absolute, a suffocating blanket that swallowed the stage whole. One second, Isla was a glittering figure in a halo of light; the next, she was gone, erased. Her scream sliced through the dark, a sound of pure, undiluted terror that bypassed my ears and went straight to my primal brain. My chest seized, a visceral reaction that had nothing to do with training. Instincts, older than any military manual, kicked in, count the steps to her last position, map the exits by memory, steady your breathing. But the soldier's calm was a thin veneer over a raw, pounding fear. I couldn't see her. In this void, I was just a man, and the woman I loved was in the hands of a monster. The professional detachment I'd clung to for weeks shattered. This was personal.

The world became a symphony of panic, shuffling feet, confused shouts, the crash of falling equipment. But all of it was background noise to the one sound that mattered: her ragged gasps. My world, which had once been defined by mission parameters and threat assessments, had narrowed to a single, terrifying point: find Isla. Every other objective, apprehend the suspect, secure the area, evaporated. The mission was her. The *only* mission was her. I was no longer a bodyguard executing a plan. I was a man hunting the predator who had taken his heart into the dark.

I plunged into the blackness, my weapon drawn, every sense stretched to its breaking point. They had taken the light, but they had also taken the shadows to hide in. And I was about to show them what a real predator looked like.

"Isla!" I growled her name into the darkness, a low, guiding sound meant to cut through her panic and lead her back to me. I shoved past disoriented crew members, my ears straining, filtering out the chaos. There! A faint, choked sob to my right. I pivoted, my boots silent on the carpeted floor, moving toward the sound like a bloodhound.

"I'm here. Keep talking." My voice was a command, a lifeline I was throwing into the abyss.

Another gasp, closer this time, followed by the scuffle of a struggle. The sound was moving. Up. They were taking her up into the balcony. Rage, cold and sharp, burned through the fear. They weren't just trying to hide; they were staging a spectacle. Maybe thinking of throwing her from the upper balcony.

Moving upward was a tactical nightmare, limited exits, a kill box of stairs. They knew what they were doing. A flicker of emergency lighting from an exit sign cast just enough hellish red glow to reveal a shadowy figure dragging a shimmer of neon pink up the carpeted stairs toward the highest balcony. Isla's brand persona was a glowing target even in this apocalypse. The sight of her being manhandled, of those neon curls flashing in the dim light, blinded me with a fury so pure it was almost calm. They were hunting her mask, but they'd taken the woman. My woman.

I stormed after them, taking the steps two at a time. The hunter was now the hunted, and I was coming for them with everything I had.

I hit the top of the balcony stairs, the plush carpet muffling my steps. The air was colder up here, thick with dust and silence. The frantic sounds from the stage below were a distant echo. My eyes, adjusted to the gloom, scanned the long row of seats. And then I saw them. A masked figure, clad in all black, had Isla pinned against the back wall. One hand was clamped over her mouth, the other held a knife, the flat of the blade pressed menacingly against her throat. Her eyes, wide and terrified over the top of the gloved hand, found mine. In them, I saw a plea that would haunt me forever.

The figure was smaller than I expected, but the grip on the knife was professional. Isla's glittery heels scraped uselessly against the carpet as she tried to struggle. The giant bow in her hair was askew, a grotesque parody of innocence in this violent tableau. My finger tightened on the trigger of my weapon, but the angle was bad. A shot risked her. Every ounce of my training screamed to negotiate, to de-escalate. But the animal part of me, the part that belonged to her, just wanted to tear the bastard apart.

"Let. Her. Go." The words weren't a request. They were a death sentence.

The masked head tilted. For a heartbeat, no one moved. We were a frozen tableau of violence, balanced on the edge of a knife.

The attacker shoved Isla aside, and she stumbled, crashing into a row of seats. The distraction was all I needed. I lunged. We came together in a violent crash of muscle and fury. They were fast, unnaturally so, and strong. The knife slashed upward, a silver arc in the dim light. I twisted, the blade slicing through my shirt and scoring a line of fire across my ribs. I barely felt it. I drove my elbow into their masked face, hearing a grunt of pain. We grappled, a brutal dance of fists and leverage. This wasn't a random fan. The moves were efficient, brutal, Krav Maga. This was training. This was personal.

We were too evenly matched, a fact that fueled my rage. I blocked a knee strike to my groin, countered with a blow to their kidney. They staggered, and I used the moment to seize their knife arm, slamming it repeatedly against the balcony rail until the weapon clattered to the floor far below. With a final, desperate heave, I spun them and drove them face-first into the wall, pinning them with my full weight. My hand went to the back of their head, grabbing a handful of fabric and hair, and yanked. The mask tore free.

It tumbled to the floor, and I stared at the face now exposed in the eerie glow. It was a face I saw every day. A face Isla trusted.

I stared, my mind refusing to process the information for a single, suspended heartbeat. The person pinned beneath me, breathing in ragged, furious gasps, was Lily. Isla's assistant. The quiet, unassuming shadow who fetched coffee, who straightened bows, who offered a sympathetic smile. The sheer, audacious scale of the betrayal was a physical blow. All this time, the enemy hadn't been lurking in the shadows. She'd been standing in plain sight, taking notes, learning routines, and whispering poisonous lies while handing Isla her morning chai. The perfect spy. The violence in her eyes now was a shocking contrast to the demure girl I thought I knew. The mask hadn't just hidden her face; it had hidden a monster.

My grip on her tightened instinctively. This changed everything. The sniper rifle, the sabotage phone, Lily didn't have the resources or the nerve for that. She was the inside woman, the source of the intimate knowledge, the creator of the psychological terror. But she was a tool. A deadly, sharpened tool, but a tool nonetheless. The mastermind was still out there, and he had just lost his most valuable asset. The fight wasn't over; it had just become infinitely more complicated. And the woman currently crumpled on the floor a few feet away had trusted this viper with her life.

I had the hand, but the brain was still operating, and it had just been tipped off that its primary weapon was compromised.

A broken whisper cut through the heavy silence. "Lily?"

I turned my head. Isla had pushed herself up from the seats, one hand clutching her throat where the knife had been. Her face was a mask of utter devastation, all color drained away. She wasn't looking at a stalker; she was looking at a friend. A confidante. The person who knew her deepest insecurities and her daily schedule. The betrayal wasn't just a threat; it was a profound, personal violation that reached into the deepest, most trusted parts of her world. Her lips formed the name again, soundlessly, as if her voice had been stolen by the shock.

I saw the fracture happen in real time. The pop star persona was completely gone, replaced by a raw, wounded woman whose foundation had just been vaporized. This was worse than a physical attack. This was a soul-deep ambush. She was replaying every private moment, every shared laugh, every time she'd cried on this woman's shoulder. Every kindness had been a calculation. Every bit of loyalty, a lie. The horror in her eyes was for the death of that trust, and it was a more painful wound than any knife could ever inflict.

In that moment, I wasn't sure which of us was more powerless, me, holding the traitor, or Isla, watching her past become a lie.

For a moment, Lily just panted, her body slack with defeat. Then, a strange, gurgling laugh escaped her. It wasn't a sound of amusement, but of madness. Her eyes, wild and unfocused, locked onto Isla.

"You had it all," she hissed, her voice trembling with a fervent, possessive energy. "The fame, the fans... him. You didn't even want it! You were going to throw it all away! They promised it to me. I'm Lily Flame. *Pure Fire*. I deserved it more!"

The words were a torrent of twisted logic and seething envy. She wasn't just a stalker; she was a fan who wanted to become the idol, to consume the life she coveted. She saw Isla not as a person, but as an obstacle to her own destined stardom.

Her gaze flickered to me with a covetousness that made my skin crawl. I was just another prize in the Isla Dove collection she felt entitled to. This wasn't just about jealousy; it was about a complete identity theft. She had practiced the role, learned the lines, and now she was furious that the original star refused to leave the stage. The "Pure Fire" she snarled was the name on the demo, the replacement. She wasn't just working for the mastermind; she believed his promise that she was the upgrade. She was a willing, fanatical participant in her own delusion.

"They said you were a problem," she spat at Isla, her voice dropping to a venomous whisper. "And I was the solution."

I tightened my hold, my knee digging into her spine to keep her still. "Who's 'they,' Lily? Who are you working with?" I demanded, my voice low and lethal. This was the critical intelligence. The name.

But she just laughed again, a soft, broken sound that was more terrifying than any scream.

"You can't stop him," she whispered, her voice dripping with a twisted sense of victory even in defeat. "He's smarter. Stronger. He'll finish what I started."

The words landed like a physical blow. *Him.* A partner. An accomplice. We hadn't just been fighting one enemy. We'd been fighting a team. And the more dangerous half was still out there, his plan in motion, his inside asset now compromised. My eyes met Isla's across the short distance. Her hand was over her mouth, fresh terror dawning in her eyes. The nightmare wasn't over. It had just multiplied.

My mind raced, re-evaluating every piece of evidence. The sniper shot, the professional sabotage,, it all made sense now. Lily was the intimate threat, the psychological warfare. But *he* was the strategist, the one with the resources and the cold, calculated will to see this through to its bloody conclusion. We had captured the scorpion, but the hand that held it was still hidden, and it was already reaching for another weapon. The real war was just beginning, and we were dangerously behind.

Lily's capture wasn't a victory; she was just a POW from an enemy we hadn't even known was there.

Chapter 24
Web of Lies

T he sound of Lily's mask hitting the stage floor was a small, plastic clatter, but to me, it was the sound of my entire world splitting open. I stood frozen, the frantic thumping of my heart the only thing I could feel. My assistant. My shadow. The one who fetched my chai tea with exacting precision, who knew my schedule better than I did, who'd held my hair back when I was sick with food poisoning last year.

Lily.

Her face, now exposed, was twisted not with remorse, but with a kind of feverish, ecstatic devotion. The bow she'd just straightened for me before I walked on stage dangled from her fist, a grotesque trophy. I looked from her wild eyes to the broken accessory, and the connection was a physical blow. The very symbol of the "Forever Innocent" brand I loathed had been wielded by the person closest to me, a tool in her twisted game. The betrayal wasn't just a stab in the back; it was a surgeon's precise incision, cutting away the last vestiges of my ability to trust anyone. The foundation of my life, already cracked, gave way completely, and I was left in free fall.

Memories assaulted me, each one now tainted. Lily giggling with me over a stupid meme on her phone. Lily patiently braiding my hair, her touch gentle and sure. Lily telling me, "You're the realest person I know in this fake town." Every shared confidence, every moment of supposed camaraderie, was now a lie constructed inside a funhouse mirror. She hadn't just wanted to hurt me; she had wanted to get close, to study me, to become an expert on her prey. The friendship I'd clung to in this isolating world had been a meticulously staged performance, and I was the only one who didn't know the script. The pain was so acute it was a vacuum, sucking the air from my lungs and leaving a hollow, aching silence in its place.

"Why?" The word scraped out of my throat, raw and broken. It was all I could manage. I needed to force the nightmare into some kind of sense, to find a logic in the madness.

Lily's eyes, those familiar warm brown eyes I'd trusted, shone with a fanatical light. They flickered from my face to Jake, who held her pinned with a terrifying, controlled fury.

"Because you had *everything*," she spat, her voice trembling not with regret, but with a fervent, possessive energy. "The fans, the fame, the spotlight... even *him*. They promised it to me! All of it! I'm Lily Flame. *Pure Fire*."

She said the name like an incantation, a destiny she was claiming. Her gaze lingered on Jake with a covetousness that turned my stomach to acid. She didn't just want my career; she wanted to step into my skin, to wear my life like one of the costumes she so carefully laid out for me. She wanted my cowboy. The sheer, audacious scale of her envy was a bottomless pit, and I was dizzy from staring into it.

The name 'Lily Flame' echoed in the silent hall. It was the name on the demo track, the one meant to replace me. It wasn't just a stage name; it was an identity she was stealing.

"I know all your songs," she whispered, a smug, secretive smile playing on her lips. "I know your keys, your vocal inflections. I practiced in your shower, when you weren't home. I sang into your microphone."

Each confession was a violation, a psychic trespass that made my skin crawl. She hadn't been my assistant; she'd been my understudy, studying for the role of a lifetime, the role of *me*, and she was ready for her debut, no matter the cost. The bile rose in my throat, bitter and hot. This was no longer about a stalker; it was about an identity thief who was willing to kill to complete the transaction.

Jake didn't just hold her; he contained her. His body was a wall of coiled tension, every muscle defined against the fabric of his shirt. He wrenched Lily upright with a force that made her gasp, his fingers like steel bands around her thin arm.

"Names," he growled, the sound low and lethal, devoid of any of the professional detachment I usually saw. This was personal now. "Connections. Who are 'they'? Who gave you the access? Who cut the wire on that mic?"

His questions were rapid-fire, each one a hammer strike. He was a predator who had finally cornered his quarry, and the air around him crackled with the promise of violence. Lily, however, seemed to feed on his rage. A strange, twisted smirk played on her lips, a perverse satisfaction glowing in her eyes. She was just a girl, but in that moment, she held a power over him, the power of the secret, and she was drunk on it. Seeing Jake, my steady, controlled Jake, vibrate with this raw, untamed fury was as terrifying as the betrayal itself. It meant the monster we were fighting was real enough to break even him.

I had seen Jake focused, I had seen him concerned, but I had never seen him like this. This was the soldier from his stories, the one who had faced down insurgents and IEDs. The civilized veneer had been stripped away, leaving only a core of primal protectiveness. And Lily, this fragile-looking girl, was staring into that storm without flinching. In fact, she seemed to be welcoming it, as if his fury was the ultimate validation of her importance. She had orchestrated a campaign of terror not just to become me, but to force a reaction from *him*. To be seen as a worthy adversary. The psychology of it was a dizzying, dark labyrinth. I was watching a deadly dance between a force of nature and a twisted mirror, and I was terrified of which one would shatter first.

Between sobs that sounded more performative than genuine and bursts of manic, girlish giggles, the story tumbled out. Lily admitted to everything with a chilling nonchalance. The notes, the roses, leaving the locket hanging in my dressing room, it was all her.

"It was so easy," she giggled, her eyes wide and unblinking. "You just leave the door unlocked for the delivery, you sweet-talk the new security guard, you wear a headset and look like you belong. You trusted everyone, Isla. It was your biggest flaw."

Each admission was another brick torn from the wall of my reality. She described watching me from the shadows, learning my routines, my fears. She hadn't just been my assistant; she had been my curator, and I was her exhibit. The "Forever Innocent" brand, she explained with a sneer, was the perfect target.

"It's so weak. So breakable. All I had to do was apply a little pressure, and the whole pretty lie started to crack." She had weaponized the very image I despised, using it as the blueprint for my torment.

As she spoke, the last year of my life rewrote itself in my mind. Every misplaced item, every creepy fan letter that felt a little too personal, the constant, gnawing feeling of being watched, it all had a name and a face now. Lily's. The time my favorite sweater went missing and showed up days later, smelling faintly of her perfume. The day I found my sheet music out of order, and she'd blamed the cleaning crew. She hadn't just been staging attacks; she'd been meticulously gaslighting me, slowly eroding my sense of safety and sanity, making me doubt myself so I'd be more pliable, more dependent. She wasn't just a stalker; she was a psychological saboteur. The brand wasn't just a bullseye; it was the weapon she used, knowing its inherent fragility would amplify every strike. She understood the product better than the product understood herself.

Just as a sickening sense of closure began to settle over me, the mystery solved, the monster unmasked, Lily dropped her bomb. Her manic energy subsided, replaced by a sudden, eerie calm. She looked directly at Jake, her voice dropping to a conspiratorial whisper that was far more frightening than her screams.

"But you'll never catch *him*," she said, a knowing smile touching her lips. "He's smarter. Stronger. He doesn't get his hands dirty with notes and necklaces." She paused, letting the implication hang in the air like poison gas. "He'll finish what I started."

The words sliced through the fragile relief, leaving a deeper, more profound terror in their wake. The partner. The accomplice. My knees threatened to buckle. Lily wasn't the mastermind; she was the instrument. The hands that had tightened the noose. But someone else was holding the rope. The betrayal wasn't just personal anymore; it was part of a larger, more sinister machinery. Lily had been the face in the mirror, but there was a shadow standing behind her, pulling the strings, and we had no idea who it was.

The pieces I had forced into a picture of Lily as the sole villain shattered and rearranged themselves into a far more terrifying mosaic. The sniper rifle. The sophisticated sabotages. Breaking into the panic room. Those weren't the work of a jealous girl with an obsession. That was the work of a someone with money and connections. Lily provided the inside access, the intimate knowledge, the psychological warfare. But *he*, the word was a cold stone in my gut, provided the muscle, the strategy, the finances, the true lethal intent. Lily was the virus, weakening the system from within, but he was the one who would eventually hit 'delete.' My betrayal was a two-headed beast, and we had only cut off one.

My mind became a frantic, scrolling feed of every suspicious moment, every unexplained event, and I tried to superimpose this new, two-faced reality onto them. The lipstick slash on the photo of Richard and me, that was Lily's dramatic flair. The roses with their threatening cards, her signature. The whispers in my earpiece, the intimate knowledge of my private fears, all her. But the cold, calculated precision of the sabotaged rigging? The sniper's red dot on my chest? The chilling, distorted voice on the phone? That was *him*. The brand I loathed had bred not one, but two distinct kinds of enemy: one driven by a twisted, personal envy, and the other by a cold, impersonal agenda I couldn't even begin to fathom. I was drowning in a sea of paranoia, wondering who else in my inner circle was hiding behind a mask, which friendly face was just waiting for a signal from the shadow in the wings.

The walls of the concert hall seemed to pulse, the faces of the remaining crew blurring into a single, untrustworthy mass. Was it the sound guy who always gave me a sympathetic smile? The new head of security Richard hired? Someone on the pyrotechnics crew going to aim something at me? Lucas DeWitt, with his slick, calculating eyes?

My breath started to come in short, sharp pants, my vision tunneling. The glitter on my costume felt like a million accusing eyes. I had been so focused on the single, defining threat of Lily that the idea of a collaborator, a silent partner, opened up an abyss of uncertainty. I was no longer just looking for a monster; I was looking for a ghost in my own machine, and the fear was a live wire, electrocuting my nerves one by one. I was losing my grip on reality, and the only thing tethering me to it was the man holding the broken girl in front of me.

As if sensing my internal collapse, Jake pulled me against his side, his arm a solid, unyielding bar across my back. The gesture was possessive, protective, and it shattered the last of my composure. I turned my face into his chest, my body trembling uncontrollably as the police moved in to take Lily from his grasp. She didn't go quietly. She kicked and screamed, a whirlwind of flailing limbs and guttural cries.

"You'll see! He'll make you see! I'm the star now! I'M PURE FIRE!" Her shrieks echoed in the vast space, the sound of a dream curdled into madness.

But muffled against Jake's shirt, the world narrowed to the scent of him, the steady thrum of his heart, the feel of his hand splayed firmly against my spine. His presence was a fortress against the chaos. He was the only thing that felt real, the only thing that hadn't been twisted into a lie. In the wreckage of my trust, he was the foundation that remained.

The cacophony of Lily's ravings and the stern commands of the police became a distant, muffled noise, a storm raging outside the sanctuary of his embrace. I focused on the rhythm of his breathing, on the rough texture of his work shirt against my cheek. He didn't whisper empty comforts. He just held me, absorbing the tremors that wracked my body, his silence more reassuring than any words could ever be. This was the man who had fought for me, who saw past the glitter to the shattered woman beneath. In his arms, the terrifying question of "who else?" momentarily lost its power. One enemy had a name, and she was being taken away. For this single, suspended moment, the war felt winnable because I wasn't fighting it alone.

The sirens faded, leaving a ringing silence in their wake. The immediate threat was gone, caged in the back of a police car. A strange, heavy calm descended upon the hall. But as Jake gently guided me toward my dressing room, a new sound began to filter in from outside. At first it was a murmur, then it grew into a familiar chant. Fans. Dozens of them, undoubtedly held back by barriers, their voices rising in a fervent, devoted chorus. "Is-la! Is-la! For-ev-er In-no-cent!" I stopped dead, my blood running cold. They'd have signs adorned with giant glitter bows. They'd have copies of my first album, the one with the "I'll Stand Tomorrow" ballad that started it all. They were chanting the lyrics. Their devotion was a wall of sound. My heart hammered a new, terrible rhythm. Lily was unmasked, but the machine she was part of was still grinding on. The brand was still out there, creating more Brians, more Lilys. They were consumers of the very product that had nearly gotten me killed, and their love felt like a cage. Jake's hand tightened on my arm like he felt it too. The danger wasn't over; it had just changed its clothes. It was no longer a single, identifiable threat, but a hydra. We had cut off one head, but the body was still alive, and it could be wearing the face of a fan. As I let Jake lead me away, the cheers felt like a funeral dirge. The enemy wasn't just in the shadows anymore; he was in the spotlight, and he was clapping the loudest.

Chapter 25
Unmasked

The slam of the police car door was a period at the end of a chaotic, screaming sentence, but the story was far from over. I watched the taillights disappear, Lily's distorted face still pressed against the window, a final, silent shriek. The easy, clean answer would be to close the book. Case solved. But my instincts, honed in sandbox alleys and mountain passes, were screaming a different truth. The dossier in my mind refused to snap shut. The sniper rifle was a professional's tool, not a stalker's keepsake. Lily was chaos and obsession; those acts were precision and strategy. She was the perfect smokescreen, a patsy with intimate access, but she didn't have the spine or the skill for the heavy lifting. Someone else had been calling the shots, someone who knew how to weaponize a fan's madness and stay impeccably, terrifyingly clean. The real predator was still out there, and he'd just sacrificed his most useful pawn. I believed Lily's tale of a mysterious *him* still out there though, god knew, I didn't want to.

My mind replayed the evidence like a tactical briefing. The cut on the rigging bolt was a single, clean saw stroke, no hesitation marks. The attack on the mansion starting with the sniper shot was tactical. It took finances and planning. Lily's methods were scattershot: notes, stolen trinkets, psychological warfare. The other attacks were... efficient. They were mission-oriented. Lily wanted to *become* Isla. This other entity, this *him*, simply wanted Isla gone. The two motives had converged, but they were not the same. Letting the police believe it was over was the strategically smart move for the real perpetrator. It made us lower our guard. It made us stop looking. And that was exactly when he would strike hardest.

Isla's dressing room was a shrine to violation. The lingering scent of her perfume was suffocated by the acrid smell of Lily's panic and the faint, metallic tang of fear. Glitter was scattered across every surface like toxic confetti, and drawers hung open, their contents spilling out like guts. While Isla sat numbly on the plush velvet couch, arms wrapped around herself as if holding her own pieces together, I sifted through the wreckage. I ignored the costumes and the makeup. I was looking for the ghost in the machine. Under a pile of discarded sequined tops, my boot knocked against something solid. I bent down and retrieved it, a laminated backstage pass on a lanyard. Crew Level 2 Access. It wasn't Lily's. Hers, I knew, was a Level 3, general assistant clearance. This one had higher clearance, granting access to the lighting rigs, the sound board, the secure storage where the chin mic equipment was kept. I held the cold plastic in my hand. The name had been deliberately scratched off, the photo rendered unidentifiable. Lily hadn't used this. Someone had given it to her. Or someone else had been here, moving freely in the chaos she created.

The pass felt like a lead weight. This wasn't just about stolen moments or planted notes anymore. This was about systemic infiltration. This pass represented a hole in our security large enough to drive a truck through, and it had been used by someone with the knowledge to exploit it fully. Lily provided the intimate, personal terror, but this pass was the key that allowed for the large-scale, technical sabotage. It connected the sniper attack to the rigging, to the chin mic. It was the thread linking the two perpetrators, and it proved that the real threat wasn't just a person; it was a position. It was someone with the authority to grant or possess this kind of access without raising an alarm.

I watched Isla from across the room. She'd shed the costume, the plastic bow, but the aura of her trauma was still wrapped tight around her. Her arms were crossed over her chest, a self-imposed straitjacket, and her gaze was fixed on some invisible point of horror on the floor. When she finally spoke, her voice was a hollow echo in the plush room.

"I can't trust anyone," she whispered, the words not meant for me, but a confession to the universe. "Not my manager. Not my assistant. Not even the fans who say they love me."

Her eyes, when they lifted to meet mine, were stripped raw. All the pop-star bravado had been sandblasted away, leaving behind the terrifying vulnerability of a woman who had seen the abyss up close. My chest tightened, a visceral reaction to her pain. I hated the machine that had done this to her, that had polished her into such a tempting target. But more than that, I hated my own powerlessness to erase the fear etched into her soul. I could stand between her and a bullet, but I couldn't shield her from the betrayal that had already pierced her heart.

The soldier in me knew this was a critical vulnerability. A client who trusts no one is a liability, unpredictable and prone to dangerous, independent action. But the man, the one who had held her while she fell apart, saw something else. He saw the first, painful emergence of a necessary survival instinct. The innocent, trusting Isla was a casualty of this war. The woman left in her place was harder, sharper, and despite the agony of that transformation, she might just be strong enough to survive what was coming. My mission was to protect her, but in that moment, I felt a fierce, possessive pride for the fighter she was being forced to become. It was a dangerous line of thought, one that blurred the professional with the profoundly personal.

Back in the temporary command post I'd set up in a janitor's closet, I spread the security logs across a rickety metal desk. The flickering fluorescent light hummed like an anxious thought. Isla sat on an upturned bucket, watching me, her silence a heavy weight. I traced timestamps, cross-referencing access codes with the moments of each attack. The night of the rigging sabotage. The window for tampering with the chin mic. My finger stopped, hovering over a single, recurring access code. It wasn't a random crew member. It wasn't a temp. The code belonged to a master keycard, one that opened every door, that granted unimpeded access to every corner of this venue, from the loading dock to the catwalks. I followed the digital breadcrumbs, and they led to one name, printed over and over with bland administrative authority.

Lucas DeWitt.

The concert producer. The man in the expensive suits with the polished smile, the one who shook my hand and called me "son." The one who controlled the budget, the schedule, the entire goddamn show. Slick. Polished. Untouchable. My instincts, which had been a dull roar, now screamed a single, clear warning.

There. The snake is right there.

DeWitt hadn't just allowed the attacks; he had orchestrated them from the director's chair. He couldn't afford to let this go. He'd invested too much in ruining Isla. He would have to make his final move himself.

The realization was a cold splash of reality. This wasn't a fan or a jealous rival. This was a businessman. This was about profit and loss. Isla's rebellion, her relationship with me, her shedding of the "Forever Innocent" brand, it was all bad for business. It destabilized the asset. And in the cold calculus of a man like DeWitt, a destabilized asset was a liability. It was cheaper, cleaner, and more profitable to write off the asset and collect the insurance, especially if he had a shiny new replacement, a "Lily Flame", waiting in the wings. The threats, the sabotage, it was all a corporate hostile takeover, and the product they were trying to acquire and dismantle was a human life. The sheer, chilling banality of the evil made it somehow worse.

I said the name aloud, letting it hang in the stale, chemical-scented air. "Lucas DeWitt."

Isla paled, her hand flying to her throat as if she could already feel the ghost of a noose. "Lucas? But... he's my producer. He's... he is the machine." Her voice was a whisper of disbelief.

"That's the point," I said, my voice low and hard. "He controls the machine. He controls the stage, the staff, your image. Taking him on means burning your career to the ground." I looked at her, really looked at her, sitting on that bucket in a janitor's closet, stripped of all the glitter and glamour. "It means choosing your life over your legacy."

Her chin lifted, a flicker of the old defiance returning to her eyes, but it was tempered now by a grim understanding. This was the final boss. Not a monster in the shadows, but the man who signed the paychecks.

My jaw hardened. I didn't give a damn about her brand, her record deals, or her Hollywood legacy. I cared about the woman in front of me. The one who laughed with a mouth full of veggie burger, who sang her sister's song with a voice that could break a man's heart, who trusted me with her shattered pieces.

"This ends at the concert. Tonight," I said, the plan already forming, cold and ruthless. "We use his stage. We set the bait. We drag the bastard into the light and end this."

This was no longer a protection detail. It was an extraction. I wasn't just pulling her from a physical location; I was extracting her from the clutches of the entire system that had created and now sought to destroy her. The concert wouldn't be a performance; it would be an ambush. My battlefield was shifting from back alleys and dark rooms to the blinding glare of the spotlight. DeWitt thought he was a master puppeteer. He was about to find out what happens when the puppet turns around, looks him in the eye, and has a cowboy with nothing left to lose standing beside her.

I pulled Isla to her feet, her hands cold in mine. The fear was still there in her grip, a fine tremor she couldn't control, but beneath it was a new, steely resolve. "He'll be watching everything," she whispered. "He controls everything."

"Let him watch," I growled. "Let him think he's still in control. That's when he'll get sloppy." I laid out the skeleton of the plan, my voice a low, steady cadge.

She would perform. She would walk onto that stage and be the perfect, glittering bait. But this time, my team wouldn't just be on perimeter duty. They'd be embedded in the crew, in the light booth, in the sound station. We would be the stagehands, the unseen technicians, turning his own machinery against him. We would monitor every exit, every communication, every flicker of the lights. We would be the trap waiting inside his trap.

She listened, her eyes wide, absorbing the danger. When I finished, she didn't hesitate. She simply nodded, her belief in me a terrifying, beautiful weight.

"I trust you," she whispered.

That vow, given so freely in the face of certain danger, cut me deeper than any shrapnel ever could. It wasn't a client's faith in a bodyguard. It was a woman's faith in the man she loved. And it made the thought of failure absolutely unacceptable.

In that cramped, ugly room, the air shifted. The professional boundary we'd been dancing around for weeks vaporized. This was no longer a job. This was a covenant. Her trust was my mission, and my protection was her sanctuary. I saw the understanding in her eyes. She knew she was walking into the lion's den. But she also knew I would be the one locking the door behind the both of us. The urge to kiss her, to seal this unspoken pact, was a physical ache. But I held back. This wasn't the time for that. It was a distraction we couldn't afford. That would come later, in the quiet after the storm, if we survived. Right now, there was only the plan, the enemy, and the fierce, burning need to keep my woman safe.

The final dress rehearsal for the second half was a ghost of a performance. Isla held on by sheer force of will, her voice thin in the vast space, her movements a half-second behind the music. My team was a constellation of quiet competence in the shadows. Harris with Belker, the retired bomb-sniffing dog, sweeping the under-stage areas. Two others posing as riggers in the catwalks. Another embedded in the sound booth, monitoring communications. We were a net, drawn tight. For a while, the only sound was the strained music and the thump of my own heart. The time flew by.

Then the doors opened to a rush of loud, excited fans heading to their seats. Everyone, crew, dancers, musicians, singers all ratcheted up to a high intensity as the countdown to the performance started. I was on comms constantly getting updates from the team. Isla was staring at me from her seat at her dressing room mirror, eyes wide, hands gripping her seat. We knew whatever was planned would take place during the next hour and a half.

A knock on the door made us both start. It was a stage assistant announcing places. Isla grabbed my hand, and we walked out to the wings. The crowd was chanting Isla's name.

"I'm going to puke." she whispered.

"I'll be right here." I said, squeezing her fingers.

"If you weren't I wouldn't even be standing." she said looking up at me.

I felt the burden then, the incredible trust she was giving me. She was the one out there in a spotlight. I knew the crowd had gone through screening but there were still a thousand things that could sneak through. A thousand ways she could be dead before I could get there. I couldn't tell her she was safe. I wouldn't lie. But if anything happened, I would obliterate whoever hurt her, consequences be damned.

"On 5." the stage manager announced in my earpiece.

And Isla turned on. Her shoulders straightened. Her smile suddenly sparkled. The band began the opening measures. The crowd began screaming. The dancers went out on cue. Isla released my hand, her eyes focused on the stage. She had don her persona. She was intent on giving a performance and I had to let her go be Isla Dove, pop princess.

She skipped out onto the stage, twirled and started right into the first song as if she wasn't petrified. I felt a surge of irrational pride at her incredible courage. She hit every note, every move of the choreography and the fans were with her all the way.

I had to stop focusing on her and keep my eyes roving, looking for anything that should not be. I kept up a steady monologue with my team, checking in on all stations. I was sure something was going to happen. I didn't know what or when, but this concert had been set up for a reason. And Lucas DeWitt wouldn't waste the opportunity.

We made it through to intermission free and clear. I escorted a sweating Isla back to her dressing room where she guzzled lemon water and got into her third costume to get ready for the second half.

"Do you think something still's going to happen?" she asked as someone redid her makeup and hair.

I nodded as I listened to the team going through their checks.

"I need drugs." Isla muttered. "All right. On with the show."

We marched back to the wings to wait for her cue. I knew there were two more costume changes in this half and a lot of pyrotechnics. I had an operative staged at both of the pyro stations to make sure nothing was tampered with. So far, they were reporting that everything there was clear with no one without clearance approaching the areas. Since I was such a trusting person, I had given each operative a code word to give me when they reported in. That way someone couldn't disable one of my guys and fake a "clear" report.

My anxiety level did not decrease as the night progressed. It increased. Because I was sure something was planned and the more time that passed, the surer I was that we were approaching time zero.

Then, Harris's voice crackled in my earpiece, low and urgent.

"Jake. Belker just went on alert. Stage left, near the hydraulic lift. We've got a positive."

My blood went cold. "Confirm."

"Confirming. Two charges. C-4. Enough to take out the building and half the block. Bomb squad is en route, ETA eight minutes. My team is handling one."

I started moving toward Isla, my body already shifting to extraction mode. Get her off the stage, get her to the armored vehicle, get her the hell out. But before I could take three steps, Harris's voice came again, sharper this time.

"Jake, stand by. Belker's alerting. Costume station, stage right. High explosives."

"Which station?" I demanded though I was nearly positive I knew. Stage right was furthest from me where Isla had gone for the final costume change.

"Isla's." Harris replied.

Of course. My head whipped around to stare at Isla. She was hardly wearing anything. Usual short sequined skirt, glitter clogs, midriff cropped top, gauzy cape-like drape and a massive glittering ornate neck collar. Wait. It was slightly different from the one I'd seen during rehearsal, the one waiting in the case. That had to be the source of the explosive positive Belker signaled.

I didn't think. I didn't breathe. I ran, dashing across the stage as the band faltered into silence at my appearance. The audience stared, confused. I reached Isla, my hands already coming up, my voice a forced calm that felt like a lie.

"Isla. Don't move." Her eyes widened in terror as I explained, my words fast and clipped. "Your collar is an explosive The bomb squad is eight minutes out. We don't have eight minutes."

I tossed my hat aside, my world narrowing to the intricate piece of jewelry around her throat, to the woman whose life was ticking away in my hands.

Chapter 26
Finale & Fire

I dashed offstage during the band's riff, holding my arms straight out for the costume change. If anyone could have watched they'd probably compare it to a Nascar pit crew at work. Off went one costume, clothes flying to the floor without a thought and on went the final bedazzled ensemble. I automatically lifted one foot, then the other for the different clogs, separating my fingers for the different jewelry, Someone else was restyling my hair, putting on a different bow to match the outfit. New bangle earrings. Make-up change. A gauzy cape. The stylists' hands were like birds, fluttering and frantic, stitching me into my finale costume. The fabric was heavy, encrusted with a thousand cold sequins that felt like scales of armor. They teased my neon-pink curls, clamping the giant, satin bow to the side of my head with an army of bobby pins. Each tug was a reminder of the cage. I stood perfectly still, arms outstretched as they dressed and made me into a mannequin. Today, I wasn't just Isla Dove the pop star. I was the lamb being preened for the slaughter, the glittering bait in a trap that felt too flimsy to hold the monster we were hunting. The "Forever Innocent" brand was my shroud, and I was letting them dress me for my own funeral.

Every beat of my heart was a frantic drum counting down the seconds until I had to dance back out there after the drum solo. This wasn't about singing anymore. It wasn't about art or connection.

It was a battle, and my voice was my only weapon, my costume a deliberate act of war. They wanted the doll? They would get her. But underneath the polish and the paint, I was sharpening my teeth. I was going to walk onto Lucas DeWitt's stage and set his perfect, profitable world on fire. The only question was whether I would burn with it.

The final touch was the neck piece. The big heavy neck collar for this Egyptian themed song and choreography. The fear was still here, a live wire in my gut, but it was now fused with a cold, clear purpose. I was done being a victim. I was done being a product. Tonight, I would be a weapon. And I would be aimed right at the heart of the man who thought he owned me.

Jake stood hovering, a storm contained in denim and worn leather. The frantic energy of the stylists stilled in his presence. He came to me, his hands, those capable, steady hands, adjusting the battery pack on my hip, checking the fit of my mic. His fingers brushed the skin of my lower back, and a shiver that had nothing to do with fear raced through me.

"Sierra has cleared the hall and I'm right off stage," he murmured, his voice so low only I could hear it, a private vow in the crowded room.

His hazel eyes burned into mine, and in their depths, I saw no trace of the professional bodyguard. I saw a man making a promise to the woman he loved. He saw past the glitter and the bow, past the pop princess facade, straight down to the raw, terrified, and fiercely determined me beneath. In that look, he gave me a sliver of his own unshakable strength. I nodded, my throat too tight for words. My heart wasn't just hammering with fear now; it was thrumming with a desperate, wild hope.

We didn't need words. The language we spoke in that moment was older, built in shared survival and whispered confessions in the dark.

His eyes said, *I will tear this building apart with my bare hands before I let him touch you.*

My silence in return said, *I know. And I will fight beside you.*

It was the most intimate conversation we had ever had. The stylists finished and fluttered away, leaving us in a bubble of charged silence. He was my anchor in the coming hurricane, my shield and my sword. For the first time, walking onto that stage didn't feel like a death sentence. It felt like walking into battle with my king at my side. And that made all the difference.

The stage manager gave the signal. A deep breath, a final glance at Jake, and I skipped back from the muted darkness of the wings into the blazing inferno of the spotlight. The roar of the crowd was a physical force, a wall of sound that hit me in the chest. Thousands of voices chanting my name, thousands of glowing phone screens waving like digital fireflies. Neon signs bobbed in the darkness: "FOREVER INNOCENT," "OUR PRINCESS." The adoration was a wave I'd ridden for years, but tonight it felt different. It felt like the last meal for a condemned woman. I forced my practiced, glittering smile, I waved, I blew a kiss. I was their idol, their perfect, untouchable dream. But inside, I was screaming. Every sequin felt like a target. Every beat of the sugary pop music felt like a countdown. I was a doll on a music box, spinning for the pleasure of a hidden audience of one, the man who wanted to break me. Tonight, I was steel. Tonight, I would not break.

My body knew the choreography by heart. It spun, it kicked, it hit its marks with a precision that was entirely separate from my mind. My mind was elsewhere, scanning the shadows of the wings for Jake's solid form, trying to see past the lights for a glint of cold calculation, feeling for the telltale weight of a wire that didn't belong. I was singing, but the words were empty sounds, the melodies a familiar cage. The audience saw a star shining her brightest. I felt like a ghost going through the motions, haunting the stage of my own life. The lie of "Forever Innocent" had never felt so heavy, so grotesque. I was a beautiful, singing corpse, and Lucas DeWitt was waiting somewhere in the wings to confirm the kill.

I threw my arms wide during the chorus, a gesture of joyous abandon that was plastered on every merch shirt in the arena. The crowd screamed louder. And in that moment, the two realities split completely: Isla Dove, the Product, gave them everything they paid for. And Isla, the woman, retreated deep inside, gathering her strength, sharpening her claws, and waiting for the trap to spring.

Song after song, I had pushed through. My voice wavered on the first high note, a crack in the perfect porcelain veneer. I saw Jake tense in the wings, his body coiled like a spring. I locked my eyes on him, using his steady presence as a vocal warm-up, as a metronome for my racing heart. I forced the note, and it held, thin but clear. The band thundered on, the dancers swirled around me, a cyclone of color and motion. I was the still, glittering eye of the storm. Every lyric about first kisses and endless summers tasted like ash on my tongue. They were the anthems of the prison he had built for me. But I sang them. I sold the dream. Because underneath the bubblegum melody, I was listening, to the creak of the rigging, to the static in my ear, for the sound of Jake's voice telling me it was time to run.

It was the most terrifying performance of my life. Each moment stretched into an eternity. A stagehand moving too quickly would make my heart stutter. A flicker of the lights sent a jolt of pure panic through my system. The pyrotechnics made my heart stutter. I was a marionette, and I could feel the hands of my puppeteer all around me, tightening the strings. Lucas was here. I could feel his gaze like a physical pressure, watching his investment, calculating his return, waiting for the perfect moment to cash out. I was singing through a smile carved from ice, my body moving on autopilot while my soul braced for impact. The music was my shield and my cage, and I was trapped inside its beat, waiting for chaos.

But with each passing second, a new emotion began to burn through the fear: a hot, clean anger. He thought he could break me with my own songs? He thought my stage was his weapon? My fans would take a *new* Isla with no doubt? The defiance that had been simmering began to boil over. Let him watch. Let him see the product fight back.

The music was a living beast, its pulse thrumming through the stage and into the bones of my feet. I was in the middle of a choreographed spin, my sequined skirt flaring, when Jake's voice cut through the private channel in my ear. It was calm, lethally so.

"Isla. Keep smiling. Don't stop singing. Bomb squad is in the building. They found C-4. No time to evacuate."

The world tilted. My smile felt like a rictus grin, frozen in place by sheer will and years of practice. I kept spinning, kept singing, the sugary lyrics about teenage dreams suddenly the most macabre poetry ever written. My eyes, wide and unblinking, found Jake in the wings. He wasn't looking at me anymore; he was a statue of focused intensity, his gaze sweeping the darkness beyond the stage lights, his body a taut wire. Sierra Bravo, disguised as stagehands, moved with a grim purpose through the organized chaos. They were a silent, deadly current flowing just beneath the surface of the performance. Every second was a lifetime, every beat of the music a tick of the clock on a hidden bomb. I was singing my heart out while men with bomb suits worked to keep it from being scattered across this arena.

It was a bizarre, out-of-body experience. One part of me was the pop star, belting out a chorus about eternal love, my voice soaring over the screams of adoring fans. The other part was a raw nerve, hyper-aware of every shadow, every flicker, every potential flash of fire that could mark the end for all of us. The two realities, the glittering spectacle and the deadly siege, existed simultaneously, layered over each other like a nightmare. And I was the thread holding them together. My voice, my performance, was the distraction, the beautiful lie that kept the audience in their seats and, I prayed, kept Lucas's eyes on me and not on the counter-assault unfolding in his own house. The anger burned hotter, fueling the performance, giving my empty smile a sharp, dangerous edge.

Watch me, you bastard. Watch your asset fight for her life. For all our lives.

I hit the final, powerful note of the bridge, holding it as the dancers froze in their positions around me. The applause was a thunderous wave. And in that suspended moment, as the sound began to fade, Jake broke from the wings. He ran; he moved with a terrifying, deliberate speed that cut through the celebratory atmosphere like a knife. He was at my side in seconds, his body positioning itself between me and the audience, his face a mask of grim urgency.

"The neck piece, Isla. Don't move." His voice was low, for my ears only, but the command in it turned my blood to ice.

I stared at him, the world narrowing to the concern in his hazel eyes. "What?"

"The one you're wearing. It was altered. It's a bomb." He was speaking so softly even my chin mic didn't carry his words to the questioning crowd.

The floor fell away. The roar of the crowd became a distant hum. I could only see his face, could only feel the cold, ornate metal against my throat. A bomb. The man had gotten to the costume. He'd switched it. I was standing in front of twenty thousand people with an explosive collar around my neck.

"Get out of here, Jake," I sobbed, my voice breaking. "Just go. Save yourself."

He didn't even flinch. His hands were already coming up, his gaze fixed on the intricate jewelry. "I'm not going anywhere. Now, I need you to sing for me."

Sing? He wanted me to *sing*? With a bomb on my neck? The absurdity of it was a splash of cold water. And then I understood. The bomb squads were busy. Jake had told me he was a bomb tech in the military. He was the only one who could do this. And my job was to keep the crowd calm, to keep Lucas thinking his plan was unfolding perfectly, and to give Jake the focus he needed. The fear was a living thing, clawing at my throat, trying to steal my voice. But I looked at him, at the absolute, unwavering faith in his eyes, and I made a choice. I would not die a doll. I would not die silent. If this was my last song, they would hear the truth. I opened my mouth, and the note that came out was shaky, thin with terror. But it was mine.

The first few notes were pure instinct, the melody of my biggest hit, the one that built my cage. But the words... the words were wrong. I wasn't singing the slick, produced pop version. The bubblegum sweetness was gone, stripped away by raw fear and a rising, defiant fury. My voice cracked on the chorus, not with technical failure, but with emotion.

Crystal skies turned into concrete
Your whispered words, so bittersweet

I was singing the song as I'd first written it in my bedroom at sixteen, after the date rape that stole my safety, the one I'd called *I'll Stand Tomorrow (I Just Can't Today)*. It was a cry for help, a confession of shattered innocence, a promise to survive even when every part of you is broken. The arena, which had been a roaring beast of adoration, fell into a stunned, reverent silence. They weren't hearing Isla Dove, the brand, the pop princess. They were hearing Isla, the woman. And she was bleeding out her truth in front of them.

You promised me a fairy tale
Then pulled the rug and watched me fail
I thought I knew the game we played
But you rewrote the rules that day
And now the world feels upside down
My pretty crown is on the ground
I'm picking up the broken pieces I have found

I saw Jake's hands, steady as granite as he worked with a tiny tool, pause for a fraction of a second. He didn't look up, but his shoulders tightened. He heard it. He heard the ghost of his sister in the stripped-bare lyrics, he heard *my* pain echoing a pain he knew too well. This was no longer a performance; it was an exorcism for both of us. The crowd was utterly captivated, sensing they were witnessing something sacred and real, something no ticket price could ever buy. The glittering stage became a confessional. I was giving them my soul, and in return, their silence gave Jake the perfect, focused environment he needed to save my life, save our lives.

Crystal skies turned into concrete
Your whispered words, so bittersweet
You promised me a fairy tale
Then pulled the rug and watched me fail
I thought I knew the game we played
But you rewrote the rules that day
And now the world feels upside down
My pretty crown is on the ground
I'm picking up the broken pieces I have found

And I heard my backup singers join me quietly for the chorus, singing with me and not in any bubblegum cadence.

I'll stand tomorrow, I just can't today
The colors all around me have faded into grey
You took my sunshine, you stole my blue away
I'll find my feet again, I'll have my say
I'll stand tomorrow, I just can't today
My reflection's a stranger in the glass
Remembering the night that passed
The trust I gave, you threw away
And left me here to face the fray
This smile I wear is just a lie
A desperate flag I'm flying high
'Cause now the world feels upside down
My pretty crown is on the ground
I'm picking up the broken pieces I have found
I'll stand tomorrow, I just can't today
The colors all around me have faded into grey
You took my sunshine, you stole my blue away
I'll find my feet again, I'll have my say
I'll stand tomorrow, I just can't today

Then my keyboardist began playing softly. I thought they would have left but they were there with us.

They tell me "shake it off," "be strong"
But what you did was oh so wrong
It's not a simple change of heart
You tore my innocence apart
This isn't love, it's just a scar
A reminder of how fragile we are

Then everyone went quiet, leaving me to finish the end of the song. My voice grew stronger, fueled by this strange, sacred exchange. I was no longer a pop princess. I was a phoenix, singing my own heartbroken dirge, praying I'd live long enough to rise from the ashes.

I'll stand tomorrow, I just can't today!

The colors all around me have faded into grey!

You took my sunshine, you stole my blue away!

I'll find my feet again, I'LL HAVE MY SAY!

I'll stand tomorrow... I just can't today...

I'll stand tomorrow...

...I just can't today.

The final, aching note of the song hung in the air, a raw, unvarnished truth that left the arena in a breathless hush. In that profound silence, I felt a final, soft *click* at the nape of my neck. Jake let out a sharp, relieved breath, his shoulders slumping for just a moment as he carefully lifted the deadly necklace away from my skin.

"It's disarmed," he murmured, his voice thick with emotion. "You're safe."

A collective sigh seemed to ripple through the crowd, followed by the beginning of a hesitant, then thunderous, wave of applause. It was a different kind of roar now, not adoration, but respect. Awe.

But the encore was not over.

From the stage-left wings, a figure stormed into the spotlight. Lucas DeWitt. His expensive suit was immaculate, but his face was a contorted mask of pure, incandescent rage. The polished producer was gone, replaced by a cornered animal. In his hand, a small, black pistol gleamed under the lights, leveled directly at my heart.

"The encore ends in blood," he snarled, his voice cutting through the applause, which died instantly into a vacuum of terror.

I froze, a statue in glitter and sweat, staring down the barrel of the gun. The crowd screamed. And Jake, who had just saved me from one death, dropped the necklace.

Time seemed to fracture. I saw the furious twitch in Lucas's finger on the trigger. I saw Jake, unarmed, begin to move with impossible speed, his body already shifting into the path of the bullet. There was no hesitation. There was only him and me and the certain, violent end rushing toward us. The spotlight that had felt like a prison now felt like a target painted on my chest. The final curtain was falling, and it was going to be red.

Chapter 27
Second Chance, Last Dance

The world narrowed to a single, glinting point: the muzzle of Lucas DeWitt's pistol, aimed at Isla's heart. The applause that had been a roar of reverence curdled into a symphony of screams. Camera flashes popped like a hailstorm, freezing the nightmare in stark, blinding still-frames. Isla stood paralyzed, a glittering angel facing a devil in a Brioni suit. Every instinct in my body screamed, a raw, animal sound that overrode all training, all thought. There was no plan. There was only her.

The roar of the crowd was a distant ocean, the frantic shouts of my team in my earpiece were meaningless static. My vision tunneled, eliminating everything but the gun and the woman I loved. The polished stage, the blinding lights, the sequins, it was all a blur. The only things in sharp, horrifying focus were the determined hatred in Lucas's eyes and the stark terror in Isla's. The professional bodyguard vanished. In his place was something older, more brutal. A man defending his own. The calculation was simple, absolute: my life for hers. There was no other math.

I saw the subtle contraction of the muscle in Lucas's forearm, the microscopic shift of his weight. He wasn't posturing. He was a businessman closing a deal, and the product was Isla's life. He was going to pull the trigger. And I was already moving.

I charged. It wasn't a run; it was a launch, every muscle in my body coiling and releasing in a single, explosive motion. I hit Lucas from the side, a brutal tackle that carried us both off our feet. The gun discharged, the report a deafening crack that echoed in the vast space. The bullet whined past, burying itself in the backdrop somewhere behind us. We hit the stage floor hard, my body taking the brunt of the impact, my arms locking around him like steel. The facade of the slick Hollywood producer shattered instantly. This was a street fight now, and that was a language I was fluent in.

He fought with the dirty, desperate moves of a cornered rat, eye gouges, knee strikes to the groin, his teeth snapping near my face. A knife, sleek and black, flashed from inside his jacket. I blocked the downward stab with my forearm, the impact jarring my bones, and twisted, using his own momentum to slam his wrist against the stage floor. The knife skittered away, but my focus was fractured. Every second I spent neutralizing him was a second Isla was exposed, standing frozen just feet away in her glittering heels. He wasn't trying to win the fight; he was trying to create an opening, a single, clear shot at his target. My Isla. Rage, hot and pure, burned through me. This man had orchestrated her terror, had put a bomb on her neck, and now he was trying to put a hole in her heart. I drove a fist into his ribs, feeling one give way with a satisfying crunch.

Lucas writhed beneath me, a guttural roar of pain and fury tearing from his throat. He bucked, using his legs to try and throw me off. My grip held, but it shifted our tangled bodies, and my heart stopped as

I saw the glint of the discarded pistol, now skittering within reach of Isla's heels.

"Isla, the gun!" I barked, my voice raw.

Her eyes, wide with shock, dropped to the floor. For a horrific second, she was a deer in the headlights. But then, something in her snapped. The fear in her eyes was doused by a surge of pure, blazing defiance. She wasn't going to be a victim. Not again.

She moved not with panic, but with a fierce, deliberate purpose. She didn't scramble away from the weapon; she stepped toward it, her glittery heel coming down hard on the slide, pinning it to the stage floor. In the same fluid motion, she grabbed the nearest object, a heavy, steel mic stand from the drum kit. She hefted it, her arms trembling not with weakness, but with the intensity of her resolve. She was done waiting to be saved. She was joining the fight. The pop princess was gone. In her place stood a warrior queen, and the sight of her, standing tall amidst the chaos, filled me with a pride so fierce it was almost a pain.

As Lucas lunged again, distracted by her movement, I saw my opening. And I saw her see it too. We were two halves of a single, deadly engine.

Lucas, enraged by her defiance, shoved against me with a fresh burst of strength, his focus splintering between the threat I posed and the new one Isla represented. It was the mistake I needed. As he tried to rise, Isla didn't hesitate. She swung the mic stand. It wasn't a wild, frantic swing. It was an arc of pure, concentrated fury. The steel shaft connected with the back of his knees with a sickening, hollow *thwack*. The sound was brutal, final. Lucas cried out, his legs buckling beneath him. His expensive facade was completely gone now, replaced by the writhing, pathetic reality of a man who had lost everything.

The blow was more than just physical. It was the sound of her "Forever Innocent" brand shattering into a million pieces. It was the sound of her taking back her power, of fighting back against the system that had created and then tried to destroy her. In that swing, she wasn't just protecting herself; she was executing the final act of her own liberation. She stood over him, breathing heavily, the mic stand still clutched in her hands like a scepter. She had drawn a line, and she had drawn it in blood. My beautiful, fierce, impossible woman. She had just crowned herself.

I stared, my own breath caught in my throat. In all my years of warfare, I had never seen anything more breathtakingly courageous.

The moment Lucas's legs gave out, the fight shifted. It was no longer me against him. It was *us*. As he collapsed forward, snarling and spitting, I scrambled after the gun, my finger finding the trigger guard by instinct. At the same instant, Isla didn't retreat. She stepped forward, using the base of the mic stand to shove him back down, preventing him from finding his footing. Her shove, my grip. Her cry of effort, my grunt of finality. We moved in a terrible, perfect synchronicity, a duet of survival. There was no bodyguard and client. No cowboy and pop star. There were just two fighters, back-to-back in the storm, their movements perfectly aligned against the common enemy. For the first time, I wasn't just protecting her. We were protecting each other.

It was the culmination of every shared look, every whispered confidence, every moment of trust forged in fire. We were two broken pieces that, locked together, created something unbreakable. Her strength did not diminish mine; it amplified it. Seeing her fight, feeling her beside me, filled me with a power I had never known. This was what it meant to not be alone. This was what it meant to have a partner. The stage, which had been a place of such isolation and performance for her, was now the ground where we stood as one. Lucas wasn't just fighting a man; he was fighting a unit, a bond that his bullets and bombs could never sever.

He had tried to use her own life as a weapon against her. Instead, he had forged us into a single, unstoppable blade. And now, that blade was at his throat.

The world, which had narrowed to the three of us on the stage, suddenly exploded back into chaotic, full-color reality. The hall flooded with armed SWAT officers, their black tactical gear a stark contrast to the glitter and sequins. They moved with a disciplined fury, swarming the stage. The few screams that were left from the audience were quickly replaced by the stern, amplified commands to evacuate. I kept my knee planted in Lucas's spine, the fight gone out of him now, replaced by the cold weight of handcuffs snapping around his wrists. He thrashed, but it was useless.

"You don't understand!" he roared, his voice cracking, the polished producer replaced by a desperate, ruined man. "The debts! The insurance! She was sinking the brand! It was just business!"

Just business.

The words were a profanity. He had orchestrated a campaign of terror, had attempted murder, had shattered a woman's spirit, and he reduced it to a line item on a balance sheet. The rage I felt was so pure it was almost calm.

I leaned down, my voice a low growl meant only for his ear. "It ends here."

There was no negotiation, no plea deal, no Hollywood ending for him. This was the final curtain on his production, and the reviews were going to be scathing. As they hauled him to his feet, his eyes, wide with the realization of his total loss, met mine. I saw no remorse, only the calculation of a failed investment.

They dragged him away, his excuses and justifications swallowed by the organized chaos of the takedown. The stage was a wreck, a battlefield littered with the confetti of an interrupted fantasy.

The sirens outside became a constant, wailing underscore to the silence that had fallen between us. The armed men, the frantic crew, it all faded into a blur. I turned. Isla was still standing there, the mic stand now leaning against her leg like a spent staff. Her neon curls were a mess, her makeup smeared by sweat and tears, the giant bow hanging by a single, desperate bobby pin. For once, she wasn't Isla Dove the idol. She was just Isla. Shaken. Raw. Unbelievably, radiantly alive. Our eyes met across the short, devastated distance. There were no words. There didn't need to be. I crossed the space in two strides, and she was in my arms, her body collapsing against mine. She clutched the fabric of my shirt in her fists, her entire frame trembling, not with fear this time, but with the seismic release of survival.

She buried her face in my neck, and I held her, my arms creating a fortress around her. I could feel the frantic beat of her heart against my chest, slowly beginning to steady. I pressed my lips to her hair, breathing in the scent of her perfume mixed with the acrid smell of fear. This was it. This was what it was all for. Not the mission, not the contract. This feeling of her, safe and whole in my arms. The line we had been toeing for weeks was not just crossed; it was obliterated. We were no longer a bodyguard and his client. We were a man and the woman he loved, standing in the wreckage of a war we had won together.

The cameras were still rolling, the world was watching, but they didn't matter. The only thing that was real was the weight of her in my arms and the silent, unshakable truth that had finally been forged in fire.

In the center of the ravaged stage, under the cold, shattered spot-lights, she lifted her head. Her green eyes, stripped of all artifice, searched mine. The noise of the evacuation, the static of radios, it all faded into a distant hum. Her voice, when it came, was a soft, broken whisper, but it carried the weight of a lifetime.

"I love you."

The words landed not as a surprise, but as a final, missing piece clicking into place, completing a circuit that had been live between us for weeks. My throat locked. Every professional protocol, every reason I had to hold back, evaporated like mist in the sun.

She swallowed, her gaze unwavering. "Don't ever let me go."

My arms tightened around her, pulling her flush against me until not even a sliver of light could pass between us. I didn't have pretty words. I had only the raw, unvarnished truth.

"I won't," I vowed, my voice rough with an emotion so vast it threatened to swallow me whole. "Never."

The cameras captured it all. The world just saw the truth we could no longer hide. The job was over. Our story was just beginning.

It was a confession that changed the very axis of my world. My purpose was no longer a temporary assignment. It was a lifetime vow. She was my mission now, my home, my everything. The contract with Sierra Bravo could burn. The only signature that mattered was the one my soul had just etched onto hers. We stood there, bound together in the blinding glare, the wreckage of our old lives surrounding us like the foundation for a new one we would build, together.

Chapter 28
Aftermath & Apologies

The roar was gone, leaving a ringing silence in its wake that was more deafening than any crowd. I sat at the edge of the stage, my legs dangling over the precipice, staring out at the sea of empty, shadowed seats. A fine layer of glittering confetti stuck to my skin, clinging to the sweat and dried tears like morbid sequins. Jake's worn denim jacket was draped over my shoulders, heavy with the scent of leather and him, the only anchor in a world that had been completely unmade. For the first time, there were no stylists, no managers, no demands. No bow. No brand. Just me, Isla, trembling in the aftermath, the ghost of a scream still lodged in my throat. The performance was over. The monster was caged. So why did I feel so completely shattered?

It was like the entire arena was holding its breath. The air itself felt thin, used up. My body was a hollowed-out shell, all the adrenaline and terror siphoned out, leaving behind a profound, aching exhaustion. I could still feel the phantom weight of the bomb collar, the cold press of the gun's stare, the bruising grip of Lily's hand. They were over, but they were etched into my nerves. I pulled Jake's jacket tighter, seeking his warmth, his solidity. This was the other side of survival. It wasn't a victory parade; it was a quiet, lonely landscape of rubble, and I was standing in the center of it, unsure of what to build next.

The stage, my kingdom and my prison, felt different beneath me. The boards were just boards now. The lights were just lights. The magic had been a lie, and the truth that replaced it was brutal, beautiful, and terrifyingly fragile.

A low, persistent buzz began to intrude on the silence, filtering through the heavy main doors. It was the sound of a swarm, the media, held back by a line of police, their voices a collective, hungry murmur. My phone, which I'd clutched like a lifeline, buzzed in my hand, the screen lighting up with a cascade of notifications. Trending hashtags scrolled like a ticker tape of my own public execution and resurrection: #ForeverPureNoMore, #CowboyBodyguard, #IslasFinalEncore, #DeWittDestroyed. I flinched. My carefully managed brand, the pristine "Forever Innocent" lie, had shattered on live television, and the world was feasting on the pieces. They had seen the doll break. They had seen the real, bloody, fighting woman underneath. And maybe, just maybe, that was the first, terrifying step toward being free.

A part of me, the part trained for a decade, recoiled in horror. The brand was in tatters. The investment was lost. My career, as I knew it, was over. But a newer, stronger part, the part that had swung a mic stand, felt a grim, defiant satisfaction. Let it burn. Let them see the scorch marks. Let them know the price of the fantasy. The pristine image had been a cage, and Lucas DeWitt had held the key. Now, the bars were bent and broken, and I was standing in the wreckage, breathing real air for the first time. The vultures could pick over the carcass of Isla Dove™. I was done with her.

I looked at the headlines, each one a nail in the coffin of my old life. The pain was there, a sharp, professional grief. But underneath it, like a seed cracking open in dark soil, was a shocking, undeniable sense of relief.

Jake was a restless storm circling me, a predator unable to settle even after the hunt was over. He checked the locked doors, peered out the narrow windows at the media scrum, his movements sharp, efficient. But when his eyes found me, they were different. The battle-fire was gone, replaced by a deep, guarded shadow. I saw the guilt there, as clear as if he'd shouted it. He thought he'd failed me. He thought by letting it get this far, by allowing me to be used as bait, by not stopping Lucas sooner, he had broken something irreplaceable. He saw the death of my career and was tallying it as his personal failure. The thought was a physical ache. He had given me everything, my life, his heart, and he believed it wasn't enough.

I wanted to go to him, to smooth the tension from his shoulders, to tell him he was my salvation, not my ruin. That he hadn't destroyed my career; he had helped me escape it. But the words felt too big, too fragile for this raw space. His guilt was a wall he was building between us, a last bastion of his professional duty, and I didn't know how to tear it down. I saw the man who had faced down a bomb and a bullet for me, and my heart broke that he could look at himself and see anything less than a hero. My hero.

He stood as my protector until the very end, even from the consequences of my own freedom. And I realized the next battle wouldn't be for our lives, but for his peace.

A commotion at a side entrance drew my gaze. Jenna was there, being led through in handcuffs, her head bowed. As they passed near the stage, she looked up, and our eyes met. The fiery jealousy was gone, extinguished. In its place was a hollowed-out shame, her face a mess of smeared mascara and stark reality.

"I just wanted my shot," she whispered, the words meant for me, a pathetic, broken confession.

The anger I'd held for her dissolved, replaced by a wave of pity so sharp it stole my breath. We were both casualties of the same brutal machine, girls who had sung the same dreams into the same microphones, only to be chewed up and spat out by the industry we'd given our lives to. Her shot had come at the cost of her soul, and mine had nearly cost me my life.

In that moment, I didn't see a rival or a saboteur. I saw a reflection, a darker, more desperate version of what I could have become if I hadn't fought back, if I hadn't had Jake. We had both been pawns in Lucas's game, pitted against each other while he profited from our conflict. The system had bred her resentment as surely as it had bred my fear. The chain of betrayal was long, and she was just another link, broken and discarded. As they led her away, I felt a piece of my own past being carted off with her, a ghost of the girl who believed fame was the answer.

We hadn't been stars. We had been gladiators in a glitter-dust arena, and the crowd had never known the difference.

Then I remembered Lily's plaintive screams.

"It was supposed to be me!" she had shrieked, her voice raw and tearing. "I'm Pure Fire! I earned it! You had him, you had everything, and you didn't even want it!"

She didn't just want my career; she had wanted to step into my skin, to wear my life, to claim the man who loved me as her prize. Her apology wasn't for the terror or the pain; it was for her own failure to successfully become me.

Her words were a violation that went deeper than any physical threat. She hadn't just been in my space; she had been in my head, studying my routines, my fears, my relationship, wanting to consume them and make them her own. The friendship I'd cherished had been a predator's camouflage. A profound cold settled in my bones. The brand I despised had not only made me a target; it had created a monster who believed my life was a prize to be won. The applause, the fame, the illusion, it was a sickness, and Lily was its most tragic, terminal patient. The most terrifying part was that in her broken logic, she truly believed she loved Jake. She just loved him like a possession, a trophy to complete her stolen set.

A different sound cut through the grim proceedings, frantic, familiar voices. "Isla!" Tony, my bass player, charged in, his loud laugh replaced by eyes wide with worry. Maya, my backup singer, was right behind him, her face streaked with tears, already cursing a blue streak about "that soulless suit DeWitt." And Rafe, my quiet keyboardist, simply walked up and put a steadying hand on my shoulder. Their embrace was a different kind of anchor, not the fierce, singular protection of Jake, but the warm, grounding weight of people who knew the real me, not the brand. They didn't love the idol. They loved the woman who brought them coffee, who forgot lyrics, who laughed until she snorted.

They weren't here for a photo op or a statement. They were here for *me*. In an industry of users and fakes, they were the real thing. Tony squeezed me too tight, Maya whispered fierce, loving obscenities in my ear, and Rafe's silent presence was a wall of support. They were the family I had chosen in this chaotic world, the ones who had seen me before the glitter and would see me after it was gone. In their arms, the hollowed-out feeling began to recede, filled with a genuine, uncomplicated love I had almost forgotten how to feel.

The machine was broken, the castle had fallen, but my tribe was still standing. And I realized that was the only legacy that had ever truly mattered.

A police officer approached, his expression grimly sympathetic. "Miss Dove, the press is... insistent. We can get you out a back way, but if you have anything to say, now's the time."

The easy thing, the safe thing, would be to run. To hide from the flashing lights and the shouted questions, to let the headlines write the story without me. I felt the old instinct to paste on a smile and give a vapid, PR-approved nothingness. But that woman was gone.

Jake stepped forward, his hand finding the small of my back. "You don't owe them a damn thing," he muttered, his voice a low, protective rumble.

I looked from his fiercely loyal face to the faces of my band, my real family. Then I looked toward the doors, behind which the machine that had nearly devoured me was waiting to feast on the scraps.

Running felt like letting Lucas win. It felt like admitting that the story was his to control, that the narrative of my life was just another asset to be managed. But I was done being managed. I was done with their stories.

Squeezing Jake's hand, I whispered, "But maybe I owe myself."

I owed myself the truth. I owed myself the final word. This wasn't for the cameras; it was for me. It was the last, defiant act of reclaiming my own name, my own voice, from the wreckage they had made of it. Taking a deep, shuddering breath, I turned toward the doors, ready to face the storm on my own terms for the very first time.

I would walk out there not as a product, but as a person. Let them see the scars. Let them hear the truth.

The moment I pushed through the heavy doors, the world exploded in a blinding, white-hot frenzy. Camera flashes erupted like a silent artillery barrage, and a cacophony of shouted questions hit me like a physical wave. I stood on the steps, squinting against the glare, Jake a solid, silent pillar just behind my shoulder. I lifted my chin. No bow.

No glitter. No fake, placating smile. Just me, Isla, raw and real and terrified. I ignored the questions about my career, about the brand, about Lucas. My gaze swept over the sea of hungry faces, and I found the lens I knew was broadcasting live to the world.

"My name is Isla Dove," I began, my voice trembling but clear. "And I'm done playing a doll."

I felt Jake stiffen behind me. This was it. The point of no return. I was about to torch the last bridge to my old life.

I took a shaky breath, my heart hammering against my ribs. "The 'Forever Innocent' brand was always a lie. It was a cage. And I'm done living in it."

The crowd roared, a mix of shock and confusion. I pressed on, the words tumbling out, a confession and a liberation. "The man you saw on stage with me... the man who saved my life..." I turned my head slightly, my eyes meeting Jake's. His expression was unreadable, a storm of surprise and something deeper, something fierce. I looked back at the cameras, my voice gaining strength. "I love him."

The silence that fell was absolute. And in that silence, I realized my confession hadn't just been about my truth. It had been a challenge to his. I had just thrown my entire world at his feet, in front of millions of people. And as I stood there, the echo of my words hanging in the air, I had no idea if he would catch me, or if I had just pushed him away for good.

The air crackled. I had stripped myself bare for him, for the world, with no promise of shelter. I had chosen him over everything, and in doing so, I had forced him to choose. Would he choose the simplicity of his old life, the clear lines of a bodyguard's duty, now that the job was technically over? Or would he choose the messy, public, complicated reality of us? I stood there, completely exposed, waiting for my cowboy to make his move, praying that the man who had fought a war for me was ready to build a peace with me.

Chapter 29
Cowboy or LA

The silence in Isla's Beverly Hills mansion was a physical weight after the screaming chaos of the arena. I paced the marble floors, the sterile gleam of the surfaces reflecting a man who didn't belong. My worn boots were too loud, my presence too rough for this world of curated perfection. Gold and platinum records stared down from the walls, and glossy promotional posters of Isla, the *old* Isla, with her neon bows and vacant, sparkling smile, felt like accusations. This wasn't a home; it was a museum dedicated to a ghost, a mausoleum for a brand I had helped kill. Every fiber of my being, bred on dirt and open sky, recoiled from the suffocating polish. I was a feral thing in a gilded cage, and the door was standing wide open.

The air itself felt processed, scrubbed clean of any real scent, carrying only the faint, floral notes of expensive candles. I missed the smell of hay and horse, of dust and honest sweat. Here, I was a square peg in a round, rhinestone-encrusted hole. My reflection in a floor-to-ceiling mirror showed a man out of time, a cowboy hat in a house of mirrors. Protecting her here had been a mission. But staying? Living in this monument to everything she was escaping? The thought was a cold knot in my gut. This wasn't my world. I was a temporary fix, a crisis manager. And the crisis was over.

I had fought my way through hell to get her back to a palace she never wanted, and now that we were here, I had no idea where I fit in the picture. The warrior had no war to fight, and the peace felt like a different kind of battlefield.

As if summoned by my thoughts, my Sierra Bravo phone buzzed on the glass coffee table, a stark, black rectangle on the pristine surface. The screen lit up with a new assignment brief. A corporate executive in Dallas, a clean, straightforward protection detail. A promotion was hinted at, a desk job, eventually. Management. It was everything I'd worked for before I'd met her. A return to the simple, black-and-white world of threat assessment and clear exits. Home. It was a path leading away from the neon glare and the screaming headlines, back to a place where a man could breathe. I should have felt relief. I should have felt the pull of the familiar. But when I looked up from the screen, my gaze traveled down the hallway, following the sound of Isla's soft footsteps as she moved through her bedroom and her voice humming. The pull I felt wasn't toward Texas. It was toward her.

The offer was a siren's call to the man I used to be. The soldier who didn't get attached, who moved on to the next mission, who slept easy because his heart wasn't on the line. Accepting it was the smart, professional, sane thing to do. It was the path of self-preservation. But the thought of walking out that door, of getting on a plane and never hearing her laugh again, never feeling her curl against me in the middle of the night, felt like tearing out my own still-beating heart. The mission was over, but I was still embedded. Not in her security detail, but in her soul. And she was embedded in mine.

The phone buzzed again, an impatient demand. I had a choice: the life I was built for, or the woman I'd rebuilt myself for.

The bedroom door opened and she emerged, and the sight of her stole the air from my lungs. She wore ripped jeans and a simple tank top, her hair a loose, messy wave around her shoulders. No bow. No glitter. Just Isla. The real one. Her chin was high, her green eyes blazing with a fire that had nothing to do with stage lights.

"I told them," she said, her voice clear and steady. "My team, the label. I'm done with the brand. I'm not doing the tour. I'm not singing those songs anymore."

Her declaration hung in the air, brave and reckless. Her team would hate it. The industry would blacklist her. She was torching a multi-million dollar empire with a sentence. And she was doing it for herself.

I saw the weight of that decision in the slight tremble of her hands, but also the unshakable resolve in her spine. She wasn't just choosing a new sound; she was choosing a new life. A life without the cage. And as I looked at her, standing there in her bare feet, more a queen than she ever was on a throne of glitter, I understood the terrifying truth. She was free. She didn't need a bodyguard anymore. She didn't need a protector. The vulnerability that had first hooked me was transforming into a formidable strength. She was choosing herself. And the unspoken question that had been hanging between us since her public confession now became a deafening roar: where did that leave me?

If she didn't need me to protect her, what did she need me for?

I gripped the brim of my hat, the familiar felt worn soft under my calloused fingers. It was a tether to who I was, to the man I understood.

"You don't need me now," I said, the words coming out rougher than I intended. "The threats are gone. DeWitt's in custody. Lily's locked away." I gestured vaguely at the opulent, sterile room around us. "I don't fit here, Isla. This world... it's not mine."

I was laying my insecurities bare, building a wall of logic and self-doubt to protect us both from the harder, messier truth. I was giving her an out. I was the hired gun, and the shootout was over. It was time for the cowboy to ride off into the sunset, alone. The thought was a physical pain, a cold stone in my gut, but it felt like the right thing to do. The noble thing.

I saw the future clearly: me, a relic in her new, authentic life. A constant reminder of some of her worst times, a rough-edged man who would always be out of place at her parties, who would never understand the nuances of her world. She deserved to build something new, clean and free, without the shadow of a broken bodyguard trailing behind her. My love for her was the one thing I was sure of, and because of it, I was willing to let her go. Her smile faltered, the fierce determination in her eyes clouding by a hurt so profound it shook me. The woman who had faced down a bomb was now looking at me as if I were the one about to destroy her.

I was trying to set her free, and all I was doing was breaking her heart.

We spent the evening in a fragile, unspoken truce. I'd made my choice. She'd heard it. The air was thick with everything we weren't saying. She curled against me on the oversized couch, her head on my chest, her bare feet tucked under my leg. She was quiet, humming a soft, unfamiliar melody under her breath, something raw and new, the sound of her future. I memorized the weight of her, the feel of her hair against my chin, the rhythm of her breathing. I was stockpiling memories for the long, empty years ahead. I told myself this was a goodbye, a perfect, final memory to hold onto. But with every beat of her heart against my side, the lie grew thinner, the future without her feeling more like a self-imposed death sentence than a choice.

This was the peace I'd fought for. This quiet intimacy, this sense of rightness, of belonging. And I was preparing to walk away from it. Every soft sigh from her, every absent stroke of her hand on my arm, was a fresh wound. I was a man savoring his last meal, knowing the famine that awaited. The cowboy who had faced down insurgents and IEDs without flinching was terrified of the quiet emptiness of a life without this woman in it. The thought of this being our last night together was a deeper, more profound pain than any combat wound. It was an amputation of the soul.

I held her tighter, as if I could imprint the feel of her into my very bones, a ghost limb to haunt me for the rest of my days.

As the night deepened and the city lights glittered like a fallen galaxy outside the window, the silence between us became unbearable. The walls I'd built, the "noble" sacrifice I'd planned, began to crumble under the weight of the reality of leaving her behind. She shifted in my arms, tilting her head back to look at me. Her eyes were luminous in the dim light, shining with unshed tears.

"I don't want this to end," she whispered, her voice so fragile it nearly shattered me. "I don't want you to go."

That was all it took. Those six words, breathed with a vulnerability that mirrored my own, broke the dam. My restraint, my stupid, misguided sense of what was best for her, frayed and snapped.

"I'm not going anywhere," I heard myself say, the words scraping my throat raw, feeling like the truest thing I'd ever spoken. "I'm all in, Isla. For you. Not the brand, not the fame. Just you."

It was a surrender. A laying down of arms. I was choosing the messy, complicated, terrifying future with her over the safe, solitary, predictable path I had always known. I was choosing *us*. The admission hung in the air, a seismic shift in the foundation of my world. I had spent my life building walls, and with one sentence, I had invited her to tear them all down. The fear was still there, a cold knot in my stomach, but it was now dwarfed by a staggering, overwhelming sense of rightness. This wasn't the end of a job. It was the beginning of my life.

The war was over. I was home.

Chapter 30
Encore of the Heart

F or the first time, I led a man into my private music studio not as a producer, a manager, or a choreographer, but as my own. Just me, barefoot on the cool hardwood floor, my hair a loose tangle, and Jake filling the doorway with a presence that felt more like a homecoming than an intrusion. The room was my sanctuary, a place of raw sound before the polish, and it had never felt more sacred. He leaned against the doorframe, his worn Stetson in his hands, his eyes, those steady, hazel eyes, watching me with a quiet intensity that made my breath catch. He wasn't just looking at me; he was *seeing* me. The woman, not the myth. And in his gaze, I felt more exposed than I ever had under a thousand spotlights, and yet, completely, utterly safe.

This was the inner sanctum, the place where I'd written the songs that became my cage and the ones that were my secret cries for help. Letting him in here was the final surrender, the last layer of armor stripped away. The grand piano stood silent in the corner, a witness to all my truths and lies. I was about to offer him the most vulnerable piece of me, my music, before it was a product. My voice, before it was auto-tuned. My heart, without a backup track. His silence was a promise that he would handle it with care.

We were no longer bodyguard and client, nor cowboy and pop princess. We were just Jake and Isla, in a quiet room, and the air between us hummed with the beginning of everything.

I settled onto the plush velvet stool, the cool ivory of the keys a familiar comfort under my trembling fingers. I didn't play one of my old hits. I played the first few, hesitant chords of a melody I'd been fiddling with for weeks, something born not from a branding meeting, but from the quiet, aching hope he'd planted in my chest. I began to sing, softly at first, my voice unadorned and shaky. The lyrics were simple, about finding solid ground after a long fall, about a love that felt less like a lightning strike and more like the dawn, steady, sure, and life-giving. I kept my eyes on my hands, too terrified to look at him, pouring every ounce of the fear, the gratitude, the wild, terrifying joy he'd given me into the notes.

This was no performance. There was no calculated breath control, no perfect pitch. My voice cracked on the high note, the emotion too big to contain. It was messy and real, the musical equivalent of standing in front of him with my soul bare. This was the song of the woman he had uncovered, the one who was scared, and brave, and so deeply in love it felt like a new kind of gravity. I was giving him the blueprint to my heart, and I prayed he could read the music.

The last chord faded into the sound of my own thumping heart. I couldn't look up. I just waited, suspended in the silence, terrified of what I would see in his eyes.

The silence stretched, a lifetime contained in a few seconds. Then, I heard his slow, deliberate footsteps. He crossed the room and crouched down in front of me, his knees bracketing mine, putting us at eye level. His work-roughened hands came up to cradle my face, his thumbs gently stroking my cheeks. His eyes were shining with an emotion so deep it stole my breath.

"That's you," he murmured, his voice a low, reverent rasp. "That's the woman I..." He stopped, swallowing hard, his gaze holding mine with an intensity that felt like a brand. He didn't need to finish the sentence. I heard it in the crack of his voice, saw it in the storm of love and awe in his hazel eyes. He wasn't just praising the song. He was claiming the woman who sang it. He was seeing every scar, every fear, every hope, and he was calling it beautiful.

In that look, a lifetime of performing, of being judged for my marketability, of being told I was too much or not enough, simply evaporated. He didn't see a project or a product. He saw a soul. And he loved it. The approval I had spent my career desperately seeking from millions was right here, in the quiet praise of one man. It was the only standing ovation I would ever need. The last of my walls, the ones built around the most wounded parts of me, crumbled to dust. He wasn't just my sanctuary; he was my absolution.

He loved the real me. And in that moment, I finally, completely, loved her, too.

The space between us vanished. I surged forward, my hands fisting in the front of his shirt, and I kissed him. There was no hesitation, no carefully constructed brand of innocence to maintain, no fear of the headlines. This kiss was a claiming, a confession, a final, desperate "yes" to everything we were. He met me with a guttural sound, his arms crushing me to him, lifting me off the stool as if I weighed nothing. Our bodies collided, a culmination of weeks of restrained looks, of barely-touches, of love spoken in the language of protection and survival. Now, it was spoken in the raw, hungry language of need.

The world narrowed to the feel of his hands roaming my back, the taste of his mouth, the scent of leather and soap that was uniquely him. It was a storm breaking after a long drought, a dam of want finally giving way. He walked us backward, his lips never leaving mine, until my back met the cool wall of the studio. The contrast of the hard surface and the soft, demanding pressure of his body was electrifying. This wasn't the gentle, tentative exploration of before. This was hunger. This was possession. This was two people who had faced death and decided to tear into life with everything they had.

He broke the kiss, his breath hot against my lips, his forehead resting against mine. His eyes were dark, his chest heaving. "Isla," he breathed, a question and a prayer. My answer was to pull him back to me, my fingers finding the hem of his shirt. The talking was done.

He didn't carry me to a bedroom. He laid me down on the deep, velvet couch in the corner of the studio, a nest of discarded lyric sheets and soft blankets. Here, surrounded by the ghosts of my old songs, we wrote a new one with our bodies.

His hands were not timid. They were sure, mapping the terrain of me as if committing it to memory. He pushed my tank top up, his calloused palms a rough, delicious friction against the soft skin of my stomach, my ribs. When his mouth followed, hot and open-mouthed against my breast, a broken sob escaped me. It wasn't pain. It was the shock of being worshipped. He wasn't taking; he was discovering. Every touch was a revelation, every sigh a psalm. He was learning the language of my pleasure, and I was his willing, eager text.

This was nothing like the fumbled, selfish encounter that had stolen my sense of safety years ago. This was a restoration. Jake's touch was a conversation, a question followed by a patient, devastatingly attentive wait for my answer. When I arched into him, a silent plea for more, a low groan rumbled in his chest.

"You're so beautiful," he murmured against my skin, his voice thick with a reverence that felt like a balm on every old wound.

He was seeing me, all of me, the strength and the fragility, the fire and the fear, and he was treating it all as sacred. In his arms, the parts of me I'd been taught to market were the very parts he cherished with fingers and kisses and tongue. I let go completely, surrendering to the current of sensation, trusting him to hold me fast. For the first time, my body was not a product or a prison. It was a gift, and he was unwrapping it with a tenderness that felt like coming home.

As his weight settled over me, a final, perfect anchor, my gaze caught on a flash of pink on the floor. The oversized bow from my old costume, must have fallen from a shelf. It lay there, a discarded symbol of everything I had been, everything I was breaking free from. A wild, reckless laugh bubbled up in my throat, mingling with a moan as he moved against me. In one fluid, defiant motion, I reached down, snatched the bow, and held it up between us.

"Jake," I breathed, my eyes locked on his.

He stilled, his gaze dropping to the bow, then back to my face, a question in his heated look.

With a surge of strength, I snapped the cheap plastic in two. The sound was sharp, final. I tossed the broken pieces aside, where they vanished into the shadows.

A slow, devastating grin spread across his face. "That's my girl," he growled, his voice rough with approval and desire.

And then he was moving again, and I was moving with him, the last ghost of the pop princess banished forever. I was finally, completely, his. And he was mine.

The act was more than discarding a prop; it was an exorcism. As the pieces of the bow clattered away, it felt like the last chain holding me to that old life had shattered. The "Forever Innocent" brand died not with a press release, but in that quiet, passionate moment, replaced by the raw, powerful truth of a woman fully claiming her desire. His approval wasn't for my innocence, but for my strength, for my rebellion. It fueled the fire between us, turning tenderness into a conflagration.

We were no longer just making love; we were sealing a pact, forging a new union in the ashes of the old.

There was no more you and me. There was only us, a single, blazing entity, burning away the past and lighting the future with our own fierce, undeniable flame.

Later, we lay tangled in the velvet dusk of the studio, the only sound our synced, slowing breaths. My head was pillowed on his chest, my finger tracing idle patterns through the blond dusting of hair there. The world outside, with its headlines and chaos, felt a million miles away. In the quiet, I began to hum a new melody, something soft and winding, born from the feeling of his skin against mine.

"We could get a place," I murmured, the dream taking shape in the air between us. "Somewhere with land. Not too far from the city, but... quiet. With a porch. And a studio for me, a barn for you." I wasn't talking about a vacation home. I was talking about a life.

He didn't tense or offer a practical objection. His hand, which had been stroking my back, stilled for a moment, then resumed its gentle rhythm.

"A barn," he repeated, his voice a low, considering rumble under my ear. I could hear the smile in it. "Could keep a horse or two."

It wasn't a confirmation, but it wasn't a denial. It was a man allowing himself to imagine a future he'd never dared to want. A future of simple, tangible things, wood and wire, land and animals, woven together with the complex, beautiful reality of me and my music. It was a dream of roots, not glitter. Of mornings, not encores.

We lay in silence after that, no more words needed. The dream hung in the air, fragile and real, a shared secret blueprint for a happiness we were both only just beginning to believe we deserved.

My phone, forgotten on the floor, buzzed insistently, shattering the peaceful quiet. I let out a groan of protest, burrowing deeper against Jake's side.

"Ignore it," he murmured, his arm tightening around me.

But it buzzed again, and again, a persistent, frantic rhythm. With a sigh, I stretched an arm down, fumbling for it. The screen was a blaze of notifications, emails, texts, missed calls. My manager's name was at the top. My stomach dropped. This was it. The fallout. The official notice that my career was over.

Hesitantly, I tapped the screen. It wasn't an email. It was a push notification from the music charts.

ISLA DOVE - THE RAW SESSIONS: #1 ON STREAMING PLATFORMS.

I stared, my breath catching in my throat. *The Raw Sessions*. It was the working title for the stripped-down, acoustic demos I'd recorded in this very room, the ones my label had called "unmarketable." Someone must have leaked them in the chaos after the concert. They weren't the polished pop anthems. They were the truth. My truth.

"Jake," I whispered, my voice trembling. I turned the screen to him.

He read it, his eyes widening slightly. Then a slow, proud smile spread across his face, crinkling the corners of his eyes. He looked from the screen back to me, his gaze full of a fierce, triumphant joy.

I laughed, the sound watery with disbelief and tears of relief. The album that had just hit #1 wasn't the product of the brand. It was the sound of it breaking. And Jake was right there, his arms around me, sharing the victory. For once, the success didn't feel like it belonged to a corporation or an image. It felt like mine. Ours.

The world wasn't applauding the doll anymore. They were listening to the woman. They were buying the scars, the shaky notes, the raw, unvarnished confession. I had finally given them *me*, and they had chosen me, not the fantasy. It was the most terrifying and liberating encore of my life. I looked at Jake, at the man who had fought for the woman behind the music, and I knew this wasn't an ending. It was the first, beautiful note of our forever.

Chapter 31
Happily Ever Encore

Jake

The Los Angeles skyline shrank in the rearview mirror, a glittering, jagged monument to a life we were leaving behind. My hand was wrapped around Isla's, her fingers laced securely with mine on the center console. Ahead, the highway unfurled toward rolling hills painted in shades of gold and green, under a sky so wide it felt like a promise. The hum of the SUV's engine was a steady, familiar song, replacing the frantic buzz of the city. In the mirror, I saw glitter and neon and chaos. But through the windshield, I saw peace. I saw home. For the first time in years, the road ahead didn't lead to another mission. It led to our future.

I glanced at her. She was watching the landscape change, a soft smile on her face, no trace of the fear that had haunted her for so long. She'd traded a mansion for the promise of a ranch, spotlights for starlight. And I was trading the solitary life of a soldier for the profound responsibility and joy of building a life with this woman. The weight of my past, the ghost of my sister, the dust of a hundred battlefields, it all felt lighter out here. It felt like I was finally bringing all the broken pieces of myself to a place where they could heal, right beside her.

I squeezed her hand. She squeezed back. No words needed. The cowboy was finally riding toward his own sunset, and he wasn't alone.

Isla

I stepped out of the truck, my scuffed boots crunching on the gravel drive. The air was different here. It smelled of hay and earth and wildflowers, a symphony of realness after the sterile, perfumed air of Beverly Hills. I took a deep, cleansing breath, feeling it fill lungs that had been breathing manufactured air for far too long. Inside the rustic barn, my piano waited, already delivered and standing proudly on the raw wood floor. My music, in a cowboy's world. It wasn't a contradiction; it was the most perfect harmony I could imagine. He gave me roots. And I hoped, with every note I'd play here, I could give him wings.

This wasn't about escaping my past but about building a new future where all the parts of me could coexist. The pop star, the broken girl, the survivor, the woman in love, they all had a place here. The glitter was gone, but the music remained, purer now. Jake's world of simple, honest things didn't diminish mine; it gave it a foundation. Here, a song could be just a song, a feeling shared between us, without a marketing plan or a brand manager. It was freedom. It was the encore my soul had always been waiting for.

I looked from the piano to the man unloading our bags, his hat tipped back on his head, and I knew I was finally home. Not a place, but a person. A life. A duet.

Jake

My phone buzzed, a group text from the Sierra Bravo team.

Heard you went native, cowboy. Send pics of the horse you're gonna buy.

I smirked, a real smile that felt good. The teasing was a lifeline, a reminder of the brotherhood I'd always have. I looked over at Isla, who was now wrestling a box of kitchen supplies out of the back with a determination that made my chest ache with pride. She was tougher than they'd ever know. I thought of my sister, a ghost I still carried, and I knew with a sudden, clear certainty that she'd approve of this woman, of this life. She'd have loved Isla's fire, her courage, her refusal to break. The family I'd lost was gone, but the family I'd found and was building was right here, standing in the sun.

For so long, my purpose had been about protection, about forgetting loss. Now, it was about cultivation. About building. The love I had for Isla didn't erase the pain of losing my sister; instead, it built a new garden around that old, sacred grave, allowing something beautiful to grow from the grief. My brothers from Sierra Bravo, Isla, the home we were making, it was all a different kind of unit. A different kind of mission. One with a heart, not just a target.

I typed back a quick reply to the guys:

No horse yet. Just building the fence.

It was the truth, in more ways than one.

Isla

My first livestream from the ranch was terrifying. I sat at my piano, no bow, no glitter, just me in a worn-out flannel of Jake's.

"Hi," I said, my voice a little shaky. "This is just me. Isla."

I played the raw, acoustic version of *I'll Stand Tomorrow*, the way it was meant to be heard. The chat exploded. Some fans were furious, mourning their "Forever Innocent" idol.

Where's the bow? This is so depressing.

But others... others were saying things that brought tears to my eyes.

This is real. Thank you for your courage. I hear you.

I wasn't selling them a fantasy anymore. I was offering them my truth. And for the first time, it was enough. It was the most vulnerable performance of my life, and also the strongest. With each note, I felt the weight of the brand finally, completely, lift from my shoulders. I wasn't their princess; I was a woman with a piano and a story. And Jake, my steady cowboy, leaned in the doorway, his quiet presence a silent cheer. He was the reason I had the strength to do this. He was the reason I knew I was worth more than a product. The mask was off, shattered on a concert stage, and the face beneath was finally free to feel the sun.

I signed off with a simple, "Thanks for listening." And I meant it. They were finally listening to *me*.

Jake

One evening, under a blanket of stars so thick it felt like you could reach up and scoop them, I pulled her close on the porch swing. The only sounds were the crickets and the soft creak of the chains. My heart was a drum in my chest, louder than anything I'd heard in combat. From my pocket, I pulled it out, her mother's locket, the one that had been stolen and returned, the last piece of her past. I'd had it cleaned, the chain repaired. Inside, I'd placed a tiny, new photo, one of her, laughing, her head thrown back, completely and utterly herself.

I fastened it around her neck, my fingers fumbling slightly. She touched the locket, her eyes wide and questioning.

I took her hands in mine, my voice rough with an emotion so big it threatened to choke me. "Marry me, darlin'."

It wasn't a diamond. It was something more precious. It was her history, restored and made new, just like her life. It was a promise that I cherished all of her, the girl she was, the woman she became, the future we would build. The question hung in the night air, simple and profound. There were no cameras, no audience, no spectacle. Just a man, a woman, and a sky full of witness stars. It was the only way it ever should have been.

I held my breath, my world balanced on the single word I prayed she'd say.

Isla

My heart didn't somersault; it settled, as if it had finally found its true, permanent home. I didn't squeal or cry out. A laugh bubbled up from a deep, joyful place inside me, breathless and real.

"Yes," I whispered, the word carrying the weight of every shattered dream and every new beginning. "Yes, Jake. A thousand times, yes."

I threw my arms around his neck, and he caught me, his own laugh a low, joyful rumble against my chest. Boots on boots, rhinestones on denim, we kissed under the starlight. I was a pop princess no more. I was a woman claiming her cowboy, her partner, her forever.

This was the opposite of a staged, public relationship. This was a private vow, sealed with a kiss that tasted of starlight and certainty. There were no contracts, no branding opportunities, no managers calculating the PR value. There was only this: his strong arms, his steady heart, and the overwhelming, glorious truth that I was his and he was mine. It was the best deal I had ever made. The only one that ever truly mattered.

I pulled back, my hands framing his face. "I love you," I said, the words an easy, effortless truth. He was my encore, my curtain call, my happily ever after, all rolled into one.

Jake

I adjusted my hat, my hands sweating. The barn was strung with fairy lights, filled with the people who mattered, my Sierra Bravo brothers, her band, a few true friends. No press. No fans. Then the music started, a simple guitar melody. I turned. And my world stopped.

Isla

I walked down the aisle of hay bales and wildflowers, not in a designer gown, but in a simple ivory dress and my favorite, well-worn rhinestone boots, my mother's locket around my neck. My something old, something new. I carried a bouquet of sunflowers. I saw only him. My cowboy, his eyes full of a love so deep it made my own eyes fill with tears.

Jake

She was a vision that brought tears to my eyes. No veil to hide behind. No glitter, just a touch of rhinestones to honor her glittery past and a damned cowboy hat to honor our future. She was real now, and she was walking toward me. Her smile was for me alone. To the world, it might look like a spectacle that should have been recorded for her fans. To me, it was the most sacred promise I'd ever make.

Isla

I reached him. He took my hand. His grip was firm, sure. I saw the sheen of tears in his own eyes, and my heart overflowed. This was it. The final bow on my old life, and the first, beautiful step into our new one.

Jake & Isla

The vows were simple. His voice was rough with emotion, promising to honor, cherish, and protect, not out of duty, but out of love. Hers were clear and strong, promising to stand by him, to sing her truth, and to love him with every beat of her heart. There were no lies in their words, no brand to uphold. There was only the raw, beautiful truth of two souls choosing each other, forever. When the officiant pronounced them husband and wife, the cheer that went up was from the hearts of those who cared about them, not from a stadium crowd.

He leaned in. She met him halfway. Their kiss was a promise, a blessing, a beginning. The music swelled around them, but all they heard was the sound of their own hearts, finally beating in time.

They kissed under a shower of sparklers, their friends and family cheering, the sound of laughter and joy echoing under the vast California sky. No masks, no fake personas, just Jake and Isla, bruised, scarred, and whole, wrapped in each other's arms. The music of their favorite song, a raw, acoustic ballad about second chances, swelled from the speakers, filling the barn.

She leaned her head against his shoulder, watching the sparks dance like fallen stars. "Encore?" she whispered, her voice full of love and a hint of playful challenge.

He grinned, that slow, devastating smile that was for her alone. His arms tightened around her, his voice a low, loving rumble against her ear.

"For the rest of our lives."

The spotlight had faded, but a different, warmer light remained, the glow of a shared life, built on a foundation of truth and forged in fire. The grumpy cowboy had found his heart. The pop princess had found her voice. And together, they had written a love story more powerful than any hit song, a quiet, enduring melody that would play on, long after the final curtain had fallen on their past. Their encore wasn't a single performance. It was a lifetime. And it was only beginning.

****

Wanna hear Isla sing *I'll Stand Tomorrow (I Just Can't Today)*? Join the Jax' Inner Circle and you'll get a copy of the song!

See the next chapter on how to join. It's free!

Want to join Jax' Inner Circle?

E very Jax Kane book has a secret code word at the end. Collect them to unlock sneak peeks, bonus chapters, and early cover reveals.

Your secret code word for *Grumpy Cowboy Bodyguard* is: TO-MORROW.

Enter it for free here to start your collection:

https://forms.gle/JTGzCbssuofe3HTp8

Hey-Jax' Inner Circle got an MP3 of Isla's song *I'll Stand Tomorrow* and an advance look at the cover. If you want a copy of the song, enter the code word into the link above to join the Inner Circle and keep the goodies coming!

A Few Final Words From Jax

Hi, Jax Friend!

I hope you enjoyed reading *Grumpy Cowboy Bodyguard*. It was fun going backstage with a popstar!

Did you know that reader reviews are largely what determine how books get ranked when someone searches on Amazon?

It is **vitally** important for indie creators, like me, to get reviews from people like you.

So, please consider heading over to Amazon and giving this book an honest sentence or two review. You can just look up the book: *Grumpy Cowboy Bodyguard* by Jax Kane or use this handy link: https://amzn .to/47TwyUm.

And if this is your first Sierra Bravo Security adventure, there are more for you to read!

Protecting the Grumpy CEO where a bodyguard has to persuade the CEO that her life is in danger and stop outsiders from stealing her world changing software! Here's the link: https://amzn.to/4pNOW pK

Locked Down with the Bodyguard: A party girl finds herself the target of a cartel. One tough ex-Marine bodyguard to the rescue!

They're stuck in a mountain cabin all by themselves. Uh-oh. Passion and gunshots soon follow! https://amzn.to/4pkBlWL

Stuck with my Ex's Brother: A plane crash strands a killer, a body-guard and a nurse on a mountain. The bodyguard and nurse escape into a blizzard to try to alert authorities. Will they freeze or get caught? https://amzn.to/4qxYvty

The best way to keep up is to follow me on my Amazon author page to get 1st notice about my new releases! Another new Sierra Bravo Security story is coming soon! Here's the address www.amazon.com /author/jaxkane and an easy link https://www.amazon.com/author /jaxkane

And if you haven't read the first book in the Sierra Bravo Security series, *Pretending with the Protector*, you can get it here for **FREE** https://dl.bookfunnel.com/ono7q131mr

Thanks for reading! Readers are why I write.

Your friend,

Jax

www.ingramcontent.com/pod-product-compliance
Lightning Source LLC
Chambersburg PA
CBHW020616110726
47899CB00002B/525